Darkness Divided

Part Two in The Unfading Lands Series

Katharine E. Hamilton

ISBN-10: 0692512136
ISBN-13: 978-0-692-51213-5

Darkness Divided
Part Two in The Unfading Lands Series

www.katharinehamilton.com

Cover Design by Kerry Prater.
Map Design by Kerry Prater.

DEDICATION

Dedicated to the strong women in the world and the incredible men who embrace them for who they are.

And to Brad, because again… I love you.

ACKNOWLEDGMENTS

Again, there are so many people to thank when trying to put together a list. I will try and do my best at remembering everyone.

My husband, Brad. I love you. I tried to think of something completely insightful to add to that, but it is just that simple. I love you, and I get the warm fuzzies just thinking about you.

Momma, Daddy, Jared, and Kerry. I'm blessed to have such an awesome family who embraces my weirdness and even encourages it.

My Beta Readers: Megan Wellborn, Annetta Hamilton, Sherrill Crisp, Kerry Prater, Megan Kruckemeyer, Macy Sutherland, Sara Wells, Pat Pfeil, and Erin Davis. Thank you for taking the time to read my manuscript and providing me with feedback. Your enthusiasm and excitement helped me shape the manuscript into what it is.

My editor, Lauren Hanson. This woman's patience… I mean…

Kerry Prater. For my incredible cover design and website designs she creates for me, usually with little notice. And how about the awesome map you are about to see???

My puppies: Tulip and Cash: They play the part of enraptured audience well. It really boosts the ego.

My friends and fellow authors in the Indie Author Support and Discussion Group. You guys have helped strengthen my confidence and my skills as a writer, and I love being part of such a wonderful group of people.

My Readers. You guys have been so awesome and receptive to The Unfading Lands series thus far, and I cannot tell you how exciting it has been to meet all of you and to hear your wonderful feedback.

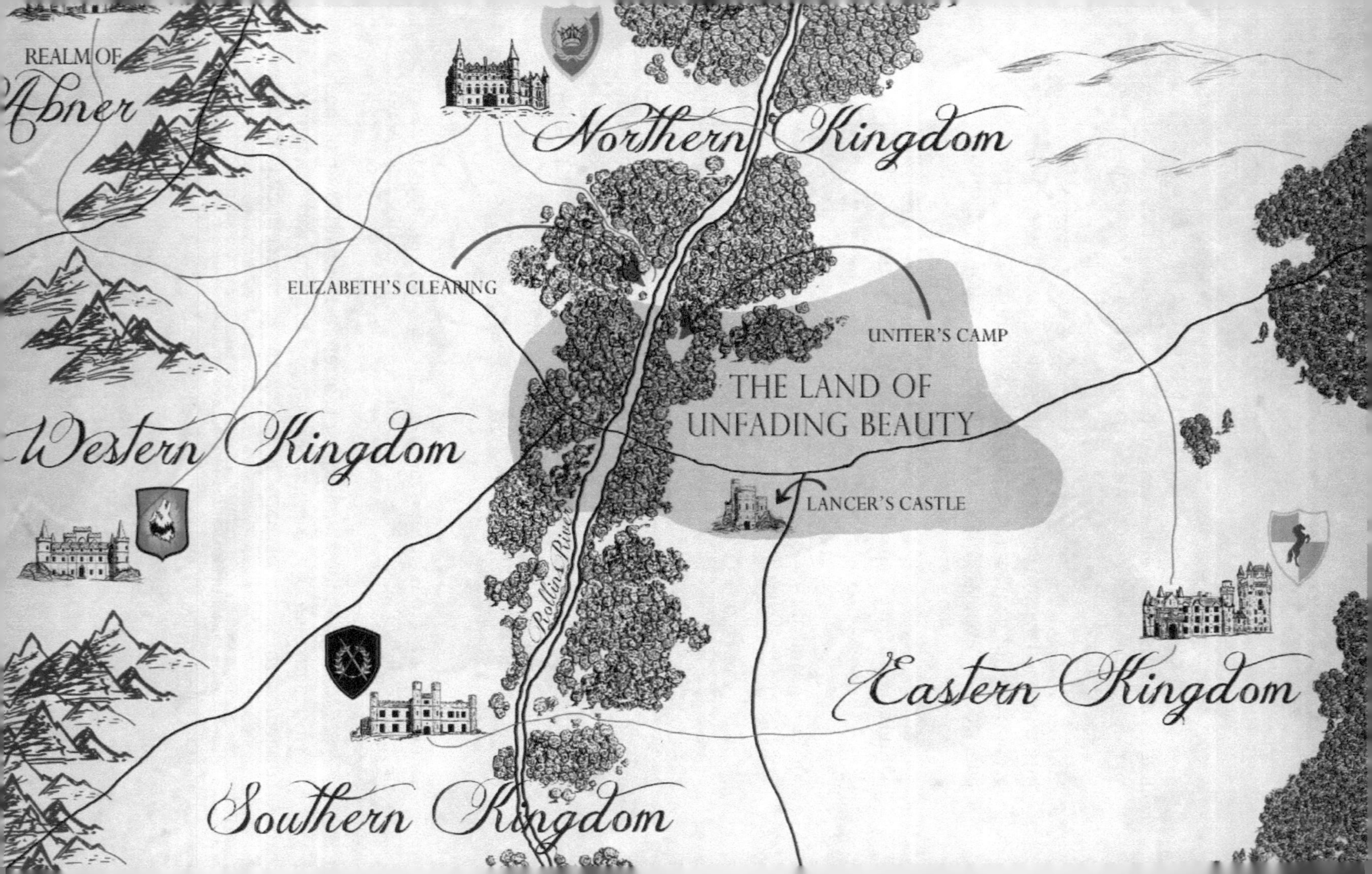
REALM OF
Abner
Northern Kingdom
ELIZABETH'S CLEARING
UNITER'S CAMP
THE LAND OF
UNFADING BEAUTY
Western Kingdom
LANCER'S CASTLE
Rollins River
Eastern Kingdom
Southern Kingdom

Darkness Divided

Part Two in The Unfading Lands Series

Katharine E. Hamilton

PROLOGUE

Nine years ago...

The sun glistened off the Rollings River and cascaded a myriad of colors atop the water's soft ripples as it wound its way through the trees. Cecilia took a small bite from the tart apple she carried in her knapsack and sank back against the tree trunk and watched as a small bundle of birds chirped away within their nest in the large willow on the other side. The other side of the boundary line. The boundary line that separated the Realm of King Granton from The Land of Unfading Beauty. A line she was taught to fear. She watched as a little blue bird was nudged out of the nest by his mother. The sporadic flapping of his little wings, the uncertainty in the feeling of air beneath his feathers, the little bird struggled until he reached mere inches from the ground. At the last second, the small creature dove upward and swiftly made his way back to the nest. *A proud mother, no doubt*, Cecilia thought with a small smile. The smile quickly faded as she thought of her own mother. How long had it been since she last felt an ounce of love from the woman who brought her into this world? She shook her head and tried to erase the feelings of hurt that washed through her heart.

Her mother had not been the same since her father's death, a death that she blamed Cecilia for initiating. No doubt even more pain came every time she looked upon Cecilia, her fair hair and sapphire eyes the spitting image of her father's. She thought of those days on the water with her father. Days to fish and float up and down the river. The feel of the sunshine on her face and the sound of crickets hiding in the reeds. Those were the best days... until her father drowned. She shook away the thought.

She caught sight of the little bird leaping from the nest on his own and testing the boundaries of the air with enthusiasm. How she wished to be free as a bird some days. She glanced down at the blisters on her palms and the dry and cracking knuckles of her hands. She helped her mother with the wash for the village. What little income they possessed came from washing other peoples' clothes and linens. Her mother took pride in the fact that she once washed the linens of Queen Rebecca of the Northern Kingdom. Cecilia took pride in nothing related to washing others' belongings. She wished for the wealth to pay someone else to do her own laundry. Maybe not wealth, she corrected herself, perhaps just enough to spare her the pain of raw hands. Lye-soaked buckets and washboards had filled her days since she was seven years old and the effects showed on her skin. Now, at twenty-two, Cecilia wished for a change. Was it her fate to end up like her mother? Alone and bitter at the life the world dealt her? Or could she change her fate?

Looking across the boundary line, everything Cecilia had witnessed the last several months had only been happiness and beauty on the other side. The people that passed by always wore smiles. The animals always pranced with an energy she envied. And a man with the most charming smile always made sure to toss a wave her direction when he passed. Her heart longed to join in the happiness.

"Cecilia! Cecilia Gale!" Her mother's voice drifted through the trees. She sighed as she stood to her feet. Duty called. It was time for her to go home and help her mother sort the afternoon drop offs. She stretched her back and picked up her knapsack. She glanced once more at the small bird that now perched upon his own branch several above his mother's nest. She could be like that, she thought. If she crossed. She would just be a mere stone's throw away from her mother, yet far enough to start her own life. A life away from the pain of loss, away from the monotonous routine of washing, drying, and folding. Away from the dull life she had come to know. She heard her name once more and tuned her mother's voice out. *No more,* she thought as the charming man stood before her surrounded by other smiling faces. What would it be like to converse with him and the other people who always seemed so happy? Sighing, she cast a tentative glance in the direction of her mother. *No, she would not go back.* She was an adult now, a woman. A grown woman, she determined. It was time for her to leave the nest, to take a leap of faith and plunge into the unknown.

Toes buzzing from the warmth of the boundary line, Cecilia took the plunge, and Cecilia Gale of the Northern Highlands stepped forward, leaving her old life behind. Embracing the hand of a handsome stranger, she crossed into The Land of Unfading Beauty.

Nine Years Later...

CHAPTER 1

Elizabeth gazed out the side of the carriage as the trees rolled by in a mass wave of green and wood, the light pine smell fluttering through the carriage and mixing with the scents of masculinity surrounding her. Her blue gaze travelled to Prince Clifton, her new husband. He glanced her direction, and she blushed before turning to gaze back out the window. What was to become of her now that she headed to the Eastern Kingdom? She had wished to speak with Edward one last time, but Clifton had carried the messages since her injury, and she had yet to venture out of the castle walls until her departure for the East. She brushed her fingertips over the elegant fabric of her wedding gown, the silver thread over the pale, blue silk felt smooth to the touch. *She was a Princess of the East now*, she thought. *A wife to Prince Clifton, the future king.* She shook her head. It was all too much to think about at the moment. Her mind wandered to Alayna and the stress she must be feeling now that she occupied the Northern Kingdom alone. Elizabeth found herself kneading her hands in her lap, worried for Alayna and the loneliness she prayed her sister did not experience.

"Is there something on your mind, Elizabeth?" Clifton asked softly, a look of concern in his meadow green gaze.

She smiled shyly. "I was just thinking of Alayna. I already miss her." She flushed at the admission and glanced down at her hands.

"I'm sure she misses you too." Clifton added with a faint smile. Nerves and worry etched his face as he tried to appear calm and confident. "It will take some getting used to for the both of you… not being around one another every day."

"Yes." Elizabeth commented softly, a hint of sadness in her voice. "Yes, it will."

Clifton shifted uncomfortably and lightly tugged at the collar of his tunic. "Mary will arrive ahead of us." He continued. "I asked her to make our quarters to your liking."

"Thank you." Elizabeth responded politely, her insides fluttering like butterflies at his usage of *our quarters*.

"I hope the Eastern Kingdom pleases you, Elizabeth. Though we will have days of reconstruction and repair ahead of us since the South's assault, I believe you may find it quite lovely."

"I'm sure I will." Her gaze travelled back out the window, and Clifton rubbed a hand over his jaw as he struggled to make conversation with his new wife. He knew Elizabeth would miss her own kingdom and sister, but her adventurous spirit had encouraged him up until today. He thought she would be up for experiencing a new journey, but her quietness and disengagement preyed upon his own nervousness and doubts.

"Do you think Prince Isaac and Princess Melody had successful journeys back to the West?" She asked quietly.

"I'm sure they are still on the road much like us. It is a full day's ride for them as it is us." He answered.

"Perhaps once we are settled, they can come visit?" Elizabeth turned to him with her question and he nodded, forcing a faint smile. "Of course."

6

He watched as a relieved smile washed over her face and her gaze travelled over him. "I meant to tell you how handsome you looked today... at our... wedding." She finished in a whisper. She watched the flicker in his eyes as they changed from anxious to relieved. He flashed his wide smile and reached for her hand. "Thank you, love. You were quite a vision yourself, and still are, as you sit with me."

They both slightly relaxed and Elizabeth lightly rested her head upon his shoulder and listened to the horses' hooves travel over the rocky terrain. Though she had spent several days recovering from her amputation, exhaustion still came swiftly, and pain... oh, the pain was still unbearable. She knew she had yet to make a full recovery, but with the latest events, her own body took secondary attention compared to the rest. She felt the sting of pain filtering up her leg and held back a wince. She sighed as Clifton leaned his head on hers. "Get some sleep, my love." He whispered. "We will reach the Eastern Kingdom in the morning."

She felt him lightly kiss the top of her head as she rested against him and her pulse raced. *Her biggest adventure was about to begin,* she thought, as she threaded her fingers through Clifton's. Though she was nervous about married life, she felt confident they would be happy. Though she missed her siblings and her friends from the West, she felt a slight thrill at the upcoming introduction to the Eastern Kingdom.

∞

Alayna hugged Princess Melody of the Western Kingdom tightly around the shoulders as both women fought back their tears. Alayna smiled and pulled Melody out in front of her. "You are welcome to visit anytime."

Melody smiled in thanks. "I just might take you up on that, my future Queen." Melody's blue gaze travelled over Alayna's shoulder to where Prince Samuel of the Southern Kingdom stood next to King Anthony.

Alayna followed her gaze and grinned. "Perhaps you can make the trip to see us for my coronation and for Samuel's as well."

"I would like that very much." Melody's blonde hair bobbed up and down when she nodded enthusiastically. She felt a hand on her shoulder and turned as her older brother, Isaac, stepped forward. He smirked and reached out his arms. "Don't I get a hug?"

Alayna rolled her eyes and briefly hugged the pompous prince. Though she had seen a slight change in his cavalier attitude, she was still not fully convinced Isaac had changed his colors. Her sister, Elizabeth, however, felt otherwise. He studied Alayna's caramel gaze for a moment. "You miss her already, don't you?" He asked quietly.

Alayna turned to him in surprise.

His lips tilted into a half smile. "You aren't the only one, Princess."

Alayna's head shifted slightly to the side as she surveyed Prince Isaac. His cheeks slightly flushed as he bowed and hurried away. His father, King Anthony, stepped forward, his red tunic crisp and bright. Her heart ached that her father, King Granton, was no longer here with her. Seeing his good friend made her wish for his company. "My dear," he began as he lightly patted her shoulder, "You are not in this alone. Please remember you have friends. Your father would want us to help you in this transition."

"Yes, my Lord, I know. I thank you for your willingness. Though my father wished for my coronation to be this week, I'm afraid everyone needs to get settled after all the excitement. Once the kingdoms are stable again, I will send word of a date."

"I think that very wise." Anthony replied. "I imagine your sister will hastily return once she and Prince Clifton have made their appearance in the East. The prince's connection with the boundary line must be utilized."

"I agree. Though I would like to give my sister time to adjust to married life prior to her coming back here." Alayna added. King

Anthony nodded with hesitation. Alayna could tell he did not wish to leave her, but his duty was to his own kingdom. She forced a confident smile. "Until our next meeting, King Anthony." She curtsied as he bowed.

She and Prince Samuel stood on the parapet and watched as the Western entourage slowly trotted away. Alayna watched the carriages until she no longer saw them on the edge of the horizon. She sensed Prince Samuel's disappointment as well.

"They'll return." She said quietly.

Hearing his quiet sigh, she smiled softly. "*She'll* return." She corrected, turning to see the soft blush work its way over the Prince's olive skin. His dark eyes and hair spoke of his origins in the South, but his character spoke of honor and sacrifice that contradicted his upbringing. *Samuel will be a noble king for the Southern Kingdom*, she thought. Though only fifteen, the boy had plenty of time to grow into the role, and with her help, and the help from the East and West, she knew he could handle the position.

She lightly patted his shoulder. "How about we eat some dinner?"

He nodded in agreement, but she caught the last disappointed gaze he flashed towards the horizon before stepping inside the castle.

∞

Edward glanced down at his palms. Nothing. He stood to his feet and surveyed Lancer's reflection chamber. All was normal now, yet he wasn't. He sensed it. Inside him. The darkness. He was different. He ran his hands nervously through his onyx hair, leaving it standing in multiple directions. His ice, blue eyes darted from corner to cranny, and though empty, he still felt uneasy. He hastily made his way to the door, opening the barricade between his old self and the new. He peaked out of the doorway, and noting the coast as clear, he slipped into the hall and quickly made his way to the stables. He had to check on Cecilia and his fellow Uniters, his army of followers who wished to see the Lands destroyed. With this new strength, he knew he could possibly pass through the boundary line and into the Realm. He needed to try, but he wished to make sure everyone was safe first.

How did he not see it before? Hatred? He wondered what hatred had consumed Lancer enough to make him wish to create his own world separated from his loved ones. *What would drive a man to such extremes? There had to be a reason*, Edward thought, and he would figure it out. With the help of Prince Clifton and the rest of the Realm, Edward would figure it out. He knew the East and West both departed from his father's castle that morning, but his communications with the Realm had just begun. With Prince Clifton's ability to cross the boundary, new ideas could take shape. It would take him several days to journey to the Eastern border of the lands, and he was not sure if he could make the trip without gathering the suspicion of Lancer. Therefore, he would hang close to the boundary line where he and Elizabeth used to meet and pray someone came to pay him a visit. If not, he would send Cecilia to the Eastern boundary line to meet with Prince Clifton.

He made his way into the clearing and made quick work of hunting down Cecilia. True to form, he spotted her blonde hair sitting alongside several other women as they prepared a campfire meal for fellow Uniters. Sensing his presence, her sweet face glanced up and a tender smile spread over her lips but then quickly vanished as her brow wrinkled. He slid to the ground and she met him half way. "What on Earth, Edward?" She asked, her hands roaming over his face and shoulders. He glanced down and it was then he noticed the charred remains of his tunic. Burned fabric clung to him as black soot covered his face and neck. "I, uh… I was in the reflection chamber." He whispered softly.

"And what happened?" Cecilia's gaze washed over him again and she led him to a log to sit. "You do not look yourself, Edward."

"Nothing happened, Cecilia." He lied. "I went into Lancer's reflection chamber to try and discover the secrets behind his power."

"And?" Cecilia prodded.

"And nothing." Edward added. "The flames enveloped me, but I did not burn, and nothing."

∞

Alayna slowly unfolded the small parchment that Prince Clifton had handed her before his departure. The wax seal showcased her father's signet ring and she traced her fingers over it until she could bear it no longer. She took a deep breath as she broke the seal and lifted the page to read.

My Dearest Alayna,

If you are reading this, then Prince Clifton must have found this letter upon my death and given it to you. I am glad he did. I know you are probably still wondering why I chose the boundary line as my deathbed, but I had to see Edward. I needed your brother to know I loved him. I know you and Elizabeth are saddened by my passing, but please do not dwell upon things lost. But look to things that are to come. Your sister's marriage to Prince Clifton will be a joyous occasion and she will need you to calm her nerves. Elizabeth may seem strong, but beneath her bravado is the tender heart of your younger sister. She will need you, Alayna. Not as queen, but as a sister.

I feel most confident in our merger with the East. I also feel confident in the change in guard. Prince Ryle will serve the Realm well, and he will guard you with his life. Together, I know you two will discover a path to defeat the Unfading Lands and Lancer. Utilize your friends of the East and West. Do not underestimate Prince Samuel of the South and his contribution either. Be open to change and suggestions. Most importantly, always choose the path your heart feels is right. Sometimes the hardest course is the one that must be taken. Know your enemy. The true enemy. Lancer, though potentially evil, is not the enemy. The darkness that consumes him is the enemy. Remember that, my dear. Should there be a way to spare his life, I beg of you to consider it. Even the most lost of people can potentially be saved. Think like a Queen in regard to the protection of your people, but think with your heart through the process.

11

The Realm is in good hands with you, Alayna. You will be a wonderful queen. My hope for you is to one day find a love like your sister and share the burden of leadership. For it is a blessing, but sometimes a burden. It helps to have a confidant and supporter by your side. I cherish the times I had with your mother, and I wish for you to have the same.

Keep your chin up, my dear. Keep your eyes on the boundary and the enemy. But keep your heart focused on hope and the goodness of our people. I love you dearly.

Your father

Alayna studied her father's handwriting a moment longer and lightly wiped away her tears. She folded it neatly and tucked it into the pocket of her emerald surcoat. *It would remain with her*, she thought, *as a silent guide.* She took a shaky breath as her mind wandered to Elizabeth and her sister's journey to the East. Her sister's injury had yet to fully heal, and Alayna knew Elizabeth was in physical pain when she left. *They had not given her enough time to recover*, Alayna feared. Perhaps Prince Clifton will insist she take it easy once they arrive in the East, and Elizabeth will have no choice but to rest. She smiled at the thought of Prince Clifton having to somehow tame her sister's rambunctious spirit. She knew he fell in love with that side of Elizabeth, for which she was grateful, but she also knew he would have his hands full with her. Sighing, Alayna stood and walked to the edge of the balcony that overlooked the main hall. This was her castle now, just her. She would be the queen in less than a month and she would rule from her father's throne. Her gaze wandered over the resolute structure below, the darkened wood carved with intricate designs that represented the Realm. *She would sit there as queen*, she thought. *Was she ready?*

She heard footsteps below and spotted Prince Ryle's dark hair as he travelled through the main hall and stopped to talk with two attendants. She felt her lips rise into a soft smile and her pulse quicken at the sight of him. *What would it be like to serve the Realm together?* Before she knew it, his piercing sapphire eyes found hers and he smiled up at her. He bowed regally as he made his way to the stairwell to rise to meet her on the landing.

"My Queen." He bowed again and stepped towards her, his hands clasped behind his back as he turned to look out over the main hall of the castle as well. "What a view you have from up here." He commented with a pleased smile. "Now I see why your father seemed to linger up here most of the day."

"Yes, it gives a great view." Alayna added. "Any word from your father or brother?"

He turned to her and a slow smile tilted his lips. "Not yet, but I am sure that is due to the fact they only left a few hours ago."

She blushed and turned her gaze back to the hall.

"I imagine we will receive a letter of their arrival once they reach the Eastern Kingdom." Ryle continued. "You miss your sister?"

"Yes, I do." She admitted. "She seemed to bring life to the castle. I didn't realize how much until now. Do you miss your father and brother?"

"I do. But I know I will see them in a few days when I travel there to renounce my claim to the throne."

"You are sure you still wish to go through with it?" She asked him, her creamy brown gaze full of uncertainty as she glanced over him. He turned with a confident smile. "Of course I do. I wish to serve you, my Queen." He saw the slight disappointment in her gaze before she smiled and nodded. "I am glad, Prince Ryle. I know you will serve the Realm well."

"We will make a great team." He added. "I spoke with Samuel, and he wishes to stay here until after your coronation. He does not wish for his own coronation until after the Realm has a new queen. He finds it an honor to have you preside over his coronation. I told him that would be fine. I figure he will be added company to you while I journey to the East."

"I see." Alayna turned to face him. "I assure you, Prince Ryle, that I do not need to be coddled. Though I am saddened by my father's death and my sister's departure, I assure you I can withstand being alone in my own castle."

Ryle pulled back slightly in surprise and his brow creased. "I beg your pardon, Alayna. I did not mean any offense. I just wished to share with you Samuel's request and that I find it befitting for him to linger because he has no family to go home to as of yet, and he is quite reluctant. I merely meant the boy wished to stay as long as possible without wearing out his welcome."

Alayna's hardened gaze slightly softened into one of pity. "I did not think of that. I apologize, Prince Ryle. You are right. Samuel is welcome to stay here as long as he wishes. I did not consider the disarray of his own household and kingdom. I wish for him to face those only when he is ready."

Ryle nodded. "Well, if you do not need me for anything else, your Highness, I am going to set about familiarizing myself with the guard. I feel a transfer in leadership might be an adjustment for them."

"Yes. You are right."

He bowed and began to walk away.

"Oh! And Prince Ryle!" Alayna called after him. He turned at the edge of the stairwell. "Thank you… for wanting to stay."

A wide smile spread over his face. "You're welcome, Alayna."

She noted the lack of formality in his response but found herself quite pleased. Instead of correcting him, she nodded and watched as he departed down the stairs.

∞

Prince Clifton restlessly adjusted as the carriage lulled to a stop and the drumming of hooves ceased. He turned to find Elizabeth still asleep on his shoulder, but her once peaceful demeanor was now

14

marred with sweat and a scowl. Her eyes were closed, yet she slightly moaned in pain. *Her leg must be bothering her,* Clifton thought. He lightly tapped her hand and squeezed her delicate fingers, her skin hot to the touch. She did not move. He then placed the back of his hand to her forehead and felt a scorching fever. He felt a slight panic rise in his chest as he lightly shook her arm and tried to awaken her. "Elizabeth." He nudged her arm. "Elizabeth, love, time to wake up. We have arrived."

Nothing. Not even a flutter of lashes. Clifton lightly lifted the edges of her formal wedding gown and pulled it up just high enough to gaze upon her false leg. Blood streamed down the sides of the wood and he lifted her petticoat higher to see the bandages soaked through, swelling, and too much blood. He swished the fabrics back over her as the carrier door opened and cheers from the Eastern Kingdom citizens erupted. King Eamon waited patiently outside the carriage for his son and new daughter-in-law.

"Father!" Clifton called, his voice edged with worry. King Eamon stepped towards the doorway and noted the pallor of Elizabeth's skin. "She is asleep. Her bandages are soaked through, she's feverish, and she won't wake up. I think an infection has set in." Clifton reported, his eyes filled with fear at the thought of losing his new bride. King Eamon slipped into the carriage and shut the door for privacy. Clifton lifted the edges of her dress again and King Eamon inhaled deeply. He tapped the top of the roof and the carrier continued onward towards the backside of the castle to avoid the celebratory welcome. "We must get her to bed immediately. I will fetch Arnos. He will see to her. She will be fine, Cliff. She will be fine."

"How can you say that?" Clifton bit back his anxiety and shook his head. "I knew she was pushing herself too hard. We should have waited a few weeks. What were we thinking rushing such mobility and stress?"

"What is done, is done, son. Now, we must tend to her." King Eamon cast a nervous glance towards Elizabeth and lightly squeezed her hand. When the carriage halted, Eamon stepped out quickly and

Clifton followed, reaching inside to lift Elizabeth into his arms. She hung limply, and all the attendants that awaited them exchanged looks of concern as Clifton's panicked face sought after one of them. Mary. Mary made her way through the crowded entry hall to his side and lightly brushed Elizabeth's sweaty bangs from her forehead. "I fear, Mary, she has caught infection. My father is fetching our healer, but I need you to help me tend to her." Clifton softly ordered, a sadness in his voice.

"Yes, my Lord. I have prepared your chambers. We must take her to the bed." Mary began leading the way through the castle halls towards a back chamber that overlooked the gardens. She had the curtains pulled back so that Elizabeth's first view would be a welcome sight of the beautiful flower gardens the Eastern Kingdom had to offer, but privacy dictated her movements of quickly drawing the drapes closed. Clifton carried Elizabeth to the large four poster bed and gently laid her on top of the covers. He then lifted the edges of her skirts and Mary gasped.

"Can you change her out of her dress, Mary?" He asked quietly.

"Yes, my Lord. Of course."

"Good. I will be just outside awaiting my father and Arnos. Please fetch me when you have her settled. Do not touch her wound. I will have Arnos take care of it."

"Yes, my Prince." Mary made quick work of untying the corset around Elizabeth's waist and carefully removed the layers of formal dress until all that remained were her underskirts. She then eased Elizabeth's body back against the pillows and placed fresh linens beneath her injury so as not to soak through to the bedding. She hastily walked to the door and opened it to the three men outside in the hall. Clifton quickly rushed to his wife's side and clasped her hand as Arnos, the kingdom's most trusted healer, made his way towards the new princess. "She is a beautiful woman, Prince Clifton. I imagine she holds quite a smile when she feels up to it."

"Yes, she does." Clifton lightly kissed the back of her hand. "Very beautiful."

King Eamon eased into a chair across the room and watched as Arnos began removing the straps around Elizabeth's waist and shoulders. He gripped the false leg around the calf and softly tugged, the peeling sound of suctioned blood and soaked bandages making Clifton's stomach roll. Arnos set it aside and unwrapped the remaining bandages. "I did not know your new wife would have an artificial leg."

"It is not common knowledge." Clifton stated. "It is an injury that happened recently, and one we wish to keep quiet."

Arnos took the silent warning in stride. "How long ago?"

"Five days, I believe." Clifton commented.

Arnos' head snapped up. "Five days?! My Lord, she should not be walking on this." He turned a nervous glance towards King Eamon. "She should have allowed the wound to heal properly first before a peg was even attached. This is most unheard of, your Highness."

"Circumstances did not allow for such a wait." Clifton explained.

"Yes, well these circumstances may just cost her her life, your Grace. The infection is severe and by the looks of her skin, I would say she has only but a few days."

Clifton ran a hand through his golden hair and flashed a terrified glance towards his father who slowly rose to his feet and walked over. "Arnos, please do what you can for the princess."

"I will, my King, but I'm just warning you that the future looks bleak."

Arnos, an older man with a slight hunch to his back and scarcely any hair on his head had been the healer for the castle as long as Clifton could remember. He took care of his mother until she passed, and he knew his father trusted him. Arnos did not fear the

17

wrath of the king, nor the disappointed glares he received at bedsides during bleak hours. Once, Clifton admired him for this, but at the moment, the crotchety old man upset him to the core with his frankness. There was hope for Elizabeth. He did not marry her and bring her with him just for her to die. No. She would live. Clifton eased his hip onto the bed and sat, and lightly threaded his fingers through hers. He kissed her knuckles and softly ran his fingertips over her pale cheek. Her lashes fluttered at his touch and a faint smile tilted his lips. "Hang in there, my love. You can fight this. You are a fighter, for that we know is true."

Eamon looked at Mary and the way she worried the small hand towel in her hands. "Mary," he interrupted the silence, "you think you could keep watch over the princess while Prince Clifton and I see to other matters?"

"Of course, my Lord." Mary bowed.

"I am not leaving her." Clifton tossed a heated gaze over his shoulder towards his father, his green eyes blazing.

"You must, Cliff. We have matters to attend to. Arnos and Mary will see to her and let us know of any change. You may come back as soon as we finish." King Eamon stated patiently. He watched as his son kissed Elizabeth's forehead and brushed his thumbs over her cheeks as if willing her to wake up. He knew the pain his son felt. How many weeks did he sit by his beloved Erica's bedside and wish for the same thing? He knew the death of a love was hard. And death is exactly what he felt was coming for dear Elizabeth. Clifton stepped towards him and he lightly draped his arm around his son's shoulders as they walked out. Perhaps he could spare his son at least some of the pain by removing him from her side during her darkest hours.

"We must send word to Alayna." King Eamon stated gruffly. "And the West. Prince Isaac would want to know."

"You giving up already?" Clifton asked in disappointment. "I do not want to send word until Arnos is finished making his assessment. I will not lose hope. She will fight this. I will fight this."

"Cliff," Eamon's apologetic tone and gentle hand had Clifton fleeing from his comfort as if betrayed. "Do not speak that way to me, Father. I refuse to lose her. Not after everything we went through to be here. She will beat this."

"I pray she does, son. I do. I just want you to realize that should Elizabeth remain… asleep for much longer, the hope of her waking is slim. Her sister, your queen, deserves to say goodbye to her sister too."

"She won't have to." Clifton barked and stormed out the castle doors and to the stables leaving his father with a worried frown and a heavy heart.

∞

Prince Isaac waltzed through the doors of his personal chambers, the deep, navy drapes drawn closed, candles lit upon every surface, and a willing woman draped seductively over his bed. He stopped in his tracks at the sight of her and waited until his eyes adjusted to the dim room. "Not tonight, Rayna."

"But you just got back." The maid pouted and slipped off the bed and to her feet to walk towards him. She draped her arms around his neck and tried to convince the prince to give in to her temptations. "I said not tonight." Isaac barked, removing her arms and walking past her into his room. "I do not wish for you to be in here."

"But you have been gone for months." She whined with a playful smile.

"And much has changed. You must leave." He tossed her dress towards a chair near the door. "And this—this display you have set up is no longer appropriate." He began blowing out candles as he reached for the oil lamp and adjusted its brightness.

The maid slipped into her dress with a frown. "Something is different about you, Isaac."

His head snapped up. "Do not address me so informally." He scolded, his dark eyes heated.

The maid crossed her arms over her chest and tilted her head to study him. "Do you have a new lover?" She asked boldly.

"What does it matter?" He asked on a growl as he opened his doors to allow several attendants to bring his trunks inside his room.

"It matters, because you are not yourself. Normally you cannot keep your hands off of m—" He cleared the room in two steps and jerked her arm as he tossed her out of his chamber door. "Do not disrespect me in the presence of attendants, maid. I will not have it." His voice was low and dangerous, and Rayna smiled as she slipped her hands to his sides. He pulled them away as if her touch disgusted him. "Leave me." He ordered.

She stepped back as if he slapped her. "Fine." She murmured. "But don't think I will be back, Prince."

He waved her away and went back into his chambers. Sighing, he sat on the side of his bed as he loosened his collar. *What had overcome him lately?* Normally, he would jump at the chance to have a woman in his bed. He shook his head. *No. Not anymore. He was the future king of the West. He did not need to settle for maids and servants. He needed to think of a future queen.* His mind wandered to Elizabeth and Prince Clifton. Now there was a pair befitting of the role as king and queen. He thought of the slight dimple to Elizabeth's left cheek when she smiled. And the light glint of mischief that lurked beneath the depths of her icy, blue eyes. His lips tilted into a smirk as he laid back against the cushions and stared at the canopy of rich, cream velvet that draped over the top of his bed. *Prince Clifton would have his hands full with that one*, he thought. *He missed them*, he realized. There, alone in his chambers, annoyed with himself for even thinking it, yet he missed them. He missed *her*. Elizabeth understood him. Yes, he was not the most respectable of men, but he wished to change. She saw that in him. That ability to be a good man. But he also knew Princess Alayna thought her sister daft for even thinking it possible of him. *Perhaps Alayna was right*, he thought. Without Elizabeth's belief surrounding him every day, what would become of him now? He thought of Rayna, naked, lying on his bed in wait of him and he felt nothing. Not even a smidgen of attraction for the one maid he had taken into his chambers multiple times in the past. He ran a frustrated hand over his face and sighed into the darkness. Sitting up, he relinquished all thoughts of sleep and decided brooding into his fireplace a better option.

He sat, a small blanket strung over his legs and stared into the flames. The hypnotic fans of orange, blue, and red taking his mind back to the Northern Kingdom. Back to the clearing by the boundary line. And back to the very moment his sword pierced through Prince Eric of the Southern Kingdom. He clenched and unclenched his fist, remembering the feel of his sword and the slight resistance that tugged upon it from inside Prince Eric's chest. *Right through the heart*, Isaac thought. He absentmindedly ran a hand over his own heart and thought of how Elizabeth had saved him that day. In more ways than one. Not only from their enemies of the South, but also from himself and his self-destructive ways. Now, back in his kingdom he felt like a stranger. No one knew of Prince Isaac the heroic rescuer of Prince Clifton and Princess Elizabeth. All that remained here was Prince Isaac the scalawag. He shook his head in disappointment. Perhaps the only means of escape from his old self was to escape his old kingdom. He pondered that thought a moment and then contemplated where he might travel. *Neighboring realms looked promising*, he thought. Or the Southern Kingdom, once Samuel took the throne. He could help the young king if Prince Ryle allowed it. He could visit the Eastern Kingdom. Elizabeth. He blinked, the vibrant flames searing through his mind and bringing him out of his revelry. No. She needed time to adjust to the East and her new marriage. He did not wish to interfere with that no matter how much he missed her companionship.

∞

Alayna read the letter in her hands and eased herself onto a chaise in the conservatory. Prince Ryle stood alert as he studied her face. "Something is wrong." He observed.

Alayna nodded, her smooth caramel gaze locking onto his. He noted the tears puddling at the corners. He quickly made his way towards her and sat, gently cupping her face in his hands. "What is it, Alayna?"

She sniffed as the first tear rolled over and down her cheek and he lightly swiped it away. The understanding in his sharp, blue eyes was almost her undoing, but she cleared her throat and slowly pulled her face away from his tender grasp. "It is Elizabeth."

"She writes of bad news? Is she not happy in the East?" Ryle asked.

Alayna shook her head. "It is not that. This letter is from Clifton. Elizabeth has fallen ill. Her amputation has become infected. She has not been awake since they left here. Prince Clifton says Arnos, your healer, feels there is not much time before she passes."

"No." Ryle stated quietly in disbelief. "We must leave at once. You have to see her."

Alayna shook her head. "I can't leave, Prince. I can't. Not with Samuel here and our kingdom still recovering from the battle with the South."

"Then I will go." He stated. "I was to ride there by week's end any way. I will just leave earlier than planned."

Alayna nodded. "Please, ride swiftly and send word as hastily as possible. I cannot bear the thought of losing another member of my family, especially my sister."

He grabbed Alayna's hand and kissed her knuckles. "I will, my Lady. I will send a messenger right away."

She watched him leave and then began a letter to King Anthony of the West explaining the situation of her sister to him and the possibility of her death. Penning the words, she cried, not just for the potential loss of Elizabeth but also the recent loss of her father. She somehow felt this never would have happened had he still been alive. He would at least know what to do, who to send for. She enquired of the Western Kingdom's healer and the possibility of sending him to the East to aide in Elizabeth's care. She swiped a hand over her face and called for her attendant.

"Jessa, I need you to take this to one of the messengers. Possibly Hector, for he is the fastest rider, and have him deliver this to King Anthony of the Western Kingdom as quickly as possible." The young woman nodded and bowed before scurrying away.

Alayna sighed as she leaned against the cool, stone wall at the top of the landing. She leaned over the edge and spotted Jessa's blonde hair and her handing the letter to Hector. He glanced up and nodded at Alayna before turning to leave. *Good*, she thought. King Anthony would receive the letter by nightfall if Hector galloped the whole way. She turned and made her way to the Council Room and drew back the heavy drapes. Maps of the Realm laid upon the large table and she briefly scanned over them. Her eyes settled upon a darkened blot in the middle of the Realm. The Land of Unfading Beauty. *It spread like a virus*, she realized. Starting in the very center, the very heart of the Realm and leaking out over the meadows. She thought of Edward and how he managed to survive all this time and his commitment to the Realm never wavering. She sensed dark days laid ahead for the Realm. Would she be able to maintain the strength of the kingdoms? Would they be able to fight Lancer and the darkness that continued to spread over their lands? *Not without Elizabeth*, Alayna thought.

Elizabeth brought everyone together in a way no else could. Her marriage to Prince Clifton had forever sealed an alliance with the East, but if she were to pass, Prince Clifton would lose his heart along with her. The East's strength was only as strong as its leaders, and the loss of Elizabeth would definitely weaken the future king. The West, her mind conjured up images of Prince Isaac, he too

23

would be upset at the loss of Elizabeth. And Alayna knew her own relationship with the West was not as solid as she wished it to be. It was Elizabeth who created strong ties to the other kingdoms, not her. She scolded herself for her lack of benevolence and sat at the head of the table to filter through parchments. She tossed them aside on an angry growl and glanced out the window. The boundary line, the light fog on the horizon, crept closer and closer. She had to stop it. She would stop it. She fisted her hands and walked to the window and stared at her unassuming enemy. "I will figure out a way, Lancer." She whispered to the air. "I will. I will destroy you and your lands."

CHAPTER 2

Edward waited at his spot on the other side of the boundary. He waited for what seemed like days for someone from one of the kingdoms to come to his and Elizabeth's spot. *Why had they not communicated with him?* Yes, much was happening in the Realm. His father's passing. Elizabeth's wedding. *But a war was still upon them, did they not realize his dangerous predicament?* If Lancer found out Edward possessed the darkness, Edward knew his days would be numbered. Yes, Lancer would see it as beneficial at first, but Edward knew the unstable ruler would dispose of him when the time was right. He glanced up as a horse stepped through the trees on the other side. Prince Samuel of the South dismounted and walked nervously to the boundary line. He waved shyly as he lifted a letter from his trouser pocket and slipped it upon Thatcher's neck. He nudged the small rabbit over the line and Edward eagerly unwrapped the parchment and read.

Dear Prince Edward,

I am sorry to be the one to come to the boundary line, when I know your heart must desire one of your family over me. However, I am afraid I am the best there is to offer at the moment. Princess Alayna does not know I have come to see you. I fear if she did, she would not approve. Though I know the future queen trusts me, I do not feel she wishes for anyone to know the news I am about to tell you. For she does not even know I overheard her and Prince Ryle discussing the matter. I am sorry for the suspense, therefore I will continue with what I had planned to tell you.

Your sister, Princess Elizabeth, has fallen ill. Her injury from this very clearing has become infected, and word has it, that she never even made it to her welcome party in the East, but that she fell asleep on her journey and has yet to awaken. My heart is saddened by this grave news. The future queen has requested Ryle to go back to the East and survey her sister's health, while she also has sent letters to the West in search of the best healers the Realm has to offer. I ask you, my prince, is there anything across the boundary that might save your sister? Perhaps you could send it to me across the line and I could take it to Prince Clifton? I know he has experienced the power of miraculous healing from the Unfading Lands, and I wish to use that same healing upon Princess Elizabeth. From what I have heard, it may be the only thing that can save her life.

He watched as Prince Edward paced on the other side and read his letter. The prince looked up and shook his head. He then sat to return a response and Samuel waited patiently. He had come to this clearing many times before the battle to spy upon Princess Elizabeth and Prince Edward. He had watched Princess Elizabeth learn the sword, converse with her brother, and even witnessed the princess enjoying her own quiet time of just escaping the castle walls. Now, as he stood in the small clearing, the peaceful sounds of the Rollings River rushing by, the leaves rustling in the wind, and the sweet scent of roses filtering through the air, he realized how perfect a spot the clearing actually was for such an escape. He glanced up as Thatcher crossed back over the line, the small rabbit not having aged but a few days over the course of the last five years. The rejuvenating effects of the Unfading Lands maintained the rabbit's youthful appearance much like it had the prince's. He grabbed the letter.

Future King,

Thank you for coming to the clearing. I have been worrying myself sick over the condition of my father's lands. I also thank you for your news in regard to my sister, Elizabeth. I had not heard the news and am deeply saddened by it. Unfortunately, the Unfading Land's healing powers do not come from a plant or creature that can cross. It is part of our atmosphere here. I cannot send you anything to help her heal. The only thing that would heal her is for her to cross, but please, do not think this a wise decision. Her safety would be greatly compromised if she did. I assure you, she is much safer in the Realm than the Lands. I wish for you to send a letter to Prince Clifton for me.

Samuel glanced up as Edward sent another rabbit across the line and with it another letter tied to its neck. He fetched it and continued with the first.

This letter must go to Prince Clifton and Prince Ryle. It contains a most valuable secret I have stumbled upon and will aid the Realm in the battle against the Lands. The battle we all know is coming. No one must know of the contents of that letter but Prince Clifton and Prince Ryle. Please show me you understand this.

Samuel glanced up and nodded passionately, holding a hand over his heart. Edward nodded in return.

Please deliver this letter personally, Samuel. Convince Alayna you must see Prince Clifton. She must not know what is in that parchment, but I only trust you to deliver its contents. Seek out the prince, give it to him yourself, and please… hurry back with his response. I will return to this clearing in a week's time. I wish to know his response then. Take care, Samuel, and thank you for your service to the Realm.

Samuel rushed to his horse and vaulted into his saddle. The wind whipped over him as he galloped towards the castle as fast as his horse could carry him. When he reached the front steps, he made his way to the Council Room where he knew Princess Alayna would be seated. He knocked and upon her voice, entered. She glanced up in surprise.

"Your Grace." He bowed, trying to stifle his heaving breaths. "I wish to speak with you."

"Of course, Samuel. Come in." Alayna invited warmly. She waved a hand to one of the chairs and he ignored it.

"My Queen," he began. "I wish to make a visit to the Eastern Kingdom."

"And why is that?" She asked, her brows rising in surprise.

"I—I wish to see Prince Clifton, my Lady. For I was wishing to speak with him on personal matters."

"Personal matters?" Alayna looked confused and Samuel fidgeted on his feet. Understanding donned on her face and she smiled. "Ah, I see. I guess it is quite difficult for you to be in the midst of growing up and not have an older brother or father to talk to."

Samuel lightly blushed. The princess thought him a mere boy needing guidance. He shrugged. *Whatever allowed him to leave*, he thought. "Yes, my Lady. And Prince Clifton and I have... a bond, so to speak."

"I understand. Say no more, Samuel. Please feel free to take a guard with you. Should you arrive before Prince Ryle departs, perhaps you two can journey back together." Alayna smiled as relief washed over the young prince's face.

"Yes. Of course. Thank you, your Grace." He bowed swiftly and made his way to the stables once more. Gathering a guard for company, Samuel set out towards the Eastern Kingdom at a reckless speed.

Clifton paced outside the door to his personal chambers. Arnos and Mary were tending to Elizabeth, and he had yet to muster the courage to go inside and find what condition his wife was in. *It had been a long night*, he recalled. He spent most of the night feeding the fire and sitting next to Elizabeth's side. Not once had her eyes opened. Not once had she awakened to find him there with her. He wondered if she even remembered making the journey to her new kingdom. He heard footsteps echoing down the hall at a fast clip and glanced up to find his brother pacing towards him. Clifton dropped his crossed arms to his sides as Ryle stepped into the light of the lantern. "How is she?" He asked.

"Not good." Clifton replied.

"I'm sorry, brother." Ryle placed a firm hand on Clifton's shoulder and squeezed in reassurance. "Arnos is inside?"

"Yes."

"And what are you doing out here?" Ryle asked.

"I—needed a breather." Clifton admitted and rubbed a hand over his tired face.

"Come." Ryle motioned for them to step inside the room. Lanterns cast a soft glow, and the fireplace maintained a warmth that under different circumstances would have been quite inviting. But the still, pale face of Princess Elizabeth lying in the bed sucked all joy from the room. All warmth. All comfort. He watched as Clifton rushed to Elizabeth's side and replaced Mary. Mary stepped away and nodded her greetings towards Prince Ryle.

"Miss Mary." Ryle greeted quietly.

Arnos glanced up and he briefly smiled in welcome. "Good to see you, Captain." Using Ryle's newest title, he turned back to Elizabeth's wound and continued changing out her bandages.

"What can you tell us, Arnos?" Ryle asked.

29

"Well, the bleeding has finally stopped. And that is a big thing in itself. She has lost quite a bit of blood, poor thing." Arnos gently tucked and weaved the bandages so they would not come untied and then slowly pulled the covers back over Elizabeth. "She broke her fever a few hours ago too."

"She did?" Clifton asked, hope lighting up his face.

Arnos held up a hand to calm his enthusiasm. "Yes, but that doesn't mean anything at this point really. Sometimes the body begins to act better before it takes a turn for the worst."

"No. She is getting better." Clifton stated, placing a kiss on Elizabeth's hand.

Arnos eyed him carefully. "We all hope so, Prince."

Ryle stepped closer and lightly laid a hand on Elizabeth's shoulder. His mouth held a straight line as he struggled to think of a way to describe Elizabeth's condition to Alayna. How would he break the news if she passed?

"Did the queen come?" Arnos asked looking around the room.

Ryle shook his head. "The Northern Kingdom is much too unstable for her to make a trip just yet. I am to report back to her as soon as possible."

"She did not come?" Clifton asked curiously.

"She couldn't, Cliff. You know she would have if possible."

Clifton shook his head. His obvious anger at the circumstances making his thoughts poison towards anyone who did not seem to grasp the gravity of the situation. "She is the queen and most importantly, her sister. She should be here."

"The Northern Kingdom is recovering, much like the East. Her presence is needed there. She knows Elizabeth is well looked after here, by you. There would be nothing for her to do here but worry.

At least in the North she can worry while also helping the kingdom recover." Ryle answered.

"Spoken like a true Captain." Arnos stated as he eased off of the bed and slipped the extra bandages into a basket by the bed. "I'm afraid there is nothing more I can do for now, Prince. We must see how she sleeps."

Clifton nodded soberly as he turned back to Elizabeth and studied her face. He lightly brushed her bangs from her forehead as she slept. She breathed deeply, the slow rise and fall of her chest making him nervous. His eyes drawn to the small movement in hopes that it would continue throughout the day and night. He heard the chamber door close and only Ryle remained.

"Alayna has sent word to the West. I imagine Prince Isaac will be here within the next couple of days." Ryle reported.

"Yes, he would want to be here." Clifton answered.

"Is that alright?" Ryle asked.

Clifton turned to him and shrugged. "Why would it not be?"

"Because he cares for Elizabeth." Ryle pointed out.

"Yes, he does. They have a friendship I only hope to obtain with her."

"Friendship? You think Prince Isaac has friendship on his mind when he is with Elizabeth?" Ryle asked in disbelief. "Come now, Cliff. Surely you can see he is in love with her."

Clifton's back straightened. "Yes, well that does not matter, because she is my wife. Prince Isaac can feel how he wishes, but nothing changes the fact Elizabeth is unobtainable for him now."

"Are you so sure?" Ryle asked.

Clifton dropped Elizabeth's hand and stood quickly in defense. "Yes. What are you trying to say, Ryle? You think Elizabeth's heart belongs to Isaac?"

"No. I'm just saying that their friendship is—odd. And I can see the look in Prince Isaac's eyes when he is with her, and friendship is not what I see."

"Isaac respects her. He respects me." Clifton barked. "He would never compromise my marriage, and he certainly would not risk harming Elizabeth's reputation or happiness."

"I'm just trying to prepare you, brother. If Isaac arrives, he will not take kindly to lingering upon the side during her recovery." Ryle explained.

"He can do as he wishes as long as it helps her heal." Clifton slid back into the chair next to Elizabeth and lightly tugged her blankets up further. Ryle shook his head. His brother could not see past his current dilemma. Ryle knew Isaac would arrive as soon as he possibly could, and he also knew the prince of the West would overstep his place in regard to Elizabeth. That's how Isaac was after all. Selfish. Though his actions in the battle with the South proved heroic, he also knew deep down that the prince's true colors could not change so quickly. He imagined him easily slipping back into his old lifestyle quite willingly. Were it anyone else on death's doorstep, Ryle imagined the prince would not bat an eye. But Elizabeth... yes, Prince Isaac would arrive quickly. And Ryle hoped his brother would become more cautious of the threat of Isaac's relationship with Elizabeth.

∞

Isaac teetered in his saddle, the movement jerking his body awake and forcing him to focus on the trail before him. He caught the amused gaze of one of his guards at having witnessed the prince almost fall out of his saddle. "Don't be so smug, Andrew." He mumbled to the man. The guard's smile widened as he nodded and flicked his reins to pull ahead of the prince towards the front of the caravan. *He should be arriving soon*, Isaac thought. They had cleared the bridge crossing into King Abner's Realm a few hours prior and he knew it was less than half a day's journey to the castle. King Abner, ruler of the valley lands, had sent a personal invitation to the Prince of the West. Isaac had hoped to remain in his own kingdom for a few days of rest before journeying out, but his father insisted Isaac make the trip. "Seven daughters, Isaac. Take your pick." His father's enthusiasm at a potential mate for his son blinded him of the fact Isaac was not actively seeking a bride. Isaac shrugged the thought away. Seven daughters. If anything, the trip could provide much pleasure. He tried to muster the excitement of beautiful princesses seeking his attentions, but it didn't come. He rubbed a roughened palm over his face and groaned at his own misfortune. His mind was only on one princess at the moment, and she was married. Not only was she married to another man, but a man he considered a friend. If Isaac did not feel like a scalawag before, he certainly did at that thought and berated himself for even thinking of Elizabeth. This trip would be good for him. He would step out of the Realm of King Granton… or now, the Realm of the future Queen Alayna, and wash away his thoughts of Elizabeth. *A purging of sorts*, he thought. Then when he travelled back to the West, his mind and heart could focus elsewhere. On his own kingdom. On his own potential bride if things went successfully here in Abner's court.

The archway into Abner's kingdom was the grandest entrance Isaac had ever laid eyes on. The smooth stone statues of knights guarding the castle gates were just as intimidating as the real ones that surveyed from the towers. *Well protected from enemies*, Isaac thought, his eyes travelling over the busy marketplace. Several peasants stopped and watched as his caravan of red and gold colors passed through the streets. He smirked as several young maidens' eyes widened at the sight of the prince from the West. He flashed a charming smile to everyone and offered a few waves as he progressed towards the castle. When his guards approached the gate to the main entrance, the heavily, iron clad doors opened, and Isaac's eyes lit up with pleasure at the sight of such splendor. Servants, attendants, and guards lined the stairs and walkways leading up to the castle doors. And standing at the top was King Abner, his wife, Queen Nora, and seven extremely beautiful daughters varying in age. Isaac pulled the reins of his horse and dismounted. He inhaled a deep breath before rounding the side of his horse and climbing the marble stairs. When he reached the king, he bowed to his knee, hand over his heart.

"Rise, my dear prince." King Abner's gravelly voice had Isaac rising to his feet to meet a warm smile in a weathered face. "Prince Isaac of the Western Kingdom, we are pleased to have you with us." Abner extended his arm in welcome.

"Thank you for the invitation, your Grace." Isaac replied. He offered a slight bow to the queen and then turned to see all the nervous faces of Abner's daughters staring back at him. He knew he was an attractive sort, he had been told many times growing up that he was a handsome child and now man. But dressed in his finest apparel, his pelt of the white wolf slung over his shoulder and the crimson tunic fitted to his broad shoulders, Prince Isaac knew he made a lasting impression. *It was not ego*, he told himself, *it was just fact*. He smiled at the line of princesses.

"My daughters." King Abner walked towards the girls and gently laid his hands on his eldest. "Katarina, my eldest." Isaac bowed politely as she curtsied. Her dark hair spilled down her shoulders almost to her waist, and her brown eyes held a kindness and silent confidence that Isaac found intriguing.

"Elora." Abner continued to the next in line and the daughter curtsied and smiled. Isaac felt Katarina's gaze following him as he made his way down the line of sisters one by one. When he turned to make his way back towards the queen, he caught Katarina's pleased gaze and nodded his acknowledgment. A small smirk tilted her lips as her father took his place beside her.

"I trust your travels went well?"

"Yes, my Lord. Very. You have beautiful lands."

"Aye, indeed. I am sorry to hear of the misfortune in your own realm. King Granton was a dear friend and ally. I am sorry to hear of his passing."

Isaac nodded stoically. "Yes. His absence has been quite hard on the realm. But his daughter, Princess Alayna, has easily and successfully filled his shoes. I have high hopes."

Abner forced a polite smile. "We will talk more, Prince Isaac. In the meantime, please allow my servants to guide you to your chambers where you may rest until dinner."

Isaac bowed. "Thank you, my Lord." Isaac flashed another charming smile at the queen and princesses before turning to head down the stairs. He sensed King Abner's slight disapproval at his words regarding Alayna, and he wondered why. A warning bell rang in Isaac's mind, and he mentally decided to take a strong note on the matter, and to read into the king's thoughts.

∞

Princess Melody grasped the edge of her chair as her father read Princess Alayna's letter aloud. She pressed a hand to her heart and felt the tears rising in her eyes at the thought of poor Elizabeth. Her father lowered the parchment and swiped a hand over his grim set mouth. "This is grave news." He stated soberly.

"Father, Isaac will have already arrived in King Abner's Realm. We must send word to him to head to the East."

"No." King Anthony stood and walked towards the window overlooking the main market square. "Isaac is where he needs to be at the moment. You must go to the East, Melody."

"Me? But you never send me on trips alone." She countered softly.

"I know, my dear. But I have just returned, and Isaac is not here to fill my stead if I were to leave. I am sure Princess Alayna would very much appreciate you going to see to her sister in her absence as well."

35

"But Isaac would want to know." Melody added, worried for her brother's devastation at losing one of his closest friends.

"Isaac is not your concern. Princess Elizabeth is. Now, see to your things, and I will have the carriage prepared. You will take a healer with you. You will stay in the East until the princess is fully recovered or until she passes."

"Father—"

"No interruptions, Melody. You will do as I say. I imagine by the time one of those two things happen it will be time for Princess Alayna's coronation and you can travel with the Eastern Kingdom to the North. I will see you then. Please send word on Princess Elizabeth's condition as it progresses." King Anthony turned from his daughter and began ordering guards and attendants to prep for her journey.

Isaac would be furious at her father for not informing him of Elizabeth. She nervously wound her hands in her lap. She needed to send word to Isaac. It was the right thing to do. Her brother had come so far in the last few months while staying at the North. While being around Elizabeth, his true champion. She brought out a side to her brother befitting the nature of the future king that he needed to be. She believed in his goodness, and Melody knew Isaac had come to believe it as well. Withholding her condition would only make him upset, and worse, lash out. Not onto her, not onto her father, or even onto their citizens of the West. But onto himself. What progress of decency her brother had made would be lost due to anger and betrayal.

Melody's warm gaze washed over her father's demanding figure, his very presence fierce and resilient. She did not wish to act without his knowledge, but her father was wrong in his actions. She would go to the East, but once there, she would send word to her brother. Defiance was new to her, unsettling, and she did not like the feel of it within her belly. But her mother had always taught her to lead with her heart, and she knew in her heart, her brother needed to know of Elizabeth's condition. He cared for the princess. Deeper than he let on. Yet, Isaac respected Prince Clifton and Elizabeth's wishes as well. They were friends. True friendship that only battles forge. He fought with both of them, and his heart was tied to the East in a way her father did not understand. Yes, she would write to Isaac immediately upon her arrival and once she had seen Elizabeth with her own eyes. He needed to know.

∞

Edward sat across from Lancer. His back aching against the uncomfortable chair and his heart pounding at the thought of Lancer possibly discovering his secret. Lancer had summoned him at the crack of dawn that morning, and for the last half hour had only stared at him. Fingers steepled in front of his mouth, lightly tapping against his lips as if he were surveying every inch and inner thread of Edward's body and mind.

"My Lord," Edward began, "Was there something I could help you with? Or that you needed? Specifically?"

Lancer lowered his hands and sighed, a slow smile spreading over his handsome face. His dark eyes twinkled as if the awkward last half hour had meant nothing. "I wished to speak with you Edward. I have not seen you as of late, and was just curious as to why that is?"

"I have been surveying the boundary lines, my Lord. With the battle of the South against the Realm now over, I wanted to check conditions along the boundary line." Edward stated confidently. "Our numbers have slightly increased due to people fleeing the fights in the Realm." He tried to sound positive in the news that sickened his heart.

"Is that so?"

"Yes."

Lancer's brows lifted with slight approval. "And how do you feel about their sudden arrival?"

"What do you mean, my Lord?" Edward asked.

Lancer stood, his lean frame taut and regal. "I mean, Edward, how do you feel about their crossing? They were fleeing. Do we want such cowards on our side of the line? Is our land to just be filled with cowards? How does that strengthen us?"

Edward inwardly sighed in relief. Power. He should have known all Lancer was concerned about was himself and the strength of his dominion. "Strength can come in numbers, my Lord. Though their hearts were weak for a moment, does not mean they are always weak."

"Weak for a moment?" Lancer scoffed in disbelief. "It is my experience, Edward, that once a man is weak, he is always weak. Weakness hides within the heart, Edward. It is not a temporary temperament. It's a root, deep within a person's very self. I have no tolerance for weakness."

"I understand." Edward studied Lancer as he glanced out of the main hall window.

"I must share something with you, Edward. Though if I do, I must ask that you not speak of it to any of the guards."

"Of course, you can tell me anything." Edward stifled the excitement in his voice. What was Lancer to divulge?

"Something is wrong with me."

"I'm sorry?" Edward's brows rose in surprise and confusion.

Lancer turned, disgust and self-pity etched upon his face. "Something is wrong with me."

"I see." Edward paused a moment and followed Lancer as he walked towards his throne and sat like a sulking child. "And what do you feel is wrong with you, my Lord?"

Lancer looked up at Edward and forced a friendly smile. "I don't know. I just feel it. Something is—off. My power is waning somehow. The Realm is weak, therefore the Unfading Lands should be strong. Yet, I feel a quiver in my heart. No darkness has come to me the last two visits into my reflection chamber. Nothing."

"Perhaps it is building up its strength." Edward suggested.

Lancer shook his head. "No. Something is wrong. This has never happened before. I am never weak, Edward. Never. The darkness always comes when I call it."

"Perhaps you are just tired from all the excitement of the Realm's battles and need your rest. Your body cannot function without rest no matter what power you hold."

Lancer glanced up at him, his chin in his hand. His eyes sparkled in amusement. "You know Edward, perhaps you are right. I knew you would make a wise choice as my captain. I will rest for a few days. Please keep me informed on the boundary crossings. I wish to come up with a plan to strengthen the cowards before they immerse within our people. We have standards that must be upheld, Edward."

"Yes, my Lord. Of course."

Lancer stood and began to walk away. Edward bowed his head until he heard the door to Lancer's personal chamber shut quietly. He then darted a gaze towards the reflection chamber. The darkness had entered him and now Lancer felt weaker. Did he consume all of Lancer's power? Or did he divide the darkness in half? He would need to try and cross the boundary line. He hesitated to try until he knew of Lancer's strength. Lancer sensed every attempt of escape, but now that he was weakened, perhaps Edward could try and he not notice it as more than just another person attempting to cross. He could try.

∞

Alayna marked her quill through the drawing before her in frustration and growled underneath her breath as she leaned her hands on the tabletop and surveyed the maps of the Realm. She

39

moved her finger around the outline of the Lands. *Why this spot?* She pointed to the center of her Realm. Why would Lancer choose a spot exactly in the middle of the Realm to create his Land? Her eyes flashed from kingdom to kingdom. The mysterious darkened stain covered mostly the Northern Kingdom's southern boundary across the Rollings River and spread to the edges of the Eastern and Western Kingdoms and the Northern tip of the Southern Kingdom. It was right in the middle of the Realm. *There had to be a significance*, she wondered. She traced around the Unfading Lands and studied it carefully. "Talk to me, Edward." She whispered to the air. "I need something to go on." Defeated for the moment, she eased back into her chair and propped her chin on her hand. Her eyes never leaving the maps. She grabbed some parchment and began to make her notes.

Lancer desires power and strength.

Targets center of Realm. Why?

Did not want Southern Kingdom's help.

Darkness? Where does it come from?

Bloodline able to cross? Must speak to King Eamon about his wife's connection to Lancer.

She set the notes aside and studied the spot again. The Northern Kingdom was the strongest in the Realm and Lancer's lands were slowly edging its borders over it more and more. Why? "Because we are the most powerful." Alayna stated aloud and leaned forward in her chair. "The South offers to help Lancer overcome the North in trade for his favor in the Unfading Lands. Lancer denies their offer. Why? Because they are the weaker kingdom." She reached for her notes once again and listed her thoughts. "He only wants power." She repeated to the empty room.

The sun began to set and Alayna found herself rushing around the Council Room lighting lanterns for light. She could not stop now. She was on the verge of something, she could feel it. She leaned on the table and looked at the map, her finger resting on the Southern Kingdom's boundary line with the Unfading Lands. "The South has no king. It is weak. Crumbling. Lancer ignores it. The East has a king and two princes willing to fight for not only their kingdom but also the Northern Kingdom, and they are attacked. The boundary line pushing further into their lands. Attracted to the power." Alayna muttered. She knew her boundary line had not shifted the last few weeks. The Northern Kingdom, though weakened by the assault of the South, remained strong. "But Lancer sees us as weak, so his attentions are diverted elsewhere... to where the power sits." She sat in her chair and smiled to herself. "You think I'm weak, Lancer." She softly giggled. "Perhaps I will just let you keep on believing that then." Smugly, she reached for the quill and marked a deep 'x' over the Land of Unfading Beauty, the ink filtering into the map and leaving her permanent mark of satisfaction.

∞

Samuel tugged his reins and slipped to the ground. Two armed guards blocked his path into the castle. *Would he ever be welcome anywhere?* He thought. "I am here to see Prince Clifton and Prince Ryle. I am Samuel, future king of the Southern Kingdom." His voice rang of confidence and Ryle stood in the shadows with a wide smile of appreciation.

The guards glanced at one another unsure of whether or not to let the teenager pass.

"My business is urgent. If you should hinder me from delivering a message from the future queen of the Realm, I assure you your resistance will not be rewarded." Samuel stood firmly, his arms at his sides and feet planted. His fists clenched, and he narrowed his gaze. "I must insist you let me pass." He barked.

The guards stood resolute.

Samuel gritted his teeth. He could not fail the queen. He had to deliver Edward's message to the princes, and also seek out Elizabeth's condition for the queen.

"You refuse to let the future king of the South pass?" Ryle stepped from the shadows and the guards stood at attention.

"Prince Ryle!" Samuel exclaimed with pleasure. "I mean, Captain." He bowed. "I must speak with you and your brother immediately. It is most urgent."

Ryle smiled in greeting. "Of course. Come Samuel." He waved his hands at the guards and they stepped aside for the two princes to enter the castle. "Welcome to the Eastern kingdom. I am sorry our guards have not received the message of your friendship just yet. I will make swift work on that."

"Yes, no problem, my Lord. That is of little importance to me."

Ryle assessed Samuel carefully. "Yes, well, let us find my brother." Ryle led him through the elaborate castle, the marble stone archways billowing higher than even the Northern Kingdom's castle. The light drapes of pale blue covered the windows, and though it was dark out, the castle interior held a lightness to it that welcomed. *Much different than his own castle*, Samuel reflected. Dark fabrics, paintings, and statues made the Southern Kingdom less inviting than his current surroundings. Ryle turned down a long hallway and up ahead stood King Eamon outside a large door that stood partially opened. He smiled at the sight of Samuel and embraced the young prince. "My dear Samuel, my is it a pleasure to have you in the East."

"My King." Samuel bowed.

Eamon continued to smile as he looked to Samuel for an explanation of his visit. "I must speak to Prince Clifton."

Ryle motioned through the doorway as Samuel entered. He immediately froze when his eyes fell upon the princess' figure.

"Come, no need to be frightened. The princess is improving. Right, Cliff?"

Clifton finally glanced up and his green eyes sparked with gratitude at the presence of Samuel coming to check on Elizabeth. "Prince Samuel." He greeted and slowly stood from his chair beside Elizabeth's bedside.

"My prince." Samuel bowed.

"It is good of you to come." Clifton reached out and placed a hand on Samuel's shoulder and Samuel did the same. He studied the tired lines of the prince's face, and the slight tinge of pain lurking in his usual kind eyes. "I hate to intrude upon you, Prince Clifton, but I have been sent on a task that only I may fulfill. It is my duty to talk with you and your brother."

King Eamon lingered in the room and Clifton turned towards him. "And what of my father?"

Samuel slightly fidgeted. "I am not sure, my Lord. He was not included. Perhaps I may speak to you and your brother first, and if you feel it necessary to share with him, we shall then?"

Clifton nodded. King Eamon quietly slipped out unoffended and shut the door. "Come Samuel, have a seat and a drink. You must be tired from your journey."

"I must say, I am quite surprised Princess Alayna sent you on such a journey knowing I had just departed." Ryle stated quizzically.

"Princess Alayna does not know the true nature of my visit, my Lord. Nor shall she, just yet."

Ryle's back stiffened. "You snuck out?"

"No." Samuel shook his head. "I just did not tell her the true reason of my departure."

"So you lied to the future queen?" Ryle stepped closer to Samuel and towered over him. Clifton reached a hand to his brother's chest. "Calm yourself, brother. Let him speak first."

Samuel turned a grateful glance towards Clifton and then took a comfortable step away from Ryle. "When you left, my Lord, I felt the need to ride to the boundary line… to Princess Elizabeth's former place. I sensed Prince Edward may be awaiting news from the Realm, and I was right. He was there. I had overheard your conversation with Princess Alayna," he looked to Ryle in apology. "I had heard you discussing Princess Elizabeth's condition. I felt her brother should know. I wrote him a letter and sent it across the boundary as I had seen you do countless times before." He looked to Clifton. "I asked for anything that might heal the princess since the Lands have healing power."

"It doesn't work like that." Clifton stated quietly.

"Yes, I know. He explained that to me." Samuel continued. "However, he did give me something else."

The two princes stepped closer in eager anticipation at the thought of a possible way to heal Elizabeth. Samuel withdrew the letter from Edward. "He asked me to give you this. Only you two. I was not told I could read the letter, therefore I do not know of its contents. It is my hope, my Lords, that Prince Edward has provided a way to heal the princess." He relinquished the letter into Clifton's palm, the strong prince suddenly weak in the knees. He sat in the chair next to Elizabeth's bed and lightly clasped her hand and kissed it in hope.

"Go on, Cliff." Ryle prodded, waiting to hear what Edward had to say. Clifton unfolded the letter and began to read, his hope slowly diminished, and a glower marred his handsome face.

My New Brother,

I hope this letter finds you well, though I fear it may not. Prince Samuel has updated me on Elizabeth's health, and I must say I am deeply saddened by the news. I know you are providing her with the best care known to the Realm, so I will not waste precious time or words on the matter more than my deepest thoughts and prayers go towards her.

I wish my letter could consist of great tidings and joyful announcements, but we do not live in such times. I wish to share with you the latest development for me in the Unfading Lands and what I have come to discover.

After the death of my father, I lost myself in grief and sadness. I ventured into Lancer's reflection chamber to try and unearth the beast responsible for separating me from my loved ones, so that I might destroy it and Lancer's power. What I found, was something entirely different. I had seen the darkness before. I had seen Lancer accept it into his own body. But I had never been able to. Until then. I found what makes it possible. What sustains the boundary line.

Hatred.

It was my hatred towards Lancer and the Unfading Lands that drove me to my knees in that chamber. Hatred opened my heart to receive the darkness. I now possess it. Lancer does not know, nor can he. But now... I have the same power as he. I have yet to test the limits of this new strength. I do not yet know if I can cross the boundary line. But I will be trying soon. I wish to speak with you soon, Prince Clifton. We must meet at the clearing. I know you do not wish to leave my sister's side, but I fear I cannot venture to the Eastern boundaries without drawing attention from Lancer. I need you to come see me in the North.

I await your response.

Edward

"What does it say?" Ryle asked.

Clifton lowered the note and ran a hand over his face and mouth. He handed the letter to Ryle who scanned over it quickly.

"He has the darkness." He mumbled, his eyes flashing over to Clifton. "This changes things."

"I am not sure if this is a good thing or a bad thing."

"Good! What do you mean it could be bad?!" Ryle beamed in excitement. "Don't you see?! If Edward can cross back into the Realm, we will have control over half the forces within the Lands and aide our armies here in an attack against Lancer."

Clifton shook his head. "But did you not read the part about hatred? Ryle, pure evil is guiding him. His hatred towards Lancer, yes, but it is still evil. We cannot join forces with darkness. There has to be another way."

"Cliff, we have searched for a way to breach the Lands. We thought it was your ability to cross by being a relative of Lancer. What if it wasn't? What if it has nothing to do with bloodline after all?"

"What do you mean?" Clifton asked.

"What if the reason you were able to cross was because of the feeling you had when you did?" Ryle explained. "You saw Elizabeth about to be killed and you lunged at the Southern guard. I guarantee you it was not love for the man that filled your heart. It was hate. Hatred is the key."

Clifton shook his head vehemently. "No. I refuse to believe that. I crossed to save Elizabeth. My thoughts were only on her, not the guard. Besides, how was I able to cross back and forth since then? I was not full of hatred the second, third, or fourth times of my crossing."

Ryle lightly rubbed his chin. "It's worth looking into."

Clifton glanced towards Samuel. "And what do you think, Samuel?"

Samuel stepped forward, his hands clasped nervously behind his back. "I think it wise to be cautious, my Lords. Evil lurks in those lands. I have seen the effect it has on men. It draws out the worst of our hearts and tempts us to act on its behalf. Whether or not

46

Prince Edward is a positive resource for us, I feel we must tend carefully to our interactions with him. Nothing good comes from darkness."

"I agree." Clifton replied.

Ryle bounced his blue eyes between the two men. "There may come a time when we have no choice but to utilize the very darkness Lancer possesses against him. Surely you both must know that."

Clifton stood and took the letter from Ryle. "Perhaps so. But until that desperate moment, I suggest we consider other options." Clifton's voice held warning, and Ryle noted the slight rise of defense against his younger brother's reprimand. He took a calming breath. "Of course. A last resort. But we must inform Father of this."

"Agreed." Clifton stated. He handed the letter to Samuel. "I trust you two can take care of that. Now, if you will excuse me, my wife needs me."

Ryle watched as Clifton resumed his seated position next to Elizabeth and lightly brushed his fingertips over her cheek. *She would not make it if she did not awaken soon*, Ryle feared. Her body could only go so long without water and food, and two days had now passed. He turned towards Samuel and lightly patted him on the back to motion him towards the hallway. "Come Samuel, let's find my father."

Samuel cast one last look at the princess' immobile form and walked out.

CHAPTER 3

Isaac awoke to the sweet smell of orchids and the faint hint of lavender circulating his room and blinked several times to acclimate himself with his surroundings. *Realm of King Abner. Seven daughters.* Isaac rubbed a hand over his stubbled chin and rose to find his attendant laying his clothes on the chaise. "Morning, Prince Isaac."

"Morning Rupert." He grumbled as he stumbled towards the vanity to wash his face. The cold water awakened him quickly and he slipped into his trousers and shirt to avoid a chill. Rupert made haste of helping him slip into his tunic and managed to clasp the buckles and belts properly all while Isaac attempted to shave his face. He ran a hand over his smooth jaw and rinsed away the soap. That would have to do, he smirked at his reflection and then walked towards his boots.

"A maid sent for you earlier, my Lord. It seems breakfast is to be served in a few minutes in the main dining hall." Rupert reported.

"They sent a maid?" He asked.

"Yes, my Lord."

Isaac tried not to be insulted. Normally the king's attendant sought out royal guests. A maid?

"You will join me, Rupert." He stated.

Rupert nodded.

Isaac never disliked Rupert, the young attendant took weeks to season into his position over a year ago, but Isaac now found him a comfort outside the realm he was accustomed to. He brought a sense of home with him, Isaac presumed, that allowed him to look past certain faults in the young man. Truth be told, Isaac was not sure how old Rupert truly was. *He could not be more than a couple of years younger than himself,* he thought. Rupert followed faithfully behind him as he rounded the corner into the main dining hall. All the daughters stood behind their chairs as their father began to seat himself. He looked up at Isaac's entrance. "Ah, Prince Isaac. Good of you to join us. Please, have a seat." He motioned to a chair next to him and across from his daughter Katarina. Isaac waited until the king and queen took their seats before sitting himself.

"Thank you." He acknowledged the servant who filled his goblet. She froze in her movements a moment as if taken aback by his kindness. He offered a warm smile as he reached for his glass. She intercepted a harsh glance from King Abner at her lingering and moved on.

"So how is your father?" King Abner asked.

"He is quite well, thank you. He sends you his best." Isaac smiled politely.

"I hear the Northern Highlands has suffered quite a bit with the uprising from the South." Abner continued.

"They did, but all is well now. The North shall make a quick recovery, of that there is no doubt." Isaac added.

"And what of this Lancer fellow? The mysterious lands in the center of the Realm. What is the story on that?"

"Your guess is as good as mine, my King. The Unfading Lands have a dark hold on much of the lands in the Realm. Though currently weakened by the merger in the East and the defeat of the South, I fear we have only seen a smidgen of Lancer's true strength."

Abner measured him with a steady gaze. "I had heard Prince Clifton of the East married Princess Elizabeth of the North. I was not sure if it was true."

"It is. They had a beautiful wedding not but two weeks ago."

"And you were in attendance?" Katarina asked intrigued. Isaac caught her gaze and nodded.

"Yes, I had the luxury of escorting the princess down the aisle."

"Well that is just unheard of." Abner protested.

Isaac's back stiffened at his condescending tone. "It is quite out of the norm, but I believe you will find Princess Elizabeth to be a free spirit and one to stray from the norm." His lips twitched into a small smile at the thought of Elizabeth in her trousers.

"I suppose with her own brother's betrayal of crossing into those dreadful Lands there was a need for a substitute." Abner interjected.

Isaac felt the heat rising in his chest at the small insults to the Northern family. "Prince Edward's departure from the North was quite a blow, but he has proved to be quite loyal despite his current whereabouts."

"Is that so?" Abner asked. "And how is that?"

Isaac's brow slightly arched at the line of questioning from the curious king. How much did this man know of the Unfading Lands and of Lancer? After all, Lancer originated from his realm as well as King Eamon's wife.

"I had heard, my King, that Lancer is from this Realm. Is that true?" Isaac changed the subject and noted the darkening of King Abner's gaze.

"Long ago, yes."

"And also, King Eamon of the Eastern Kingdom's wife." Isaac continued. "Her kinship to Lancer was not known until just recently. Are they from one of the neighboring kingdoms in the Realm or this one? I would love to see their lineage whilst I'm here."

"I fear you will not see much. All that is left of Lancer's family is a memory." Abner stated, his tone slightly edged with hardness.

"He has no relatives?"

"No."

"Oh, that is surprising. I was under the assumption he had quite an extensive family here." Isaac appeared nonchalant but knew something brewed beneath the surface of their conversation and that King Abner did not want him knowing.

"Most people assume incorrectly. As do you. He has no family left in these lands."

Isaac leaned back and caught the warning gaze of Katarina from across the table. The servant came to claim his plate. "Thank you. Please send my regards to your cook." Her eyes widened in surprise again and she nodded with a slight blush to her cheeks.

Katarina's brows disappeared beneath her hairline in astonishment as well. Isaac caught her cursory gape and smiled warmly. "I wonder, King Abner, if I could receive a tour of your gardens by your lovely daughter?" He nodded towards Katarina and Abner nodded.

"Of course. Katarina would be most pleased."

Katarina stood and offered a shy smile as she led the way. Isaac followed. Once outside, he inhaled a deep breath of sunshine and free air. "Feels much better out here, doesn't it?" He asked, his boldness catching the princess by surprise. She offered a warm smile in return. "The castle can get quite suffocating sometimes." She admitted.

"Have you ventured beyond your father's walls?" Isaac waved a hand around the vast area, every inch guarded by royal guards.

She shook her head. "No. I wish to, but my father is quite adamant about us staying within the protection of the castle."

"The world is not as dangerous as it may seem." Isaac countered.

"To us it is." She replied quietly, glancing around to make sure no one heard her comment. He tilted his head and surveyed her. He extended his arm and she slipped hers through his. "And why is that?" He asked.

She shook her head. "Long story."

"From what I gather, we have time."

She shook her head again. "I'm sorry, my Lord, but I cannot speak of our affairs to a stranger."
"I see. You mean you cannot speak to me unless your father allows it." He corrected.

She flashed a stunned look his direction and he chuckled. "Don't look so surprised, Princess. I see the way your father guards his castle, much less his secrets."

"Is that why you have come? To learn his secrets?" She asked in a hushed whisper.

Isaac laughed. "No. I came because I heard King Abner had seven beautiful daughters and my father wished for me to see if any of them were to my liking."

She blushed at his response and he found it charming. "Yes, well my father does pride himself on his collections."

"Collections?" Isaac turned to her in amusement. "Are you a piece of art?"

"Yes. Sometimes." She answered truthfully.

"Aren't all women a piece of art?" Isaac complimented.

She looked away and glanced towards the guards upon the parapet. "Art because we are beautiful or art because we can be owned?" She asked, a slight harshness lying in the undertones of her soft voice.

"Because of beauty. No one can be owned, Princess."

She turned to him then, a light of appreciation in her eyes. "Your Realm sounds most intriguing, my Lord. The Princess of the North taking over as Queen has been a heated topic of conversation here as of late."

"I'm sensing your father does not approve of that either." Isaac spoke frankly, his casual tone leaving the princess speechless. He chuckled. "I apologize. In the Realm of future queen Alayna, we are able to speak more freely."

"Apparently." Katarina replied. "Forgive me for being out of practice."

Isaac grinned as she came to a stop next to a stone bench and sat. He sat beside her and lightly plucked a rose from one of the shrubs next to his shoulder. He sniffed it thinking of Elizabeth's chambers in the Northern Kingdom and the light scent of rose she always carried with her. He twirled the small bloom in his fingers and Katarina watched him closely. "You miss your realm already, don't you?"

"Aye. It is home. I am reminded by small things of how lucky a man I truly am to be a part of it, no matter how insignificant a role."

"You are a prince, a future king. If that is insignificant, I hate to see what servants rank." He chuckled at her wonderment and shook his head. "I did not mean it like that. I just... have an interesting position at the moment."

"Life is all about position." Katarina stated. Her voice sounded like a recital of an ancient text that had been ingrained upon her from birth, and Isaac found it most stimulating.

"Is that what you are taught here?"

"Yes." She replied. "Since the Overcoming, my father has taught that as our main guide to live by."

"The Overcoming? What is that?" Isaac asked.

She turned to him with a quizzical brow. "You do not know?"

"Clearly not." He waved his hand for her to continue.

"Did you not sense my father's hesitation in discussing Lancer?"

"I did, but I assumed it was because Lancer is evil, and to be honest, no one in any Realm likes discussing the man."

Katarina sighed and shook her head. "You come to visit blindly then."

"You have lost me, Princess." Isaac handed her the small rose and she accepted it with a hint of a smile at the corner of her lips at the thoughtful act.

"Lancer's father used to rule this Realm."

Isaac's eyes widened. "What?"

"Yes, before my father. Lancer is the son of the rightful king to this Realm."

Isaac turned away from her and stared blankly into the gardens. *Lancer was royalty?*

"What happened?" Isaac asked.

"There was a war. My father was the king of the Valleylands, the most Southern point in the Realm. He was not happy there. He had become king at an early age and found he did not wish to be ruler of the smallest kingdom in the Realm. Lancer's father was older, much older, and Lancer himself was quite young at the time. My father formed an army and overthrew two kingdoms in the Realm. All to become a stronger enemy against the aging king. It was assault after assault."

"Was Lancer's father ruthless? Was he an evil King?"

"No. From what my mother told me, he was a loving king. But it was greed and selfishness that drove my father. He wanted to be powerful, and to be powerful he needed more. More land. More influence. More people."

Isaac, baffled by the Princess' story, listened intently.

"My father spent his younger days contemplating different ways to overthrow the king, but he could not just overthrow the king, he had to rid the Realm of all his heirs as well. Otherwise the Realm would just pass to his son."

"Lancer." Isaac finished.

She nodded. "Lancer. Lancer was young, maybe three plus twenty at the time, and his younger sister Erica was but eighteen."

"King Eamon's wife."

She smiled softly at him. "Yes. See, when the king feared my father's advances, he made it his goal to marry off his daughter. King Eamon of the East was seeking a bride, and one sight at Lancer's sister, and the man was enraptured. He married her within three days' time."

"Sounds familiar." Isaac muttered softly.

"Lancer was furious at his father for sending his sister away. In Lancer's mind they could protect the realm from my father. He wanted to fight and rule, as was his right. But his father was old and barely alive at the time. Lancer had never had any military experience, he was a—child in his father's eyes. A spoiled child at that. He had never faced a tough decision in his life. He had never had to fight or work for anything. He was furious with his father. He was furious with King Eamon. He was furious at my father."

"Why would he be upset with King Eamon? Surely he could see his sister had a chance at happiness."

"No. In Lancer's eyes, she was stolen from what was rightfully hers. She had the right to help rule a Realm, not just a single kingdom in a neighboring Realm."

"So what happened?"

Katarina glanced around nervously before continuing. Her voice lowered and Isaac leaned forward to hear. "My father attacked the Realm and killed Lancer's father. Lancer fled to the Eastern Kingdom in the Realm of King Granton."

Isaac's eyes widened. "Lancer sought refuge with his sister."

"Yes, but he did not find it. King Eamon refused to let him stay. Called him a coward for not defending his lands. King Eamon did not want to lure my father's armies to the Eastern Kingdom by housing the one man standing in my father's way to rule. So he sent him away."

"Well that explains how he ended up in our Realm, but how could he create The Land of Unfading Beauty? What could possibly give him such supernatural power to create his own Realm?" Isaac scratched his chin in thought.

"That is what no one knows, and it has plagued my father for years. My mother warned me to never speak of this to anyone. My father does not know I know of his past."

"The Queen seems quite compliant with his persona it would seem."

"The current queen is not my mother, my Lord. My mother died years ago."

"I am sorry." He saw the brief flash of pain she hid in her eyes. "Yes, well, she taught me to remain strong and so I have."

"Yes. I would say so. You live under the hand of a ruthless brute."

"He can be friendly." She defended weakly.

Isaac shook his head. "Thank you for sharing this with me, Princess. I must admit it sheds great light on Lancer and his interactions within my Realm."

"You must not tell anyone I told you, my Lord. Please?"

"Of course. I would not betray your confidence." Isaac held her kind gaze a moment longer and then squeezed her hand. "To new friendships."

She flushed at his touch and nodded.

Isaac opened his mouth to speak when Rupert raced towards him in a panic. "My Lord!"

Isaac and Katarina stood quickly to their feet. "What is it Rupert?"

Rupert thrust a letter into his hands, panting from his sprint. Katarina watched as Isaac's face fell from concern to sadness and he sunk to the bench in shock.

"My Lord? Is everything alright?" Katarina knelt next to him and lightly touched the back of her hand to his forehead. Isaac blinked to clear his thoughts and focused upon her kind brown eyes. "I must go. It is urgent."

He stood and began running back towards the castle.

∞

Samuel sat on the side of the awning, his long legs draped over the stone and dangling in the air. He leaned against the castle wall and surveyed the people down below. Two days had passed and no change in Princess Elizabeth. He had sent word to Princess Alayna, and now he sat wondering if Elizabeth would ever wake up or if she would continue to waste away. Her cheeks had begun to sink in and her body looked frail. Prince Clifton sat with her most day and night and rumor had spread to the villagers why there had yet to be a formal welcome party and ball for the newly married couple. A cloud of gloom hung over the kingdom and Samuel feared it followed him wherever he went.

A gloomy day for a birthday, he realized. He tampered down his disappointment and scolded himself for the selfish thought. There was no reason for him to think of celebrating himself when the princess' life hung in the balance. He felt older than his sixteen years. Perhaps the last few months had forced him to leave his childhood behind quicker than was usual. All he knew, was that he wished to serve the Realm as king of the South and aide his new friends, his new family, in protecting the lands from Lancer's power. His dark eyes found their way towards the horizon and he squinted at the sight of two horses coming up the long road. Then he saw it. The red roof of the Western royal carriage and his heart leapt. Prince Isaac had come. Just like everyone knew he would and with him would come the Western healer to help Arnos. He jumped to his feet and sprinted through the castle and towards the main entrance.

"Samuel, what is it?" He passed a surprised King Eamon and Prince Ryle on his way and heard them trying to catch up to him.

When he pushed open the main doors, the carriage had stopped in front of the main steps. "Prince Isaac has arrived." He turned towards the Eastern rulers with a wide smile and cleared the steps quickly to open the door to the awaiting carriage. He pulled back quickly as if bitten. Princess Melody slowly eased out of the carriage, accepting the hand of an attendant until she found her feet. Prince Ryle and King Eamon smiled in welcome and she turned a warm grin towards Samuel. She enveloped him in a firm hug, his arms embracing her quickly and then releasing her. He blushed at the interaction and bowed. She then lifted her skirts and embraced both Ryle and Eamon on her way up the stairs. Once inside, she shed her crimson outer coats and handed them to her attendant. "I must see her." She stated.

Ryle nodded and began leading her towards Elizabeth's chambers.

"Your appearance is most welcome, Princess." King Eamon stated. "Has your brother arrived as well?"

"My brother is not here yet, my Lord. I fear he does not know of the Princess' condition. He had already set out to King Abner's realm when the news came to us in the West. However, I have sent word via messenger on my way here. My father did not wish for him to know just yet."

"Why is that?" Ryle asked. Melody turned towards the two of them before entering the chambers. "My father feels Prince Isaac would only interfere at the moment. Though I feel differently. He would want to know and to be here. I apologize if I offend, but I sent word to him immediately. For Princess Elizabeth is very dear to him."

"You did the right thing, my dear." King Eamon lightly patted her shoulder as he opened the door. Clifton glanced up, his tired eyes and lack of decorum breaking Melody's heart. She rushed towards him and hugged him tightly. "My prince." She greeted.

She cupped his face and shook her head. "You must not give up on her now." Clifton smiled, his sadness evident and his eyes red from tears he must have shed during the night. He himself looked like a shadow of the man that once graced the Northern Kingdom. "I am pleased you have come." He squeezed her hand and then allowed her to take his seat beside Elizabeth. She studied her a moment, her hand lightly touching her forehead and her fingers.

"I have brought our healer with me. Though I know you have the capable hands of Arnos with you already, I felt it imperative we utilize all the help we can." She looked to the three men and then smiled when she spotted Mary walking into the room carrying a wash basin.

"Mary!"

Mary glanced up and tears of joy sprang to the attendant's eyes at the sight of the sweet princess. She placed the basin on the vanity and rushed to embrace the princess in a desperate hug of reassurance. Both women cried and smiled as they gazed upon one

59

another. King Eamon, pleased with the brightness the Princess of the West had brought with her, bowed towards her and slipped out of the room quietly.

"Isaac, Melody?" Clifton turned towards her. "Did he come?" He asked.

She shook her head and watched as the prince's face crumbled into defeat.

"He does not know yet, my Lord."

Clifton's stormy gaze found hers. "I don't understand."

"Isaac is currently in the Realm of King Abner. My father sent him there to potentially pick out one of the princesses as a suitable bride. He has yet to hear of Elizabeth's misfortune. I assure you that when he does, he will come. You are his friend, my Lord. And Elizabeth is as well. He would wish to be here for both of you."

Clifton glanced towards Ryle who stood with his arms crossed in disapproval.

"Good." Clifton replied. "I feel Elizabeth needs all her friends close by for when she wakes up."

"Cliff." Ryle began and halted when his brother's ferocious gaze landed upon him. "She *will* wake up, Ryle!"

Melody placed a steadying hand on Clifton's arm and he struggled finding his composure. "Prince Clifton, why don't you allow Mary and me to wash Elizabeth and change her into some clean clothes while you go do the same? You look as if you have not left her side."

"I haven't." He stated grimly.

She smiled tenderly at him and cupped his cheek in her hands. "She would not want you to overlook your own well-being on behalf of her. Please, tend to yourself and we will have her freshened up for you by the time you return."

He clasped Melody's hand in thanks. "Thank you for coming, Melody. Truly."

She nodded as he and Ryle exited the room. Melody turned towards Mary. "How long has she been like this?"

"Going on four days, ma'am."

"She will not survive much longer if we do not get fluids or food in her. She must wake up." Melody helped lift Elizabeth into a sitting position and eased behind her as Mary began switching out her bed robes and sponge bathing the princess' limp body. "She feels so frail."

"Yes. I hate seeing her like this myself." Mary stated quietly. "But we must not give up hope. Prince Clifton is only surviving on hope right now."

"The poor man." Melody's heart pained at the sickened sight of the handsome prince. His heart torn and completely bare and lying out on the floor for everyone to see his pain. It would not be long before he lost himself to his grief.

She smoothed Elizabeth's damp hair away from her face as Mary washed her delicate neck. "Hang in there, Elizabeth. Hang in there, my sweet friend."

∞

Alayna tossed the letter to the side and continued her perusal of the maps before her. She had barely slept, eaten, or left the Council Room since Samuel's departure. Now, two days later, she sat again in the stately chair her father once occupied and rummaged through her notes and maps to find a way to defeat Lancer.

"Your Grace?" Tomas bowed as he entered, the messenger following closely on his heels. "Did you not wish to respond to Prince Samuel's letter?"

Alayna looked up, her hair slightly standing on end from the use of her hands. Frazzled did not begin to describe her appearance as she smoothed a hand over the front of her skirts. "Yes, I have prepared a letter there." She pointed to the letter at the edge of the table. "I gave instructions to bring my sister back here to the North if her condition has not changed by the time Hector gives the letter to Prince Ryle."

"My Lady," Tomas stepped forward in surprise. "The princess should not be moved if she is in delicate condition."

"Did I ask for your approval, Tomas?" Alayna barked and then placed a steadying hand to her forehead and closed her eyes. "I am sorry, Tomas. I apologize for my outburst." She took a deep breath. "I know, but if she is to remain asleep until she passes, she should be here with me. Everyone should be. We should never have split up. There is too much at stake. Too much at stake." She mumbled as she dismissed them with a wave of her hand and began sifting through parchments again.

Tomas and Hector stepped into the hall and closed the door. "She is not well, Tomas." Hector whispered. "She has been in that room for far too long."

"It brings her comfort." Tomas stated.

"Tomas--"

"Enough. Now take this letter to Prince Ryle in the East."

"But her orders, Tomas. They are not wise."

"That is not for us to decide. She wants her sister here. She is the future queen and we must do her bidding. Now on with you." Tomas waved him away and cast a worried glance towards the Council Room doors. Granton would be proud of his daughter for focusing upon the needs of the Realm, but he certainly would not want her neglecting herself in the process.

∞

Isaac stormed into the castle and raced up the stairs to his chambers. "Pack my things. Quickly." He ordered as he grabbed his sword and sheath and belted it around his waist. "Have my horse saddled. I will ride ahead with Rupert and two guards. The rest of you come as quickly as possible. I do not have time to waste traveling with a carriage."

"Yes, my Lord." His attendants rushed around the room as a knock sounded on the door. He opened to find King Abner looming in the doorway.

"Yes, my Lord?" Isaac asked.

"May I ask the reason for your abrupt departure? You have only been here a day and a half."

"I apologize, my Lord, but urgent news has found me. Princess Elizabeth is gravely ill, and I must go to her at once."

"The Princess of the North?"

"Yes, though she now resides in the East."

"Ah, yes, Prince Clifton's new bride. Ill you say?"

"Yes. I shall return for a visit once I know her condition has been remedied." Isaac explained as he grabbed his satchel and pulled it over his head.

"And why must you go, Prince Isaac?"

Isaac stopped his pacing around the room and looked to the man. "Because she is a dear friend. She and Prince Clifton both. I must be there for the both of them through this hard time. I can only imagine what Clifton must be feeling-" He cut off his words and shook his head. "Never mind me, your Grace. I thank you for your hospitality and I hope to visit again soon."

"You are traveling to King Eamon's kingdom?" Abner asked again, his contemplative tone sending warning tingles up Isaac's spine.

"Yes."

"To help his son deal with the pain of possibly losing his wife?"

"Yes." Isaac repeated.

Abner waved his fingers over his shoulder and two guards walked into the room. "Please allow my guards to accompany you."

"Oh, that is not necessary, my Lord. I have plenty, and I must make haste."

"It is not a request, Prince Isaac."

Isaac hesitated a moment at the smug smile of Abner and then nodded. "Of course, your Grace. Thank you."

Abner nodded and stepped out of Isaac's way. Katarina awaited him at the base of the stairs. He stopped briefly and squeezed her hand. "Take care, Princess." She stepped towards him and cupped his face in her hand, knowing her father would suspect a budding relationship between the two of them. She leaned towards his ear. "Do not trust his guards, my Lord." She whispered quietly. Isaac pulled away to peer into her nervous gaze. "You will be alright if I leave?" He asked quietly.

She nodded. "Yes. I will. But you must be careful. Please."

He lightly kissed her cheek. "I will. Thank you, Katarina." She closed her eyes at the sweet gesture and did not open them until she heard the hooves of his horse galloping down the path.

"He will be back." Abner appeared beside her and Katarina forced a smile.

"I hope so. He is a kind man."

"That is the weakness of Granton's realm. They are all kind men."

"You see kindness as a weakness, Father?"

"Yes. The reason I sought the Prince from the West is that I had heard he was quite the opposite. Though after meeting him, I think him as weak as the rest of them."

Katarina shook her head. "I do not think so, Father. There's more to Prince Isaac than you know, I believe."

He turned towards his daughter and chuckled. "We shall see. How about you await him in the dining hall for dinner tonight, and you shall see how strong he is."

"Meaning?"

"Should he return for dinner, then he is just like the rest of them and was unable to beat my guards. I do not wish to offer King Eamon or his children any kindness, whether it be through my kingdom or Prince Isaac's return."

"You are going to kill him?"

"No. The guards are to bring him back here. If he is here by dinner then he is a weak man who found it easier to agree than to fight."

"And what if he does not arrive?"

"Then I underestimated him. I rarely underestimate people, my dear." King Abner lightly tugged on the edge of her hair. "Do not get too attached to the boy, Katarina. He is merely a pawn." She nodded at his retreating back, but then rushed up the stairs to her chambers praying Prince Isaac made it safely to his Realm and did not show up for dinner.

∞

Lancer trudged along the boundary line facing the Southern Kingdom. *He was never nervous about crossing, why was he nervous now?* He scanned both directions before stepping further towards the line. Taking a deep breath he stepped into the fog. Ripples of heat and pain flashed through his body as he was thrust back into the Unfading Lands and landed hard against the trunk of a tree. He groaned as he slowly stood to his feet. His horse nervously hooved the green earth and whinnied. He lightly patted a hand over its snout and glared at the boundary line. There was no reason for him not to be able to cross. He clenched his teeth and growled as he sprinted towards the line again, only to find his body flying through the air with even more force and landing upon his back on the ground in his own Land. He swiped a hand over the blood that trickled from his mouth. *He bit his tongue*, he realized, and allowed the taste of lead to fuel his anger. He took a deep breath and sprinted towards the line again with the same result. Again, and he flew into a tree. Again, and he landed against the legs of his horse and received a terrified kick to the ribs. Again, and crashed his skull against a large stone. When he awakened, again he tried. He attempted over and over again to cross, but to no avail. He sat, legs outstretched and hands in his hair as he struggled to comprehend the lack of his power. That is how Edward found him.

"My Lord!" Edward halted his horse and leapt to the ground running towards him. He knelt beside him and surveyed the weary expression upon Lancer's face. "Are you alright?"

"No." Lancer grumbled. "I am not alright, Edward!" His voice rose into a piercing yell and Edward stood with wide eyes of concern. Lancer pushed himself off of the ground and ran towards the boundary line again and flew past Edward towards the veil and then landed on the ground. Edward rushed towards him to help him up, Lancer shoving away his help. "I cannot cross!"

"At all?" Edward asked curiously.

"Did you not just see what happened?!" Lancer screamed, his eyes blazing and his appearance terrifying. *He was cracking*, Edward thought. The usual calm and collected man was completely losing his mind.

"This cannot be happening, Edward. I do not understand." Lancer raced towards the boundary line once more and his body retracted quickly, landing a few feet away from Edward. Pain laced Lancer's face, but he stood to his feet. "Something is wrong. The Lands must be weak. It's from all the cowards." He glowered at Edward. "The people that fled into our lands, the people that crossed to avoid death have lost me my strength! They must go, Edward. They must die. We must gain back our strength. I told you they would make us weak!" Lancer shoved his hands against Edward's chest and pushed him back a few feet.

Edward held up his hands in forfeit of a fight he did not wish to have. Lancer snarled and leapt into his saddle. "I will be in my reflection chamber, Edward. Should anyone need me, I will remain there until this problem is resolved."

Edward nodded as he watched Lancer ride away. He considered the boundary line a moment and then stepped towards it with a cautious hand raised. He inserted his hand into the fog and felt the shock and slap of energy pulse through him as his body was tossed back several feet. He could not cross either. Disappointment washed over him as he struggled to keep his temper in check. He did not wish for this darkness inside him just so he could stay here in the Lands. He just knew he would make it across to see his family.

Stupidity, he thought. Stupid of him to think he could just cross back over as if nothing happened. It was more than the darkness that allowed Lancer to cross. Yes, hate and evil maintained the boundary, but coupled with something else. Lancer's blood. The Lands started with him, it was his oath and seal that set the lines. Edward was merely a thorn in the side of evil. Pretty soon, Lancer would know what held him back, and when he found out, Edward's life would be over. Slumping his shoulders, he pulled himself into his saddle and set out towards his fellow Uniters. Confidence gone, he did not know what was in store for them all now. *How could he help the Realm if he was not able to cross?*

CHAPTER 4

Princess melody sat slowly weaving her needle in and out of the cream linen that rested in her lap. She intended to embroider a baby's toss towel for Princess Elizabeth. Several, in fact. Though Elizabeth was not with child just yet, Melody knew it was only a matter of time now that the Princess was wed to Prince Clifton. A royal baby. Melody's heart sighed. Oh how she longed to have children one day. Her mother had taught her the art of embroidery and Melody had mastered the skill at an early age. She also enjoyed the art. It took concentration and a detailed eye to create stitches into patterns. She sat quietly by Elizabeth's bedside and continued her work. *Perhaps I should have chosen a different pattern*, she thought. Prince Clifton and Princess Elizabeth had yet to even experience marriage, much less think of children. She sighed as she continued the routine. Hope. That is what Clifton needed. To hope. And she would, even if she was the only one. She continued with the pale blue pony stitching and thought of happier events. The royal wedding and the sight of her brother escorting Princess Elizabeth down the aisle. How hard it must have been for Isaac to hand over the woman he loved to another man. She shook away the thought. Her brother was more honorable than most gave him credit for, even himself. She could sense Prince Clifton knew of her brother's heart, but he did not seem upset by the inclination. Perhaps he knew Isaac would never overstep. Or, perhaps he knew if Isaac did, he would never step foot back into the Realm without being killed. That worried her.

She also worried about his journey back from King Abner's Realm. He should be arriving later in the evening if she timed it correctly. She gasped as she withdrew her finger from beneath the fabric and stuck it in between her lips to suck the small bead of blood the needle withdrew. Satisfied it had stopped, she went back to her stitching. A soft moan fluttered through the air and her gaze snapped up to Elizabeth. The Princess' brow beaded with sweat and Melody quickly jumped to her feet to find a damp cloth. She rang the bell on the bedside and watched as the doors opened and Arnos and Mary hurried inside.

"She moaned." Melody reported, lightly dabbing Elizabeth's head with the cool cloth.

Arnos leaned over Elizabeth's face and lightly rubbed his fingertips around her jaw line and behind her ears. He then reached for her wrist to check her pulse. A soft moan escaped her lips again and had them all lightly tending to her. "Fetch the prince." Arnos told Mary. "Our princess is waking up." Excitement laced his words, and Melody felt joy leap into her heart. She continued coddling Elizabeth with words of affirmation and tenderness until she heard the booted steps of Prince Clifton rushing through the door. "Out of my way, out of my way." He nudged around Arnos and sat on the edge of the bed leaning over his wife. "Elizabeth, love." He lightly traced his fingers down her cheek. "Can you hear me? Wake up." Elizabeth's lashes fluttered and a soft whimper slipped from her lips. Tears began pouring down Prince Clifton's cheeks as he cupped her face in his hands. "Come now, Elizabeth." He whispered and kissed her cheek. "Wake up, my love. Wake up." He gently laid his forehead upon her chest and no one bothered him. Ryle and King Eamon walked into the room, their expressions changing from joy to pain. "Did she pass?" Ryle asked Mary.

Mary shook her head. "No, my Lord. She is wanting to wake up, but having trouble."

Ryle stepped closer along with his father, who laid a comforting hand on Clifton's back as he spoke to his wife. Her lashes fluttered and slowly her eyelids opened to the ice storm in her eyes. Ryle smiled and choked back a laugh of relief. Elizabeth blinked several times in confusion and her hand slowly rose from her side and rested upon Clifton's hair. A soft smile tugged at her lips when she recognized whom it was that laid on her chest. Clifton's words silenced at her touch and his head popped up immediately. Joy instantly flooded his face as he grabbed her hand and kissed her knuckles.

Mary rushed forward with a glass of water and slowly helped Elizabeth take a few sips. She eased her head back against the pillows once more, her eyes struggling to stay awake. "She needs air." Arnos barked, stepping closer to her. Elizabeth's brow furrowed at the sight of the older man and she caught the amused expression of King Eamon. He nodded. "Nice to have you back with us, Princess." She reached her hand towards Clifton's as he sat watching Arnos tend to her. He felt her fingers brush over his and he quickly grabbed her hand and kissed it again. Her eyes warmed at the sight of him and he leaned forward and lightly brushed his lips over hers. "I have been worried about you, love." He brushed his fingers over her cheek and she closed her eyes to savor the feel of him. "H-how long have I been asleep?" Her voice was raw and crackled from lack of use and Mary offered her another drink of water that she consumed greedily.

"Almost a week." Ryle stated.

She eased her head back again out of breath. "What happened? Where am I?" She looked at the bed coverings and the drapes perplexed.

"You are in the Eastern Kingdom, my love. With me." Clifton brushed her hair back from her face. "We were journeying here after our wedding and your leg took a nasty infection that caused you to fall into a feverish slumber for a bit."

She searched his face and softly brushed her fingertips over his cheek and lips. "Have I been the only one?"

Ryle and Eamon laughed causing Elizabeth to softly smirk.

"No, Princess, your husband has just neglected his personal hygiene so as to never leave your side." Ryle teased.

Clifton turned a surprised glance towards Elizabeth and caught her weak smile. "You look… tired." She told him.

He brushed a hand over his bearded jaw and realized he could not remember the last time he had shaved. He remembered bathing the night before with orders from Melody, but he had not shaved. Now he wished he had.

Elizabeth attempted a small laugh but it came out as more of a sniff. "You are still handsome." She whispered. His green eyes sparkled as he bent to kiss her lips again.

Arnos stepped forward and waved a clean bandage wrap. "Okay, enough of that. You will have plenty of time for all that mushiness once we have gotten some food in her."

Clifton smirked and backed away so Arnos could check Elizabeth over. "I am Elizabeth." She introduced herself surprising the older man and he offered a smile. "I know who you are, my princess. I am Arnos, the healer for the Eastern Kingdom."

"My thanks to you, Mr. Arnos." She leaned forward and lightly kissed his cheek. The other men grinned as the older man blushed and fumbled with his tools. "Yes, well it was not just me. There have been several tending to you." He stood and began bustling about the room. Elizabeth's gaze settled upon Melody and she smiled and reached for her friend. "Melody." She whispered, a tear slipping from her eye. "I am so happy to see you."

"And I, you." Melody squeezed her hand.

"My sister?"

"She could not leave the North, my Lady." Mary stepped in and provided the answer they feared would upset Elizabeth, but she only nodded. "And Isaac?" She turned towards Melody.

"He does not know of your illness yet, my friend, but I assure you I sent a letter and he will be here as soon as he can." Elizabeth smiled at that news and looked to Samuel who appeared in the doorway.

"Is that the future king I see?"

Samuel bowed and nervously walked to the edge of her bed. "I am pleased to see you, your Grace." She waved away his formality. "A hug, Samuel." He walked forward and delicately hugged her. She eased back into the pillows and her smile was tired. "I am so full of joy at the moment. To see all of you."

"You must get some rest now." Arnos stated. "Everyone out, you can see her soon."

Clifton turned towards Arnos and Arnos rolled his eyes. "You can stay, but she needs her rest. I will send food up." Clifton nodded and watched as everyone exited and quietly closed the door.

He sat in the chair beside her bed and Elizabeth turned to face him. "Why do I have a feeling you have been occupying that chair a great deal lately?"

Clifton's lips cracked into a sad smile. "You had me worried."

"Worried? Over this?" She nodded in the direction of her leg. "Come now, my Prince, we have been through tougher things than this."

"No, Princess, we have not. I thought I was going to lose you." He kissed her hand and held it to his rough cheek. "I never want to feel that way again."

Elizabeth sighed and leaned her head back into her pillows. "We are married now." She stated to the ceiling.

"Aye, we are."

"I did not make a very good first impression with the East, now did I?" She smirked, and he shook his head. "Don't even think of that. There is plenty of time for that, my love."

"I had high hopes of it being quite different. I am sorry to have caused such chaos and worry."

"This is not your fault. We pushed you too hard. You should have rested for weeks and yet we had you walking around and abusing your body and preventing your leg from healing." Clifton eased onto the side of the bed and sat next to her. "It is I who should apologize, Elizabeth. I should have seen to your care better."

"Then we are both to blame. I am not one to be idle and did not give myself the needed time. But now, I am here, and I am awake, and I am your wife." She smiled as she pulled him towards her and kissed him sweetly on the lips. "And I would like you to bring me food."

He laughed as her eyes sparkled and he grinned. "I will check on that for you, my wife." He kissed her again and walked to the door as Arnos walked in carrying a bowl of broth. Clifton intercepted it and brought it back to her. He eased the tray over her legs. "Would you like me to help you?"

"I wish I could be stubborn and say I wish to do it myself, but I fear I feel rather weak." Elizabeth admitted.

"Yes, you will feel that way for a few days, I think. Your body needs nourishment. Perhaps we can get you strong enough so that by the time Prince Isaac arrives you will have your wits about you to deal with that man." Elizabeth giggled as she accepted a spoonful of broth. "That is delicious."

"Only because you have not eaten in a week." Clifton stated, making her smile.

"I may not have eaten in a week, but I have had very vivid dreams in my slumber."

"Have you now?" He asked curiously. "And what did you dream of?" He spooned her more broth and she sighed as the warm liquid settled comfortably in her stomach.

"I dreamt of you and me. For some reason we were in a field of flowers." She closed her eyes as if to draw the dream to life again in her mind. "Silly notion, I guess. A girl's dream of her love."

"I like your dream." Pleased she had thought of him, Clifton spooned her the last of the broth and set the tray aside. "You should probably rest now, my love."

She nodded as he turned to leave. "Are you not staying with me?"

He stopped and looked at her. "I was going to clean up a bit." He brushed a hand over his roughened face and she smiled. "Perhaps you could leave it a while longer and stay with me?"

He nodded and walked towards the chair beside her bed. "Is this to be our room?" Her gaze travelled around the fine furnishings and the stately bed. He nodded. "It is. Though you may change whatever you wish when you are up to it."

"I wouldn't change a thing." She stated confidently, her blue eyes landing on him once more. "Except…" She continued.

"What is that, my love?"

"Except I would have you lie next to me and hold me." She smiled at him and the flash of relief that crossed his face as he kissed her firmly on the lips warmed her heart. "I think I can do that, my love." He eased onto the bed and Elizabeth turned to curl into his embrace. Mere minutes later, they both fell asleep.

∞

Later that evening the dining hall was alive with happiness at Princess Elizabeth's awakening. King Eamon raised his glass and toasted to health. Ryle glanced at the empty chair of his brother. "Should I retrieve Cliff?"

"No. Last Arnos checked, your brother was asleep next to his wife. He needs his rest as well." Eamon reported.

"Ah, and here we are." Eamon grinned as he waved a hand for the servants to enter, and everyone cast confused expressions towards the elaborate cake set upon the table.

"A cake, Father?" Ryle asked. "Yes, it is a joyous occasion, but to celebrate without Elizabeth and Cliff?"

"This cake is not for Elizabeth or Clifton. It is for Samuel."

Samuel straightened in his chair and turned in shock towards the kind king.

"It is his birthday."

Ryle and Melody both smiled at the shy prince as he bowed his head in thanks.

"I did not realize anyone knew." Samuel stated.

"Of course I knew." King Eamon boasted. "Now let us celebrate, not only our princess waking up, but also our kind friend's birthday. To King Samuel." Eamon raised his goblet along with the rest of them and soaked in the image of happiness that surrounded his table. A shuffled gate rounded the corner as Clifton emerged. "Celebrating without me?" He rubbed a tired hand over his face and slid into his chair.

"I thought you would still be asleep and did not wish to disturb you." Eamon replied.

"Aye, well Arnos was bustling about and sleep was hard to come by. Elizabeth is resting though, and that is what matters."

"Yes," Eamon answered. "We are celebrating Samuel's birthday, son."

Clifton turned and offered a kind smile. "Well now, that is something worth celebrating." He lightly patted Samuel on the back as he accepted his plate of dinner and began eating heartily.

"I wish I had known it was to be your birthday, Samuel. I would have brought you a gift from the West." Melody slipped a piece of cake in her mouth and smiled at the sweetness of the baked treat.

"Your presence was gift enough, my Lady." Samuel replied, his eyes holding hers for a long pause until Melody lightly flushed and looked away. The other men exchanged amused expressions as they watched the exchange.

Arnos ventured into the dining hall and cleared his throat. Clifton bolted to his feet. "Is she alright, Arnos?"

"Yes, my Lord. Please be seated. I just wished to inform you she was awake."

Clifton stood again and Arnos waved him back to his chair. "No, my Lord. She asked me to tell you to stay and enjoy dinner with your family. For she wishes to have a warm bath drawn and a plate of food brought to her. Mary is assisting her with the bath and will retrieve her dinner soon. I just wished to report that she is doing well. I will check on her once more before calling it a night."

"Thank you, Arnos, for your attentive service." King Eamon waved him towards a chair. "Join us."

Arnos' mouth opened in surprise, but he quickly closed it and eased into a chair. His mouth watered at the sight of the warm cake on the pedestal in the middle.

"It is the future King Samuel's birthday." Clifton explained, following Arnos' gaze.

"Aye, happy wishes to you." Arnos nodded towards Samuel.

"Thank you, sir." Samuel replied.

Clifton reached to hand Arnos a plate of bread when a loud thunder of voices boomed from the main hall. Eamon's brow furrowed as he waved his guards and attendants to go see what the commotion was about.

∞

Isaac guided his horse through the thick forests of King Abner's Valleylands at a pace unmatched by Abner's guards. He had lost them at the last bend and intended to leave them all together. He prayed they did not stop the pursuit of his carriage further back. Rupert rode beside him, easily keeping stride and both hunkered down against the strong winds that carried the promise of rain to come. He heard the pounding of hooves behind him and the two guards of the Valleylands emerged from the tree line. Isaac slapped his reins harder and gritted his teeth as his hands ached from his tight grip. Branches snagged against his cape and tunic and several scraped along his face as he and Rupert trudged through the forest. He felt the ground shift from forest to rock and the unstable terrain took his horse by surprise. The stumble cost them both and Isaac found himself thrown from the saddle and rolling down a sharp, rock encrusted hill. Rupert halted and dismounted, sliding and sprinting his way to the valley to retrieve him. Abner's guards followed quickly behind. Isaac groaned as he slowly rose to his feet. He withdrew his sword and forced Rupert behind him. "Stay here."

Abner's guards held up their swords as well.

"Gentlemen, I do not wish to create enemies here. I must leave. I promised King Abner I would return. What is the meaning of this?" Isaac called out to them.

"Our orders are to bring you back to the king." One of the guards called.

"I am afraid we are at an impasse then. I must leave for my own Realm. It is dire." Isaac stepped forward and felt the blade of one of the guards hit his own and soon a battle engaged. He thwarted off the hits and lunges with expertise, and his fury grew with each passing stroke. He ran and slammed his shoulders into the man's middle and sent them both to the ground. He heard his own guards battling the second man. He held his sword at the guard's throat. "I do not wish to kill you." Isaac spat. "But I will, if you keep me against my will."

The guard's eyes were wide with fear, his obvious assignment not turning out how he planned. His grip on his sword loosened and it dropped next to his side. Isaac smirked in approval as he pulled the man to his feet and shoved him away. The swords behind him stopped and he turned to find Abner's other guard slowly retreating towards his partner. Isaac stepped closer to them, his eyes narrowed in rage. "Please tell your king I will not be detained like some prisoner. I am the Prince of the West, and my allegiance is to my own realm. Should he hinder my journey any further, I will kill any guards he sends after me."

The guards shuffled back a few steps and Isaac turned towards Rupert.

"You trust they will not follow the caravan?" Rupert asked nervously.

Isaac turned to the two guards. Shaking their heads in fear, Isaac walked over to the first guard. "I apologize, but my attendant is right to question. How can I be sure King Abner will not attack my caravan? I must send him a message and unfortunately, you are my message." Isaac brought his blade down quickly, slicing through the man's flesh, his hand falling to the ground as his screams disrupted the quiet forest. Isaac took a deep breath as he eyed the other guard. "Take him to your king," he barked, as he bypassed them and climbed back into his saddle. "Come Rupert, we have much ground to cover."

Isaac heaved a small sigh of relief when he finally passed into the Realm of Alayna. His eyes set upon the Eastern Kingdom, he had a ways to go. He would make it by nightfall at the earliest. Abner's small delay had cost him precious minutes, and he would never forgive the selfish king if Elizabeth passed away before he arrived to see her.

∞

Ryle rose to his feet as the calamity of chaos began filtering closer towards the dining hall, his hand resting on the hilt of his sword until a familiar voice rang through the air. "Get your hands off of me!" He watched as Prince Isaac stepped through the doorway with a scowl at the Eastern guard who followed his every step. Clifton turned and his face split into a smile as he stood. "I was wondering when you would arrive." He walked towards Isaac and placed a greeting hand on his shoulder, his smooth gaze washing over the Western prince's obvious injuries. "I have had quite a journey."

"It looks like it." Clifton replied. "I'm glad you have come."

"How is she?" Isaac quickly removed his pelt and cape and handed them to Rupert.

"She is awake and slowly gaining her strength back."

Isaac's shoulders dropped with relief and he smiled. "That is great news. May I see her?"

Clifton nodded. "Come with me."

Without greeting the others in the room, Prince Isaac hurried after Clifton towards Elizabeth's chambers.

Mary stood outside the door and she smiled warmly at the sight of Prince Clifton. Her smile slightly faltered at the sight of Prince Isaac.

"Miss Mary," Clifton greeted. "Is my wife ready to receive company?"

"Arnos is with her now, my Lord. I am sure he would not mind."

Clifton opened the door and Elizabeth smiled up at him. "How was the feast?" She asked, her eyes searching his hands for a plate of her own. "Did you not bring me some dinner?"

"Is food all you think about now?" Clifton teased. She grinned and nodded. "I feel as if I could eat a horse."

Arnos shook his head sternly.

"Okay, perhaps not a horse, but at least a warm roll with my broth."

Arnos nodded in approval and Elizabeth lightly patted his hand.

"Say I brought you something much better than a horse?" Clifton offered with a small smirk and a wink.

"Oh?" Elizabeth asked, as she situated comfortably against the pillows.

"Yes." Clifton turned towards the door and Isaac entered. Elizabeth's smile widened as Isaac stood like a statue and studied her. Clifton saw it then, what Ryle had tried to tell him. The love on the prince's face was undeniable. He turned his attention to his wife and though excited, he saw only warmth and friendship in her gaze. Of that he was grateful.

"I would say he is *much* better than a horse." Elizabeth beamed up at Clifton and squeezed his hand. "Are you just going to stand there Isaac, or might I have a welcoming embrace?"

Isaac placed a hand over his heart as he rushed forward and enveloped Elizabeth tightly in his arms. He lightly inhaled the scent of rose and closed his eyes in gratitude that she was alive. He released her and eased into the chair offered by Prince Clifton. "I will leave you two to catch up. My wife wishes for some delicious dinner." He winked at Elizabeth. "I will bring you a plate as well, Isaac."

"Thank you." He nodded at Clifton, an undercurrent of mutual understanding passing between the two men.

"You look quite rough, Prince Isaac. What happened?" Elizabeth's concerned gaze washed over him and he lightly clasped her hand. "I ran into a bit of a squabble."

"A squabble? You? Why, I would never have thought such a thing." She teased.

His lips twitched with a small smile as his warm observation surveyed her frail frame. "You look… delicate." His voice was low and pained by what he saw and Arnos shot a curious glance towards their interaction.

"I have lost a bit of weight recently… then again I guess that is what is to be expected. Arnos is making quick work of making me feel like my normal self though." She flashed the old healer a sweet smile. "And Clifton has been fluttering over me quite attentively."

"I imagine so." Isaac stated. "It pains me to see you like this. I am sorry I did not arrive sooner."

"Why would sooner have been better? I was asleep." Elizabeth pointed out. "If you ask me, your arrival was perfectly timed. Now tell me, why are you so scraped up and bruised?"

Isaac sighed as he leaned back in the chair and crossed his arms. "I took a trip to the Realm of King Abner."

Elizabeth leaned forward in interest. "Really? What's it like? Is he as friendly as my father said?"

"Quite the contrary, actually." Isaac stated. "He seemed friendly at first, but he did not wish for me to leave and had obstacles placed in my path to prevent me from crossing back into our Realm. I have learned much from the trip. His eldest daughter, Katarina, was quite open with me about the realm's history."

"Katarina. That's a pretty name." Elizabeth commented.

Isaac nodded. "I fear for her life as well as her sisters'. Their father is a vicious man it would seem."

"You care for her?" Elizabeth asked with a hopeful smile.

Isaac shrugged. "I only spoke with her a few times. I had only arrived there the day before yesterday. Not much time to establish relationships of value."

"Yet you worry for her." Elizabeth pointed out.

"Now listen here Princess, I did not come all this way to talk of me. I came to see you." Isaac playfully tried to change the subject but Elizabeth defiantly crossed her arms making him laugh.

"Fine. You have seen me. I am slowly gaining my strength back and before you know it I will be walking around this castle and able to parry blades with you like before."

"Is that so? That confident, huh?" Isaac smiled smugly as Clifton entered. "Your wife is threatening to beat me at the sword soon, Prince Clifton."

Clifton's face sobered. "Elizabeth, it will take time for you to heal, my love. Much time. I do not wish you to even attempt such a thing until we know you are fully healed."

She swatted Isaac's arm for making Clifton worry and then squeezed her husband's hand. "I know, Clifton. Isaac is just baiting me. Come, sit with us. Isaac was just telling me of his trip to King Abner's Realm and his beautiful daughter, Katarina."

Clifton's brows rose in interest.

Isaac shook his head and caught the pleased smile of Elizabeth of placing him on the hot seat in regard to a woman. "Yes, King Abner may be a threat, I'm afraid. I do not think he is pleased with my departure. And I am certain he will not approve of the message I sent back with his guards."

"Why is that?" Clifton asked.

"Let's just say, he should be wary of toying with the Western Kingdom for quite some time. I have much to report. Though I feel the future queen needs to hear what I have to say. I do not wish to divulge anything without her present."

"She is not here." Elizabeth explained. "Alayna remains in the North for now. But I'm sure she would love your company should you feel the need to report your news to her in person."

"I just arrived, Princess. You already trying to toss me out?"

Elizabeth laughed, the sound smooth and inviting and healthy. Clifton grinned at his wife.

"Now, I know it would not be that easy to get rid of you, Prince Isaac."

He nodded.

"Once I am allowed to move from this bed, I imagine we will make great haste in arriving in the North to see my sister's coronation. Right?" She turned to Clifton as he nodded.

"Only when Arnos says it is okay for you travel." Clifton replied, nodding towards the healer who lingered at the edge of the bed.

"I am sure Arnos will clear me soon." Elizabeth commented. "I feel significantly better already. We should be able to reattach my falsey in the next day or so and be on our way."

Isaac and Clifton shared amused smirks at her strong will as Arnos stepped forward immediately to dissuade her conversation. "No, my Princess, you will not be able to do so. It will be weeks before I allow such a thing. You may be able to travel soon, but walking upon your—injury— will take much needed time."

"Then it is settled. I do not need to walk just yet." Elizabeth nodded in affirmation of her plan as she tore a piece of bread from Isaac's dinner plate. Her eyes caught the small dish of sweet cake set to the side. "Is that milk cake?"

"Yes, it is." Clifton nudged it towards her and she slipped a small bite into her mouth and sighed in pleasure.

"It is in honor of Samuel's birthday."

Her tanzanite eyes sparkled. "His birthday?! How exciting!"

Arnos stepped forward and handed Elizabeth a small goblet of medicine. She snarled her nose at the smell and looked at him. "It is necessary, my Lady."

She swallowed the bitter drink and cringed as it made its way to her stomach. "She still needs her rest." Arnos warned the two men.

Elizabeth's eyelids began to droop, and her breathing began to slow into steady deep breaths. "I wish for you to stay a bit longer." Elizabeth mumbled, her words slurring as she fell asleep. Clifton removed the tray of food from her lap and pulled her blankets further around her for comfort. Isaac watched carefully. "She is frail."

"Yes, very. She does not realize it, but she is much weaker than she believes." Clifton added.

"You have tended her well. Melody spoke of bringing our healer here with her. Has he been of use?" Isaac looked to Arnos.

"His knowledge in medicine has helped with the healing process." Arnos reported, nodding towards the goblet.

"Good." Isaac stated. He stood and lightly brushed Elizabeth's hair from her forehead and gently placed a kiss on her soft skin. Clifton walked with him to the door. "Thank you for coming, Isaac. I want to hear of your journey to Abner's Realm, but fear I, myself, am too tired at the moment."

Isaac patted him on the back. "No worries, my friend. You have been through much the last few days. I am grateful Elizabeth has you to look after her. She is special to me."

"I know." Clifton replied.

Isaac shifted on his feet. "I want you to know, Clifton, that… I know I have been a harsh man in the past. And even somewhat— immoral. But I do care for Elizabeth. She has helped me a great deal. But I also want you to know, that I would never overstep the bonds of friendship."

Clifton shook his hand and smiled. "I know."

His simple answer set Isaac's heart at ease.

"Now go get some rest yourself, Isaac. You look as if you need it."

Isaac nodded and turned to walk towards the main dining hall once more to find his sister.

∞

Two weeks passed, and Alayna found herself anxiously awaiting the arrival of her sister and the rest of the Realm's allies. She knew it was much to ask of her sister's transport, but she had to see her. She turned to Jessa, her attendant. "I need you to make sure Princess Elizabeth's chambers are properly suited for her and Prince Clifton. Drapes should be opened to overlook the gardens."

"Yes, milady." Jessa bowed.

"And make sure the third level chambers are properly dressed for the Western royals." Alayna continued as she made her way down the winding stairwell to the main hall. She heard the rustling of the heavy drapes being drawn and light fluttered into the castle and brightened, not only her mood, but also the interior halls. "Fresh bouquets in the conservatory and dining hall." She turned to two maids who awaited instruction. She pressed a hand to her forehead and turned towards the kitchens. Gretchen rushed by and Alayna lightly grabbed her arm. "Please make sure there are plenty of desserts for this evening. I want it to be a celebration."

"Yes, my Princess."

Alayna glanced up as the first sound of hooves filtered through the open castle windows. Hooves on cobblestones, she could not remember the last time she had longed for that sound. She excitedly rushed across the room as two guards opened the front castle doors. A smile split her face as she spotted King Anthony descending from his carriage. Without invitation or formality, she rushed forward and embraced the older man. Laughing, he pulled away from her and smiled proudly. "It is good to see you, my future Queen."

"You as well, King Anthony. I hope your journey was swift and comfortable."

"Indeed. Am I the first to arrive?"

"Yes, I fear I do not know when everyone else will arrive."

"No worries dear. I am glad to be the first and to receive such a warm welcome." King Anthony studied Alayna's strained features closely not revealing his notice of the fact the princess showed signs of exhaustion.

"Well, you must be tired from your ride. Please come inside and feel free to rest. We have set up your quarters in the same landing of the castle as before, if that suits you." Alayna turned to escort him inside when they heard hooves traveling up the front entrance. Glancing in the direction of the sound, Alayna's eyes lit with pleasure as Prince Ryle entered the market square and headed towards the castle entrance. When Ryle dismounted, Alayna ran and jumped into his arms, taking everyone by surprise, including him. He smiled as he enveloped her in return and swung her in a brief circle, her feet dangling above the ground. He gently set her on her feet and she pulled away with a wide smile of welcome and relief. "It is good to have you back."

He nodded. "Aye, it is good to be back." His blue eyes remained on her face as her warm brown gaze studied him a moment, they then travelled to his horse and she tenderly pet its snout. "I am so happy for everyone returning." Alayna waved for the two men to follow her inside, King Anthony casting a welcoming nod to the Eastern prince.

"How much further behind are the carriages?" Alayna asked as she escorted them into the conservatory.

"Should not be too long now. I imagine your sister and my brother will be the last to arrive. I fear Arnos, our healer, had many misgivings on her traveling. His worry somewhat delayed them." Ryle explained.

"As long as they are coming, I am perfectly fine." Alayna beamed. "So tell me, did Samuel make it safely and enjoy his journey to the East? I hear Princess Melody and Prince Isaac also joined you there."

"Yes, my future Queen, they did. It was a nice surprise." Ryle smiled reassuringly at Alayna as she toiled with her cuffs at her wrists. King Anthony sat talking to Mosiah, the former Captain of the Guard, completely unaware of the undercurrents of attraction floating about the room.

"You seem well." Ryle continued, looking Alayna over with a critical eye. "Tired, but well."

"Why thank you, Captain. A woman loves to hear she looks tired." Alayna scoffed in surprise at his gumption and lightly blushed as she turned back towards the Western king.

"I did not mean to offend you, my Queen. I-"

"Future Queen." Alayna corrected.

Ryle cleared his throat. "Of course. Future Queen. I just meant you looked as if you have been working hard on something. I'm assuming within the walls of the Council Room."

Her brow rose slightly, and she tilted her head, a rogue blonde curl slipping from its pin and lightly draping over her shoulder. "I guess you will find out once we convene."

He crossed his arms over his broad chest and narrowed his gaze. "I guess so, unless you would like to tell me now."

"I would not." Alayna quipped. "It is best to share with everyone at the same time. Less breaths that way."

"But I am the Captain of your guard. I should be the first to know of any information or advances within the Realm." Ryle's back stiffened as he awaited her reply. Instead of the acquiescence of a response, Alayna laughed and waved his comment away. "I assure you, Captain, that I will keep you informed, I just wish to focus upon other things at the moment." Her smile remained, but her eyes held a silent demand for him to back down. He uncrossed his stance and sat regally in an open chair across from King Anthony and Mosiah. Mosiah's rich eyes bounced between the two in amusement.

Alayna reached over and squeezed his hand. "So tell me Captain Ryle, what did my sister think of the Eastern Kingdom?"

He smiled warmly. "It is a beautiful place. I feel she has found it quite welcoming. It is so full of light, the very halls of the castle feel like ballrooms filled with happiness now that she has awakened."

"I have never experienced the Eastern Kingdom myself," Alayna added. "Though I aim to soon. I have heard of its beauty since I was a child. It warms my heart to know my sister will have a beautiful place to live."

"The Northern Kingdom is quite beautiful too, future Queen. I noticed the lands have recovered quite well and the rebuilding has been quite successful."

"Yes," Alayna replied. "We have been most vigilant in making sure the villagers have been able to create new homes and reestablish their lands. We are fortunate to have such a loving and helpful people. Everyone is helping one another, it seems."

"As they should." King Anthony interrupted and nodded his two cents into the conversation. "A kingdom is only as strong as its weakest link."

Alayna's back straightened. "Weakest link, my Lord?"

"Yes. The villagers. If your people are weak, the kingdom is weak. It is always encouraging to see a quick recovery after a war. That means your people, your kingdom, is strong."

"I see." Alayna replied, casting a curious glance towards Ryle to make note of King Anthony's comment. "And how were things in the west, my Lord? Was your kingdom happy for your return?"

"Quite." Anthony shifted in his seat and cleared his throat. "Everything was as it should be. Though I sent Isaac to the Realm of King Abner upon our arrival."

"Yes, Melody had explained that to us in the east." Ryle supplied, his tone indicating he wished to know the reasons behind the king's decision.

"I think it will do Isaac well. Abner has been a peaceful neighbor for years and it is no secret he has a plethora of daughters. I wished for Isaac to travel to his kingdom and seek a bride."

Alayna's surprise could not be hidden as she listened to the king.

"I have yet to hear word of his journey, but knowing Isaac he has delved straight into his task with a happy mind."

"Actually, my Lord," Ryle began, "Your son's trip to Abner's Realm was cut short, so to speak."

Anthony's face tightened. "Did something happen to my son?"

"No, my Lord. Sorry to worry you." Ryle relaxed and forced a polite smile. "It's just that, well, when Isaac heard of Princess Elizabeth's condition, he came immediately to the east."

"Princess Elizabeth?! Who would tell him of her affliction?"

"Princess Melody, your Grace."

"Melody?!" King Anthony's face turned to a deeper shade of pink as anger flooded from his every pore. "I specifically told her NOT to inform her brother. How could she deliberately disobey me? She will be punished. There is no excuse for her actions."

"My Lord, she knew Prince Isaac would want to know." Ryle interjected. "Princess Elizabeth is mighty dear to him. He would have been devastated if something fatal had happened and he did not know."

King Anthony glanced from one face to another. "No. Melody knew my wishes. She was to go and see to the princess alone. Isaac was to be left to his vices in King Abner's Realm. He was to find a wife. He was to find a distraction!" The king angrily rose to his feet and began to pace, muttering under his breath of the scolding Prince Isaac would receive upon his arrival.

"A distraction?" Alayna asked, interrupting his gait and causing a lethal gaze to shoot her way.

"Yes. He needed to go someplace Princess Elizabeth did not exist. He needed to forget about her."

"W-why would he need to forget about her?" Alayna asked quietly.

"Isn't it quite obvious, Princess, my son is in love with your sister." King Anthony barked in disgust. "He needed to go away and rid himself of those feelings."

Alayna inhaled several deep breaths. Her stomach tightening at the announcement of Isaac's feelings. "He told you of his feelings?"

"Of course not!" Anthony bellowed. "But it is written all over him. Why else would his actions change?"

"Perhaps your son's mentality was altered by the battle against the South." Alayna answered. "My father used to say that character was defined on the battlefield."

Anthony studied Alayna a moment and then glanced to Ryle, his patience clearly gone. "I do not wish to speak of this anymore."

He straightened his tunic and quickly walked out of the conservatory.

"My goodness." Alayna mumbled softly. "Can you believe such words? Poor Prince Isaac... being sent away so soon after arriving home."

"I do not believe King Anthony's perceptions are too far from the truth, my Princess." Ryle stated softly.

Alayna turned to him in surprise. "What do you mean?"

"I too, have sensed Isaac's feelings towards your sister. I believe he cares for her more... more than he lets on."

"That is absurd." Alayna stood and brushed a hand over the front of her dress. "Prince Isaac is one of the most flirtatious and philandering men I have ever met. Though I do believe his character has changed but a smidgen, I still believe he is the same incessant womanizer as before. He and Elizabeth do have a friendship, a strong one, and yes, she believes him to be a changed man, but he is NOT in love with her."

Alayna's caramel gaze bounced between Mosiah and Ryle, both holding the same doubtful face.

"Y-you think this too, Mosiah?"

Mosiah slightly tugged at the collar of his emerald tunic and sighed reluctantly. "I do not know, your Grace. I do not know the prince as well as the rest of you, but I do sense he cares for her deeply."

Alayna looked to Ryle again. "And how does your brother, Prince Clifton, feel of Isaac?"

"He senses something, but does not seem worried about it. Though I have warned him to be watchful."

"Warned him to be watchful?!" Alayna held a hand to her forehead as if the topic at hand was beginning to cause a dull ache. She then looked to the two men. "I do not want to hear another word of this… this-this-this topic of conversation. Elizabeth and Clifton are married. Clifton does not need doubts of his wife's affections. And I assure you my sister loves Clifton. She is only a friend to Prince Isaac."

"We did not say the princess carried feelings, my Lady." Mosiah interrupted. "Just that we thought Isaac did."

"I don't care!" Alayna's voice rose as she scolded him. "Neither of you are to say anything to anyone on the matter. It sleeps, never to rise again. Is that understood?"

"Alayna," Ryle rose and stepped towards her, "You must not turn a blind eye to this. Due to Prince Isaac's unpredictable character, we must at least keep an open eye towards his intentions and interactions with Elizabeth." He lightly squeezed her hand and she jerked it away.

"Not a word." She reminded them forcefully, pulling her skirts in a swish of movement as she stormed away belting orders for more flower arrangements for the grand hall.

CHAPTER 5

"How are you feeling?"

Elizabeth blew a breath of exasperation. "I am fine. I am the same fine I was two breaths ago when you asked me." She glanced at Clifton and he smirked.

"I am just worried we are pushing your recovery too soon." He lightly clasped her hand and squeezed, pleased she accepted the gesture.

"I assure you, Clifton, that I am feeling almost my old self. Though I do not have my falsie attached, I feel fine." Elizabeth's tone was final, and she caught the amused grin of Prince Isaac across from them. "Don't look so smug, Isaac."

The Western prince laughed and brushed a palm over his forbidden smile. "I am not smug, Princess, I am amused."

"Amused? By what?"

"By your hard head."

Elizabeth's eyes widened at his statement and she felt Clifton stifle a chuckle at her astonished face. She crossed her arms and tilted up her chin. "I see. Well, it is because of my *hard head* that I was able to pull through like I did."

"That is true." Isaac pointed out. "But must it be so hard for you to accept the fact your husband cares for your wellbeing?"

Elizabeth shifted her gaze from Isaac to Clifton. "I know my husband cares for me, and I appreciate his concern, but I am also not a child. I do not need to be coddled."

"I am sorry if I have made you feel that way." Clifton softly spoke, his words near her ear and sending chills up her arms. She turned to him and saw the uncertainty in his eyes. She briefly claimed his lips in a light kiss and turned back towards Isaac. The Western prince refocused his attention out the side window of the carriage as they journeyed on, his thoughts traveling over the lands to Abner's Realm and Princess Katarina. He hoped her father did not learn of her providing him insight. He aimed to return to Abner's Realm as soon as he finished in the North. Perhaps he should send a letter. *No. He could not guarantee the safety of the messenger.* He sighed as he glanced at his hands in his lap, slowly rotating his thumbs over one another. His father would be furious with him for leaving so abruptly. He would probably kill him if he knew the full extent of Isaac's behavior and attack on Abner's guard. *Best to keep that to himself,* he thought, as his gaze shifted over to Prince Clifton and Princess Elizabeth, the happy newlyweds. His chest tightened at the thought of never having such a relationship. Elizabeth had made him see that. Though he knew he could not have her as his bride, she had awoken a new desire in his heart. He actually wanted what she represented. A partner. A wife. A queen. He could see the love between the two, the care and the tenderness. Prince Clifton was a good man before, but his love for Elizabeth and the love from Elizabeth had only made the man stronger. Isaac wanted that. *Was it possible for him to find such a relationship? Was he even worthy of such a thing after all he had done in his life?* His attention then turned to Elizabeth's words as she pointed out the side of the carriage.

"We should all make a trip to the clearing to see my brother."

"We will see." Clifton added sweetly, as he nodded towards Isaac.

"No, we will go." Elizabeth corrected. "Though I cannot walk, I can still ride. I need to see Edward. And I guarantee he needs to see that I am alive and well."

"Let us arrive and rest and see how you are feeling. Then we can determine if a trip to the boundary line is to be made." Clifton's voice held a slight tone of finality that Isaac had never heard from the prince. Apparently, Elizabeth had never heard it either, because her dark brows rose slightly into her hairline at the prince's obvious frustration. Clifton glanced out the opposite window avoiding his wife's probing gaze.

Isaac caught Elizabeth's surprised blue eyes and shrugged his shoulders. He saw the small flash of hurt in her eyes at her husband's annoyance, but true to Elizabeth form, she rolled back her shoulders, tilted that ever so slightly pointed chin and glanced out the window. Isaac shook his head. Prince Clifton had met his match. Elizabeth was stubborn, but he agreed with Clifton. If she did not look out for her own wellbeing, they would do it for her. Though she was able to make a trip in a carriage, she was still healing and recovering.

∞

"You seem quiet, my Lord." Melody broke the silence as Samuel sat across from her, his shoulders slightly jostling with the movements of the carriage.

"I am just thinking, I guess."

"About what?"

Samuel's cheeks slightly flushed, and his shoulders shrugged.

"About your kingdom?"

"Yes." He admitted. "It will not be long before I must go back. I wonder if my absence has gone on for too long and the south is beyond recovery."

"Of course not. I am sure the future queen has seen to it that your borders are secure and your people are eager for your return." Melody reached across and lightly squeezed his hand in reassurance, the action causing them both to stiffen and her to quickly retreat.

"How was your journey back to the West?" Samuel asked.

"Quite well. My father and I fell into our usual routine quite smoothly. It was rather lonely without my brother, but thankfully I was sent for from the East before I was to be too lonely." She smiled. "I am so glad Elizabeth has recovered. I could not imagine the Realm without her presence."

"She is quite the bond." Samuel agreed. "I know the future queen was quite nervous of her departure from the North."

"I imagine so." Melody added. "The two sisters are quite close. I imagine it will take some getting used to. As well as the princes from the East. They too have never been separated for longer than a month."

"Though Prince Clifton will now have Princess Elizabeth." Samuel explained. "I am sure they will keep one another company quite well. And Captain Ryle seems very eager to please the future queen, so I do not see either of them becoming lonely either."

"And what of you?" Melody asked. "Once you are back in the South?"

He shrugged again, a habit, she realized, that made the young, future king more endearing. "I do not know. I do fear that my positive new relations will become strained, due to lack of familiarity once I depart. But I also hope to be more present amongst the Realm than my father was. Though he ran a tight regime, the South was secluded. I wish to embrace the friendship of the other kingdoms in hopes that, not only will I not be lonely, but that my kingdom will not be lonely either."

"You have a good heart, Samuel." Melody smiled warmly.

"As do you, Princess."

"I hope to visit the South once you are king. I aim to visit all the kingdoms regularly. I also wish to maintain familiarity amongst the Realm. I have found the last few months, though devastating in some regards, have been quite wonderful in building relationships amongst one another." She brushed a hand over the red silk of her dress and smiled at him. "Perhaps you could give me a tour of your kingdom when I come visit."

Samuel's heart pounded at the thought, and he caught the small, uncertain smile of Melody as her dark eyes sought his.

"I would be honored." His voice lightly wavered and he cleared his throat as the carriage pulled to a halt and the sound of hooves ceased.

"Have we already arrived?" Melody asked, leaning towards the small window. Samuel lightly placed a hand on hers as she reached to open the door. He slowly reached for the hilt of his sword. "No, my lady, we have not. Our stopping is suspicious. Please, stay put." He hastily retreated from the carriage and Melody worried her hands in her lap at the possibilities of a halting entourage. Robbery, assault, attack, her mind whirled with dark scenarios. She gasped when Samuel's face appeared in the small opening of the window. "All is well, Princess." He opened the door and extended his hand inside. She grabbed it and allowed him to help her down the small stepladder to the forest floor. She glanced up to see Prince Clifton holding Princess Elizabeth in his arms and easing her to a small stool. Elizabeth's face split into a smile as she spotted Melody.

"Why have we stopped?" Melody asked, looking from one face to another.

"We decided to stretch our legs a bit, sister." Isaac explained.

"Make that, *they* decided to stretch their legs." Elizabeth corrected with a wink.

Isaac glanced down at the Eastern princess and rolled his eyes at her remark, knowing she attempted to make light of her injury, while also being slightly disappointed she could not walk around like the rest of them.

Rupert walked up, his hand on his sword. "Only a few more minutes. I do not like us being so exposed."

"We are fine." Clifton remarked. "We are already in the Northern Kingdom's borders. We are safer here than anywhere."

"Yes, well I still wish for us to remain cautious. We may not have enemies from the South, but the verdict is still out in regard to Abner." Rupert nodded towards Isaac and he shrugged.

"I feel we will see more of his presence, but not right now. I think he is still wondering if I shall return. Which I will… just not at the moment." Isaac confirmed. "I do not intend to visit that man until I have had my fill of the North."

Elizabeth tilted her head as she surveyed him. "And how long might that be?"

"As long as I am needed, Princess."

"Good. Alayna needs support, I'm sure. It worries me that I have not heard from her." She waved her hand. "Yes, I know I was asleep. But all of you have corresponded with my sister, and I have not. I am eager to see her face."

Clifton lightly ran his hand over his wife's hair and gauged her temper with his probing gaze. She caught his survey and lightly squeezed his hand. "I am fine. I just miss her." A tender smile washed over his face and he nodded.

"Alright, my legs are stretched." Isaac stated, interrupting the quiet. "Let's get a move on. I would like to be there by sundown."

Everyone exchanged amused expressions at his elite attitude. He stretched his arms over his head and twisted his waist until a pop sounded through the air. He then caught their stares. "What?"

Elizabeth giggled as she shook her head.

"I'm just saying it would be nice to get there before the castle has fallen asleep for the evening." Isaac explained.

Clifton scooped Elizabeth into his arms and settled her within the carriage. Isaac climbing in after them, his words following him as he continued explaining himself. Rupert glanced to Samuel and Melody. "You two content with your carriage?"

They both nodded. He flashed a relieved smile as Isaac reached to close the door to the carriage ahead of them. Rupert waited until everyone was settled before finding his way to his horse at the front of the small precession. He flashed one more careful glance behind them before clicking his tongue and guiding his horse forward.

∞

Alayna crumbled the parchment in her hand and tossed it over her shoulder adding to the small pile that now sat behind her on the green grass in Elizabeth's clearing. She had come to pen a letter to Edward, but not having seen her brother in five years had made the task quite difficult. Despite her knowledge of his letters to Elizabeth and his interactions with Prince Clifton, she found herself speechless. She stared across the boundary line and studied the Land of Unfading Beauty. Other than the sheer fog that encircled the mystical land, there were no signs pointing to its differences. She picked up a rock and tossed it as hard as she could through the veil and watched as it landed on the other side with no theatrics. She frowned. Had she hoped for there to be some sort of response? Yes. Yet she found herself slightly comforted that there had not been one as well.

Sighing, she shelved her chin in her hand as she rested her elbow on her knee. *This must have been the stump her father had sat upon. And Elizabeth,* she thought. *A good thinking spot,* she concluded. Though the Rollings River rushed by to her right and the leaves rustled overhead, the clearing held a peaceful tranquility that she had not experienced in quite some time. Her thoughts were interrupted as she spotted a movement in her peripherals. A blonde head emerged on the other side of the boundary. A woman, not much older than Alayna had stepped forward and lifted a delicate hand in hello. Alayna stood slowly, her steps measured as she slowly walked towards the boundary line. The woman's face lit into a smile as she curtsied. She then held up a piece of folded parchment. Her gaze fluttered around the ground and she smiled as she spotted a small rabbit feasting in the clovers. *Thatcher,* Alayna thought. The woman tied the letter to the rabbit's neck and nudged it across the boundary line motioning for Alayna to retrieve her correspondence. Reaching down and gathering the downy furred animal, Alayna unfolded the letter.

Greetings,

My name is Cecilia. I know you must have come to this clearing to see Edward, but I fear I must disappoint you. Edward is currently detained in Lancer's castle. He sent word to me just this morning that he is fine and well, but that his presence is needed there. Lancer is having quite a difficult time with his decrease in power. Edward worries he may attempt an attack of some sort, so he remains there to persuade him otherwise. Have you news from the Realm?

Alayna glanced up and watched as the delicate blonde sat on a tree log and anxiously wound her hands in her lap. Alayna hurriedly responded and sent Thatcher back over the line. Cecilia scooped up the small rabbit and began to read.

Cecilia,

I must say it is nice to put a face with a name. I have heard much about you. I am Alayna, Edward's sister. I am sure he has told you about me. I came to the clearing today to hopefully see him. It seems most everyone else has, but me. That aside, I wished to discuss military matters with him, but I suppose those can wait. In your letter you speak of Lancer's power decreasing. How so? And how did it happen? I must admit I am quite surprised to hear that considering the boundary line still holds strong in all of our kingdoms.

Alayna watched as Cecilia began to respond, her head popping up and tilting to the side as if she heard something. She quickly nudged Thatcher across the boundary line and darted into the trees. Alayna watched as two men on regal horses patrolled the line. One man, dressed in red and gold, and the other a typical guard's armor. She watched as their eyes swept over the clearing on the other side and then glanced towards her. She stood straight, chin held high. The royal man dismounted, and a slow smile spread over his lips as his eyes surveyed her attire. He bowed. He was a handsome man. Dark hair and bright eyes with a radiant smile. She returned it and curtsied in response, the action making his smile grow even wider. She noticed the lines around his eyes and mouth were friendly, yet strained. As if he had not slept for days. His eyes held slight relief as he gazed upon her. He motioned her towards the boundary line and she stepped closer. She felt a slight hum of energy tease her toes, and she stepped back again. He reached into his tunic pocket and withdrew a small knife. He walked over to a small thicket and cut several blooms. He then lightly kissed one of the rose buds before lightly tossing them through the veil. Alayna bent to pick them up. As soon as she did, they turned black as night and deteriorated in her hand and fell in crumbles to the ground. She glanced up to see the man laughing as he narrowed a disgusted look upon her. He mounted his horse and then drew his finger over his throat in a slicing manner before he spat on the ground beneath him and turned away. Alayna stood insulted. Her temper flaring to her cheeks, she reached for a rock and tossed it with all her might at his retreating back. It hit her mark, square in the middle of his shoulder blades, and had him turning around quickly. Venom shot from his eyes as he slapped his reins and quickly galloped towards the boundary veil. His horse lunged at the boundary and Alayna ducked behind the stump for protection, but all she heard was a thunderous clap and witnessed the man flying forcefully off his horse and landing on his back on the other side of the veil. His horse, however, crossed the boundary freely. It came to a halt not far from the line as if confused of its location. Alayna saw the fury engraved upon the man's face, a man she could only assume was Lancer. She bit back a smile as she slowly made her way to the mare and gently ran her hand down its snout. The man bolted to his feet and stepped as close to the boundary as the veil would allow, his mouth moving in shouts as she took the reins of his horse and began leading it out of the clearing. She tossed one more pleased smirk over her shoulder as she watched him pace in a tantrum on the other side. "It was nice to meet you, Lancer." She murmured, as she stepped through the trees and out of sight.

∞

Ryle paced in the entry hall, his steps echoing through the quiet room as he eagerly awaited the arrival of his brother's carriage. He knew they should be arriving soon, and he prayed they did. By his calculations, they should have arrived just a day after himself. The fact they had not, had him worried. He had withheld the knowledge of Edward's letter from Alayna long enough. He needed to speak with her about it, but he did not want to betray Clifton's confidence. He had told his brother he would wait for his arrival and he intended to. He glanced up at the sound of shoes on the stairway. Mosiah descended and offered an encouraging smile on his way down. His sapphire eyes flashed to the West castle halls as Alayna emerged, removing her riding cape. His brow furrowed. "Were you out for a ride?"

"I was." She reported as she handed Jessa her cape.

He noticed a sparkle to her dark gaze and wondered what had the princess so elated.

"I have interesting news." She continued. "I met Cecilia."

"You went to the boundary line?!" Ryle's voice boomed through the hall and bounced off every stone, amplifying his shout and making both Mosiah and Alayna cringe.

Alayna held up her hands for him to lower his voice.

"Did you take a guard with you?"

She shook her head.

"NO GUARD?!" He bellowed.

"Calm yourself. I spoke of my plans with Mosiah earlier. All was fine."

Ryle ran a frustrated hand through his hair and began pacing again. "You go to Mosiah. That is why you needed to speak with him? Why did you not tell me of your plans? I am your Captain now. I am to protect you. What were you thinking?!"

Alayna's back stiffened and Mosiah quietly shuffled out of the room and towards the conservatory, knowing he did not want to be present for the argument that was about to ensue.

"You forget your place, Captain Ryle." Alayna stated formally, her chin tilted high. "I am the future queen. I may call upon whom I please. My venture to the boundary line was for me to visit my brother, privately."

Ryle shook his head in dismay. "I am just saying, Princess," he stressed, "that I cannot protect you, if I do not know where you are. What if something had happened?"

"Nothing did."

He shook his head. "You sound just like your sister. Throwing caution to the wind. Well look where that got her. Why do you not learn from her example?! Maybe then you will keep all your limbs!" He regretted the words as soon as he spoke them. Alayna's horrified expression and the hurt that flashed briefly in her eyes swamped him with guilt. He lowered his voice. "I apologize, Alayna. That was out of line. I just... I worry. I wish to keep you safe. And if I do not know your whereabouts, that makes my task much more difficult."

Alayna nodded. "I understand, and your apology is accepted. However…" She paused and stepped towards him, her caramel eyes molten with restrained anger. "Speak to me that way again, Ryle, and you will no longer be my Captain."

He lowered his head and sighed heavily in disappointment as she turned towards the front entrance. "Carriages were arriving as I walked in from the stables." She announced as she waved for the guards to open the doors. "I believe our siblings have arrived."

Ryle felt her coldness towards him, but he also felt relieved that she now knew where he stood when it came to his role in her protection. Perhaps the learning phase for their new roles was almost over for the two of them. A smile illuminated Alayna's face at the sight of the Eastern carriages pulling up to the steps and Ryle felt his heart flip inside his chest. *He would protect her, whether she requested it of him or not*, he told himself. It was his duty. And by Heaven, he knew it was his heart's wish as well.

Alayna waved happily as she lifted her skirts and darted down the front steps towards Elizabeth's carriage. Prince Clifton stepped out and she flung her arms around his neck in a tight hug. He laughed as he returned it, and she leaned through the doorway of the carriage to see Elizabeth.

"It is about time you arrived." Alayna teased.

Elizabeth grinned as she reached forward and hugged her sister. The two women cried as they held one another and Isaac sat back and watched with a small smirk. Alayna found his gaze and her eyes widened. "Prince Isaac. I did not realize you were in this carriage as well." She retreated and swiped the tears from her eyes as Clifton leaned into the carriage and lifted Elizabeth into his arms and eased her onto her foot beside him. She balanced, one legged, against him, her arm around his waist as Alayna hugged her again. Alayna stepped back and surveyed her sister closely. "You look thinner, but that is nothing Gretchen can't fix."

Elizabeth laughed. "Oh how I have dreamt of Gretchen's jelly tarts." She waved towards Ryle as he made his way down the steps, and she noticed Alayna's small scowl at the Captain's presence. Curious, Elizabeth turned towards Clifton to see if he noticed as well. He lightly shrugged his shoulders in response and then greeted his brother warmly.

"I was worried. You should have been here yesterday." Ryle stated.

"Aye, we got a late start. Seems my wife was not quite ready to leave as planned." Clifton lightly squeezed Elizabeth's side as she playfully rolled her eyes. "He exaggerates, Captain. Your brother was reluctant to let me travel and attempted to make every excuse under the sun to postpone the trip."

Clifton flushed at the truth to her statement and Alayna chuckled. "Well I am glad to see he is looking out for you, then. Come inside."

She watched as Samuel stepped out of the other carriage with Melody and she beamed as he turned around. "Samuel." She curtsied and then hugged him warmly. She then embraced Melody. "It is so wonderful to have everyone back."

Isaac hopped out of the carriage and glanced around. "Is my father here?"

"He is." Alayna offered. "Though I would postpone a meeting with him if I were you. He is not pleased with you at the moment."

Isaac smirked. "Are you looking out for me, Future Queen?"

Alayna ignored his statement and began walking towards the castle entrance. When she reached the door, she watched as Clifton scooped Elizabeth into his arms and carried her over the threshold. "Are you still not able to walk?" Concern laced her voice as she watched her sister lean her head on her husband's shoulder.

"Not yet. Arnos said I still need a week or two before my falsie is attached again." Elizabeth kissed Clifton's cheek. "But don't worry Sister, I have the best transport there is."

Clifton winked at his wife as he turned to see King Anthony enter the room. The king greeted everyone warmly except his two children. Annoyance seeped into his gaze as he watched Melody retreat from his presence to stand closer to Samuel. "Good to see you, Isaac and Melody."

"Father." They both greeted.

Samuel turned in surprise when Melody accidentally bumped into his arm. He took a cautious step away from her but noticed she moved with him, keeping herself close to him. *Not that he minded*, he thought, but he could tell her father was not pleased.

"You all must be famished. I have dinner in the great hall in an hour. I think that will be plenty of time to rest." Alayna announced. "Please, make yourselves comfortable."

Elizabeth nodded and smiled as she pointed to the stairwell and for Clifton to carry her towards her old chambers. Mary followed closely behind. Clifton gently set her on the chaise near the fireplace and removed his traveling cape and handed it to Mary. Elizabeth handed him her cape as well and then he sat next to her. "You tired, love?"

"Not really." Elizabeth sighed in pleasure as her gaze wondered around the familiar room. "It's odd."

"What is?" Clifton asked.

"That this is my old chamber and I am now sharing it with a man." She softly giggled as he buried his nose in her neck and nuzzled. She lightly pulled his face away and stared at him. "I am grateful for you, Clifton. Truly."

His eyes softened as he kissed her, and he lightly tucked her dark hair behind her ear before hugging her to him. "Rest, love.

Though we may not need it now, I have a feeling we will have a long evening."

Content, Elizabeth sighed and allowed her eyes to close as her thoughts filled with images of Edward and the clearing and the longing in her heart to see her brother.

∞

"You deliberately disobeyed me!" Anthony began his tirade as soon as Isaac and Melody entered their wing of the castle. He tossed his formal wolf pelt to his attendant and turned towards his two children. Isaac's brow furrowed, unsure of whether it was himself that was to suffer this wrath of their father or Melody. His father caught his confused expression and pointed a finger at Melody.

"I am sorry, Father, but—"

"You are not sorry, Melody. You went against my wishes with purpose. This is so unlike you. What were you thinking?"

Isaac slipped onto the lounge sofa and his eyes bounced between the two opposing figures before him. He smirked, finding the fact his quiet sister had somehow disobeyed their father amusing. *Good for Melody*, he thought.

"I was thinking that Isaac deserved to know about Princess Elizabeth." Melody countered, her back stiffening as she tilted her chin up into the air. "It was unfair of you to keep such information from him, therefore I took it upon myself to reach out to him."

Isaac shifted and turned to look at his father. "You did not wish for me to go to the East?"

"No." Anthony confirmed adamantly. "I wished for you to serve your purpose to our kingdom. You are to find a bride. Had Melody not interrupted your stay at King Abner's you may be well on your way to doing that."

"Wait," Isaac stood, his hands outstretched in front of him as he tried to wave off what his father was saying. "You did not want me to know about Elizabeth, because you knew I would neglect my duties in Abner's Realm?"

"Yes."

"Did it ever occur to you that Abner's Realm is not where we should be looking in the first place?"

"Do not try to weasel your way out of this, Isaac. I gave you a task, and you failed because of Elizabeth. You will always fail because of Elizabeth if you do not distance yourself from the girl." Anthony's annoyance and disgust at his son's actions had Isaac's tan face transforming to a deep shade of crimson. Melody cautiously stepped back and eased onto the sofa, readying herself for what she assumed would be a volcanic eruption.

"How dare you." Isaac's voice was low, almost a whisper, his hands began shaking as anger slowly overtook him. "How dare you!" He screamed at his father. "Elizabeth is important to me."

"That is the problem." Anthony added, unamused by his son's outburst.

"Do not interrupt me!" Isaac challenged stepping closer toward his father, and inwardly pleased when his father's brows slightly rose, and he retreated a step back. "I went to Abner's Realm at your request. I met his daughters. I met him... the *kind* and *jovial neighbor* everyone believes him to be. I saw what his Realm is like. I learned about him as a ruler. I learned his history. And most importantly Father, I learned what kind of man Abner truly is. He is not what we think. AND, mind you, I also found out that Lancer is the true heir of Abner's Realm. But do you care about any of that? Do you care about anything other than your son marrying? No."

"What are you talking about?" Anthony crossed his arms as he surveyed his son.

108

"I was to fill in the remainder of the council tonight. My stay at Abner's was most enlightening, but you best not be disappointed that it was cut short. For Melody had every right to write to me of Elizabeth's condition. Every right! And if she hadn't, I could very well be dead." Isaac sat, his body tense and radiating strength, Melody feared offering a comforting hand would send her back with a stub.

Anthony eased onto the chair opposite his children. "My concern, Isaac, is that you are too attached to Princess Elizabeth. We all see it. My only aim was to try and sever the hold she has over you."

"She has no hold over me. You make her sound like an evil enchantress. Did it ever occur to anyone that I would have travelled to the East should the role have been reversed and placed on Prince Clifton? Or Prince Ryle? I would have hurried back for Princess Alayna or even Prince Samuel. But no, for some reason my heart and feelings are to be dissected by everyone but myself, and I am presumed to be a love-sick puppy trailing after the princess."

Melody watched as her brother slowly deflated and her father's anger dissipated. She knew neither man knew what to say now, a moment she wished to relish in peace, but she also recognized the need for reconciliation. "I feel as if we have all bypassed one another in some form or fashion. I apologize for writing to Isaac behind your back, Father. However, I feel we both owe Isaac an apology for assuming his intentions with the princess. Perhaps we have all been in the wrong but could possibly move passed this?"

Anthony nodded. "It seems that is the only choice, Melody. I am glad to hear of your loyalty to our Realm, Isaac, that you have strong friendships with each and every leader. I just wish for you to find a match so that the Western Kingdom has its future leader balanced and supported by a queen. It has been ages since the West has had a queen to look up to."

"Mother cannot help it." Melody whispered.

"I know, but the need in the kingdom is still the same." King Anthony stated. "Now, let us go to dinner and then we shall discuss what you have learned of Abner and Lancer." He stood and straightened his red tunic before leaving his two children. When he exited, Isaac reached over and squeezed Melody's hand. "I'm proud of you, Sister."

"For?"

"Standing up to father. For writing to me against his wishes. The old Melody would never have done that." Isaac gently tugged on one of her blonde curls and smirked as it bounced back up into place next to her cheek.

"Yes, well, I believe we have all grown over the last few months. Our roles are more important now than ever."

"Indeed, they are." Isaac agreed. "You are valuable, Melody. And not just to me."

Melody slightly blushed as she stood brushing the wrinkles from her dress. "Come. I imagine we will be the last to be seated."

Grinning at his sister's slight embarrassment, Isaac stood and followed her out.

∞

Alayna sat at the head of the table in her father's former chair and watched as everyone took their seats for dinner. She sighed happily at having everyone back and noticed Ryle's watchful eye. She nodded to him and he responded in kind, his thoughts mirroring her own. "I am so pleased to have everyone back." Alayna held up her goblet. "To friends." Everyone toasted their glasses and sipped. "I noticed your father did not come with you." Alayna turned towards Clifton.

"Aye, my father will be joining us for the coronation ceremonies, but until then he was seeing to a few things in the East." Clifton explained.

"Have you set a date for the coronations?" Elizabeth asked.

"Yes. A week's time. Everything is on schedule. We will first have the coronation here in the North and then travel to the Southern Kingdom for Prince Samuel." Alayna looked towards the future king as he and Melody spoke quietly to one another. Everyone exchanged smiles at the two oblivious royals.

"Alayna is wonderful at planning events." Elizabeth doted. "I'm sure everything will turn out lovely. Is there anything you would like me to do?"

"Not that I can think of at the moment, except help keep my nerves calm." The two sisters smiled at one another.

"You have nothing to be nervous about." Elizabeth stated. "The entire Realm has been expecting your coronation since before Father's death. As soon as Edward crossed the boundary line, you have been next in line. You will be a wonderful ruler."

"Thank you, Sister."

Clifton lightly squeezed Elizabeth's hand under the table, pleased that his wife encouraged her sister. He released his hold as servers began bringing their plates before them.

"Eat up everyone, we will need our strength for the Council Room." Alayna forewarned as she took a hearty bite of her roasted duck.

"Such mystery." Isaac baited.

"There is much to discuss." Alayna replied studying the Western Prince. "I wish to hear of your travels. Captain Ryle tells me you had an unfortunate incident with King Abner's guards."

"Yes. I did. Speaking of Captain Ryle," Isaac turned an amused glance towards the former Eastern Prince. "Is it custom for the Captain of the Royal Guard to eat with the royal family?"

"Isaac!" Melody scolded across the table.

He shrugged.

Alayna turned towards Ryle. "I never quite thought about it." She admitted. "It is true that Mosiah rarely ate with us. However, Captain Ryle's position is a bit different. He's also a royal."

"Not anymore." Isaac pointed out. "He denounced his claim."

Ryle stiffened in his seat. He knew Isaac was just being his typical self, trying to stir up a commotion, but his observation was unsettling. Mosiah never did eat with the family. It was not the role of the Captain to be included in such matters. Was he to be sent away?

"It does not matter. He is a former prince of the East. Therefore, he has a unique position. He is both royal and servant of the crown. He will remain at the table." Alayna's tone brooked no argument, and Isaac flashed a playful grin towards Elizabeth over seeing both Ryle and Alayna shift uncomfortably under everyone's scrutiny. Elizabeth shook her head, but Isaac caught the small tilt to her lips as she turned back to Clifton and continued their conversation.

CHAPTER 6

"Sit down please, Edward." Lancer motioned for Edward to take a seat within his personal chamber and immediately had a servant filling Edward's hand with a drink. "I have much to discuss with you."

Edward took a sip of the offered refreshment, hiding his distaste with a quiet gulp of revulsion.

"Edward, I met your sister."

The cup on its way to Edward's lips froze. "My Lord?"

"Your sister, Edward. The future queen. I met her today."

"Alayna?"

"Yes."

Edward set his cup upon the small table and tried to calm his rapid heart rate. How had Lancer met his sister? "Um… how, my Lord?"

"At the boundary line. I decided to patrol the boundary line today and she sat upon the other side. She is really quite beautiful, Edward. I had no idea."

"How do you know it was her?" Edward asked, praying there must be some confusion as to why his sister would even dare to approach the boundary.

"She wore the formal gowns of the Northern Kingdom." Lancer explained. "It was not hard to deduce, Edward."

"I see." Edward lowered his head to hide the concern in his gaze and tried to contemplate an explanation of her presence.

"I feel your sister is planning something, Edward. That perhaps the weakening in my power comes from an elaborate scheme in the North to overthrow the Lands."

"But my Lord, it is impossible for them to cross and return. How could she plan something without risking the lives of her people?" Edward asked.

"Think Edward. First, we receive all the cowards fleeing from the fight. That weakens me. Then I can no longer cross the boundary line. That weakens me. Then, I find Princess Alayna, future queen of the North sitting alongside my boundary line as if she had no care in the world!" Lancer rose and began to pace. "I was so angry I charged at her!"

Edward's eyes widened at that announcement and he feared what happened to Alayna.

"BUT!" Lancer continued. "Due to my weakening power, I was tossed from my horse! My horse crossed, mind you, but I did not." Lancer shook his head in disgust and frustration. "She stole my horse, Edward!" He turned a pointed gaze towards Edward and awaited a response.

Edward sat stunned. "She stole it?"

114

"Yes! She grabbed the reins and had the nerve to smile at me as she took it away! How dare she steal from me! How dare she think I will just stand by and let her take what belongs to me!"

"What do you plan to do, my Lord?" Edward asked.

"First we need to figure out what she has planned. So you are going to go to that boundary line and sit there until she comes back, and you are going to ask her!" Lancer demanded.

"My Lord, how will I do such a thing? No sound carries across the boundary." Edward played naïve as he waited for Lancer to reply.

"I don't know, Edward! Think of something. But you will not leave that spot until you know what your sister is planning. My Lands will NOT be overcome!" Lancer stormed out of the room, the large wooden door slowly closing behind his retreating footsteps. Edward heard the slam of the door down the hall to the reflection chamber. It was then he allowed a slow smile to spread over his lips.

"Good job, Alayna." He whispered. "Good job." He sighed in relief as he stood and straightened his tunic and walked out. He would make quick work of his special task. What better way for he and the Realm to partner in this fight than him being assigned by Lancer himself to converse with them? It was perfect. And it just might be the very upper-hand they had been needing. If he kept the darkness within him, Lancer would remain weak and would require Edward to fish for information from his family. Meanwhile, his meetings would have a different nature all together. Perfect.

∞

"I have Lancer's horse." Alayna announced as everyone sat in his or her respective seats within the Council Room's walls. Her excited smile beamed as she caught the stunned expressions of most everyone in the room. She noted the look of appreciation coming from her sister and winked.

"How did you manage that?" Prince Isaac asked with amusement.

"I went to the boundary line and he happened to see me."

Ryle's back popped to attention. "He what?!" He stood abruptly. "You said you did not encounter any danger."

"I didn't." Alayna waved him back to his chair. "He could not cross." Several whispers fluttered about the room at that newest revelation and Samuel raised a hand. "My Lady, Lancer can cross willingly. I have seen this with my own eyes."

"And I am saying, he is not able to cross anymore." She almost squealed in excitement but withheld the action.

"How can this be?" Elizabeth asked.

Clifton and Ryle exchanged a glance. A glance that did not go unnoticed by the two sisters.

"Wait a minute." Elizabeth crossed her arms over her chest. "What do you two know that you are not sharing?" She fixated a firm glare upon her husband and he nervously ran a hand through his golden hair as he prepared to share the news of Edward's letter.

Ryle held up his hand to Clifton to pause his explanation and rose to his feet again. "Your brother sent Clifton a letter." He announced.

"How?" Elizabeth interrupted.

Ryle began to speak but Samuel stood quickly to his feet. "By me." He admitted to everyone's surprise. "I had overheard Princess Alayna and Captain Ryle discussing your condition, Princess Elizabeth. I felt your brother should know, and I had hoped to obtain a means of healing for you from the Lands. I knew Prince Clifton had been healed and thought perhaps there was something that could do the same for you. So I ventured to your clearing and met your brother there. He informed me there was nothing he could give me to heal you, but that he had an important message for Prince Clifton and Captain Ryle and that I must give it only to them." Samuel then sat and nodded toward Ryle to continue his portion of the explanation as Elizabeth sat with an open mouth at Samuel's response.

"That is why you requested to go the East?" Alayna asked Samuel.

His face slightly blushed at having misled the future queen as he nodded.

"Oh Samuel, you are such a dear friend." She commented as Ryle cleared his throat and began speaking again.

"Samuel delivered the letter and the contents, I am afraid, may be rather surprising."

"Oh, get on with it." Isaac muttered, frustrated at the suspense. He caught the annoyed expression from his father and waved an impatient hand.

"Edward possesses the same darkness as Lancer." Ryle stated.

Everyone gasped. "What?" Elizabeth asked. "How is that even possible?"

"I do not know." Ryle continued. "He speaks of his venturing into Lancer's reflection chamber and lashing out. He was so angry at the loss of your father, the condition of the lands, and he just... lost his head for a moment, I suppose."

"No." Clifton stated with regret. "We must tell them everything, Ryle." Clifton turned a pointed gaze towards the rest of the room. "Edward realized that his hatred towards Lancer is what sparked his transformation. Hatred is what allows him to possess the darkness. He is guided by hate."

Elizabeth leaned back into her seat, her face slightly pale as she tried to comprehend the news.

"So he hates his enemy." Elizabeth stated with a slight shake to her voice. "Should that not be a good thing?"

"Aye, but to hate your enemy so much that you give yourself over to evil itself?" Clifton lightly clasped her hand. "That is not a good thing, my love. Edward has essentially become just like Lancer. Yes, he wishes to use this darkness for our gain, but I do not think it wise."

"Neither did my father." Alayna added with a fresh understanding of her father's last words to her.

"Father?" Elizabeth asked. "How do you know?"

"The letter Clifton gave me. Father had written us letters before his passing and mine is quite detailed on how we should not use the darkness in any shape or form. We must never choose to use such evil for our own gain."

"A letter?" Elizabeth asked. "I have a letter?"

Alayna's brow rose as she turned towards Clifton. He adjusted in his seat to face Elizabeth as she flushed with anger when she realized he had withheld her letter from her father.

"And why have I not received such a letter?" She stared at him, her blue eyes blazing.

"I had hoped to give it to you once you were fully healed, Elizabeth."

"I am fine now. Perhaps my letter has helpful information as well. Have you read it?"

"No." Clifton replied. "I did not wish to intrude on your father's private thoughts to you. I just held onto it a little longer so that you might heal first."

"Give it to me now." Elizabeth ordered, her hand outstretched.

"I do not think it wise just yet, Elizabeth." Clifton softly spoke.

"Now, Clifton." She ordered. "You should not have withheld something so precious from me."

He sighed as he reached in his tunic pocket. "I was only looking to protect you from further harm, my love. I feared the contents of that letter would spark a vengeance within you and you would aim to rush your healing to participate in action. I am sorry."

Elizabeth snatched her letter from his hand and slipped it into her own skirt pocket.

"What else did your letter say?" King Anthony asked.

"Just that we must remember that our true enemy is the darkness, not Lancer. We must defeat what consumes him. If Edward contains the darkness as well, I fear that his life is now linked with its destruction." Alayna dropped her forehead into her hand as despair settled around her heart. She lifted her chin and looked to those around the table. "We have much to figure out the next few days. Coronations will presume, but our main focus will need to be on the boundary line. Lancer is weaker. This must mean that by Edward consuming some of the darkness he has weakened Lancer as a result. We did not gain ground but have just divided the darkness into two targets now. We must be watchful. Prince Clifton, you and Samuel will journey to the boundary line tomorrow morning and meet with my brother. I wish for you to be fully armored on the off chance my brother is hostile. If he appears to be himself, I wish for you to find out more on his status."

Clifton nodded in understanding.

"Captain Ryle," She continued, "You will commence with Mosiah on training of our guards. We need to strengthen our numbers in preparation." She looked around the room once more. "I wish to share more information with you all as well. When I went to the boundary line, I encountered Cecilia. She sent me a letter across. She confirms the truth that Lancer cannot cross the boundary, but she has no idea about Edward's status, because she did not mention it. She just mentions she is worried about Edward. That he has not been acting himself as of late. I believe she has her own suspicions of Edward as well. Though Edward seems to be our ally in this, I think we may have found another. Cecilia."

"I wish I could have spoken with her." Elizabeth sighed, but this time not in annoyance.

"She seems sweet but aware." Alayna acknowledged. "I also experimented with the boundary line."

Ryle began to stand again but she waved him down. "Not like you think, Captain." Alayna assured. "Considering I had yet to venture to the line I was unsure of what the limitations were. So I tossed a rock through the veil and it landed on the other side."

"What? A rock?" Elizabeth asked.

Alayna nodded. "Yes, it seems objects can pass through the boundary line. Has this always been the case?"

Elizabeth and Clifton shook their heads. "No," Elizabeth answered. "It must be due to Lancer's weakened power. The line must not be as strong. That is definitely interesting news. If a rock can pass through freely, perhaps arrows can as well." Her right brow rose as thoughts of potential battle fluttered through her mind. Seeing the wheels turning in his wife's head, Clifton lightly placed his hand over hers. "An interesting observation that I will ask Edward about." Clifton added. "If he knows of any other breaches in the line perhaps we may have just found our way in."

Alayna inhaled deeply and allowed a small smile to spread over her face. "Lancer underestimates us, friends. Greatly. I want him to realize his folly."

"But we must remain wise." King Anthony interrupted. "All this new information is wonderful, but we must think on it. We must first take care of our own realm then we may worry about our interactions with the Unfading Lands."

"You are right, King Anthony." Alayna agreed. "Coronations will continue as planned."

Isaac lifted his hand.

"Yes, Prince Isaac?"

"I wondered, Princess, if I might obtain an invitation for Princess Katarina from King Abner's court for the coronations. I fear I left their kingdom in quite a rush and not on such great terms."

"And why is this Katarina of importance?" Alayna asked.

Elizabeth grinned, and Isaac pointed at her to stop with the suggested smirk. "Katarina is the one who educated me on Lancer's lineage, my Lady. All of which is of major importance. However, I do not feel we should discuss that matter until King Eamon arrives. I feel he may be able to shed more light on the subject. I feel that Katarina may be at risk within her own kingdom, and I would like to extend a friendly invitation for her to visit here as relations with her father may heat up."

"You wish to have a princess from another realm come to visit here because you upset her father?" Alayna clarified.

"Yes, and because I wish for her to see what our realm is like. She seemed quite astonished when I spoke of it. Plus, it may prevent her father from acting upon any more threats towards us."

"I will think on it." Alayna stated.

"Thank you." Isaac dropped the subject and caught Elizabeth's small smile as she watched him fidget in his chair at the attentions from around the room.

"I know you all must be tired." Alayna stood. "Thank you for meeting with me on your first night here. Please, let us all get some rest and we will reconvene tomorrow. King Eamon should be arriving and we will finally have the entire realm fully represented." Her smile warmed as she looked at each individual person. "It warms my heart to see you all again. Good night."

Everyone slowly rose. Clifton scooping Elizabeth into his arms. Alayna waved at her sister as she watched Clifton carry her out of the room. Ryle lightly ran a hand down her back. "You should get some rest too, Alayna."

She forced a smile. "I plan to. Though there are a couple of other things that need sorting out tonight. Good night, Ryle." His eyes held uncertainty as they washed over her. Alayna felt the warmth spread in her chest at such attention but contained the small butterflies in her stomach. Reluctantly, he stepped away and out of the room.

∞

The next morning Isaac reached the stables early. His intentions of overseeing the care of the caravan's horses was abruptly halted when he saw Alayna brushing the tip of a black nose protruding from one of the stables. He hung back long enough to hear her whispers, his presence unnoticed by the future queen.

"Should I send you back?" She asked the dark mare. "Surely he is not loving towards you. A man so evil must not be capable of love." The horse nuzzled her hand and she smiled. "Okay, I will keep you a bit longer. Did you see his face when I led you away?" She giggled softly as she hugged the horse's neck. "He has no idea who he is dealing with, does he?"

"Does anyone?" Isaac interrupted, causing Alayna to jump to attention. She turned, and a small flush washed over her cheeks at being overheard. "Prince Isaac." She greeted stiffly. "I did not hear you come in."

"I can see that."

"Do you make it a habit of sneaking up on women?"

"I used to." He winked. "Though I must say, that habit has changed."

"And why is that?" She asked. Her eyes squinting as she studied him. "I have heard moral debates on your character from various people. Some believe you a changed man, others do not. What say you to that?"

He shrugged and walked up to Lancer's horse and rubbed a hand down its snout. "I say they are welcome to believe whatever they wish. Though I also believe there are more important issues at hand than my conduct."

She smiled appreciatively. "A wise statement, Prince."

"I have my moments." He smirked as she studied him a bit longer before turning back to the horse. "So this is Lancer's beast?"

"It is." She confirmed. "A marvelous creature, don't you agree?"

"I do. Very marvelous. Firm shoulders, thick muscles. I would say he is quite majestic." Isaac added.

"Do you think me crazy for snatching him?" Alayna asked, and for the first time Isaac realized she wanted an honest answer from him. From *him.*

"I think it quite daring, actually. I did not realize you were made of such firm guts, Princess."

She grinned and happily stepped back from the stable door. "I have my moments."

They both chuckled at her repeating his words and he nodded. "Perhaps it showed Lancer that you are ready for your role as queen and his threats mean nothing to you."

"I wish they didn't." She admitted. "But I hope he did realize I am not weak. I know he thinks I am. I know several people think I am. But I am not. I hope to prove that. I am ready to destroy him and the Lands. And I know we can do it."

"It is hard living with a preconceived notion on your character, isn't it?" Isaac asked.

Alayna lifted her gaze to his and nodded. "I am sorry, Prince Isaac, for not believing in your change."

He waved her comment away. "I am used to it. You, however, should not have to deal with such a notion. You are the future queen. The title itself should strike fear in your enemies.

Lancer's weakness is not just his lack of strength, Alayna. It is his lack of faith in yours."

She wrung her hands in front of her and shifted from one foot to the other. "You are kind, Isaac. Thank you. It is my hope that Lancer's underestimation in us all is what will defeat him. We have new knowledge that I believe can only make us a fiercer enemy. I do not believe he is ready for what I have in store for him."

Isaac placed a hand over his chest and grinned devilishly. "I fear for the man myself, now."

Alayna laughed, and Isaac realized it was the first time he had ever heard a laugh escape the middle sibling of the throne.

"Perhaps we should head back to the castle. I have hopes that Prince Clifton and Prince Samuel have set out for the boundary line already, but I would like to make sure."

Isaac nodded and turned to walk with her. "I will come as well. I had only come to check that the caravan horses had been seen to. My purpose was fulfilled by someone else I suppose. Everything seems in order."

They walked in companionable silence and Alayna realized that the Prince of the West may be another hidden strength within their realm. A strength and weapon that even their own realm underestimated, and she felt a slight ease in the pressure of her chest. *They would win this fight,* she thought. *With men like Ryle, Clifton, Samuel, and now Isaac... there was no way Lancer could overcome the Realm.* She smiled to herself as they walked under the portico towards the castle doors and felt the finality of her thought as the heavy wooden doors latched behind them.

∞

Clifton surveyed Edward closely. He had yet to cross the boundary until he felt assured in the prince's demeanor. Edward waved him over, a paranoid glance over his shoulder had him pausing his motion for a brief moment. But then he waved again. Clifton turned to Samuel. "I will cross."

"You think it wise, my Lord?" Samuel asked.

Clifton placed his hand on Samuel's shoulder. "There's only one way to find out. I won't be long."

Clifton inhaled a deep breath as he felt the familiar buzz along his boots and through his core as he crossed over into The Land of Unfading Beauty. Edward greeted him warmly and with a firm hug.

Clifton smiled as he accepted the gesture, and Edward paced back and forth in excitement at their meeting. "I am so glad you have come. There is much to discuss. I see that Prince Samuel delivered my letter." Edward nodded towards Samuel in thanks as the young prince perched on the large boulder across the line and waited patiently.

"He did." Clifton stated. He studied Edward's movements, his eyes, and his words. "You seem rather different." He began.

Edward smiled widely. "Yes. I dare say I am. The darkness has a unique power to it, Clifton. Very unique. It sustains me in such a way that I can go days without eating or drinking anything. I haven't slept in two days' time, yet I feel as if I am fully refreshed."

"And this is a good thing?" Clifton asked hesitantly.

Edward shrugged. "I do not know. All I know is that I have weakened Lancer. He has no clue I possess the darkness. It's quite brilliant I think."

Clifton shifted his weight on his feet as he watched the prince bounce with energy. "I would be lying, Prince Edward, if I did not tell you that we are all concerned for you. Taking in the darkness… well, even your father warned that it would not be wise."

Edward paused. "But don't you see? My taking in the darkness has weakened Lancer. His defenses are down. It is the perfect time for the Realm to act."

"And how would we accomplish that? Any ideas are welcome." Clifton's abrupt attitude had Edward pulling back slightly.

"You don't trust me, do you?" He asked in surprise.

Clifton held up a hand to stop his line of thinking. "It is not that we do not trust you, Edward. We do not trust the darkness. Look what it has done to Lancer. It has corrupted him. Are you positive it will not do the same to you?"

"I can fight it." Edward stated adamantly. "I will fight it. I only succumbed to it for the sake of the Realm."

"That is what has us worried." Clifton admitted. "The fact you even have to *think* of fighting against it within yourself is an issue. At what point do you tire of such a fight? At what point does the darkness become too much for you and you give into it?"

Edward's face blanched at Clifton's words. "You think me weak? You think me so weak that I cannot fight against the very enemy I have sworn to hate?"

"Edward," Clifton's voice remained calm though he could see the Northern prince's fists clinching. "We do not see you as weak. We see the darkness as too strong for any one man to contain and fight against. It has corrupted Lancer. It will corrupt you eventually, and then where will your true loyalty be?"

"Loyalty?" Edward's eyes glowered at the Eastern Prince. "Loyalty?!" He yelled, storming straight to Clifton and pounding a fist into the man's chest. "I have risked *everything* for my Realm! Do not speak to *me* about loyalty!"

Clifton held up his hands as he saw Samuel rise to his feet on the other side of the line. "Stay calm, Edward. I am just trying to share with you our concerns. If the roles were reversed, I think you could admit to possibly having the same thoughts. Your family loves you. Hearing of your consumption of darkness has them worried. They worry for your safety."

Edward took a few calming breaths and rubbed a hand over his mouth as he looked around. "I understand, Clifton. I do. But please, convince them I can handle this. I will fight to my death for my father's realm. I do not want Alayna or Elizabeth questioning my loyalties to them. I only wish for them to be free of Lancer's threat, and if allowing the darkness to enter me weakens Lancer and aids the Realm, then so be it. I am willing to risk my life for the sake of the Realm."

The two princes considered one another a moment. Clifton gave a curt nod. "Alright. I will speak favorably of your sacrifice. But you must know I still do not agree the darkness is a tool we must utilize. I like that Lancer is weakened, but we must not use the darkness for our own gain. It remains in you for the sole purpose of weakening Lancer and that is it."

Edward released a relaxed smile. "Deal. Thank you, Cliff."

The two men shook hands and Clifton waved to Samuel that all was well. "Now tell me, how are other things?"

Edward eased onto a log and waved his hand over the clearing. "They are well. The Uniters have grown to great numbers. It is getting harder to keep their motives secret. I fear if we should have any more cross or convert Lancer will find us out. Any idea when the Realm plans to act?"

"No. There are still too many uncertainties. However, Alayna has recently discovered that objects may now pass through the boundary line as well."

"Objects?" Edward asked.

"Yes. Rocks in particular. But if rocks can cross—"

"Then weapons can cross." Edward finished with a slight edge of anticipation in his voice. "Would the Realm be able to provide weapons to the Uniters?"

"We have not discussed that possibility yet." Clifton continued. "As of right now we are still getting used to the idea that battle is even possible. Honestly we haven't even thought about utilizing the Uniters."

"That's what we are here for." Edward replied automatically. "We serve the Realm. Should you need an army on the inside, we are here."

Clifton stood and slowly walked back towards the boundary line. "I will make note of it and bring it up at the next council meeting. Our time of reprieve may be short-lived."

"Also," Edward added. "Lancer wishes for me to investigate the reasons behind his weakening power. I am to spy on the Realm for him. He has given me permission to patrol the boundary and converse with you all. When he faced Alayna, he did not like that he could not speak to her and see what was on her mind. I am to find out."

"I see. Well perhaps we can utilize that role of yours as well."

"Is there anything I can tell him?" Edward asked.

Clifton pondered a moment and then a small smirk tugged at his lips. "Yes. Tell him we have found out his origins and that King Abner has been most informative."

"Abner? As in Abner's Realm?" Edward asked the name causing slight recognition to surface within his eyes.

"Yes. Prince Isaac visited and found that Abner's Realm is where Lancer originally resided. I do not know more than that just yet but see how he reacts to that news. Isaac is to explain his visit tonight at the council meeting. I will bring you more information as I receive it."

"Lancer has not spoken of Abner before, so I will see what I can find out. Gauge his reaction to the name."

"Good." Clifton nodded. "Until tomorrow, Prince." They bowed towards one another and Clifton crossed back into the Realm. With a final wave, he and Samuel made their way out of Elizabeth's clearing.

CHAPTER 7

Clifton and Samuel emerged back in the castle and wound their way to the conservatory. Alayna stood immediately. "Well, how was he?" She rushed towards them eager for a response.

"He is fine." Clifton stated, his gaze searching the room for Elizabeth.

"She is in the gardens." Isaac reported, knowing full well the look in Clifton's eyes. Clifton nodded his direction in thanks.

"I wish for a full report this evening."

Clifton bowed towards Alayna in acknowledgment. "Aye, and you shall have one. If you will excuse me?"

He hurried towards the exit and out to the gardens in search of his wife.

"Was Edward really well, Samuel?" Alayna asked, her worried expression ceasing when he nodded.

"Yes, my Lady. He and the prince conversed for quite some time. Prince Clifton assured me that as of right now Edward seems to be immune to the darkness within him."

Alayna placed a hand over her heart in relief. "Oh, that is good news."

"Indeed." Melody agreed.

Samuel seated himself next to Isaac across from Melody and smiled shyly in greeting. Alayna and Isaac exchanged knowing glances and attempted to hide their own grins.

"Is your father well this morning?" Samuel asked.

Melody nodded. "Yes. He is answering a few letters from the west and shall join us shortly after."

"Is Princess Elizabeth well this morning?"

"She is." Alayna added. "She just wished for some time alone, as is her old habit." Alayna turned and glanced out the window and spotted Clifton walking towards Elizabeth's back as she sat on a bench in the rose gardens. A heavy sigh escaped her as she prayed her sister would receive his interruption kindly. After Elizabeth's outburst in the council meeting over their father's letter, she hoped Elizabeth could forgive Clifton for his added care.

∞

"I thought I might find you out here." Clifton's melodic voice filtered over Elizabeth and had her face breaking into a welcoming smile.

"And I was anxiously awaiting your return. How was Edward?"

Clifton eased onto the bench beside her and immediately wound his hand with hers as he nodded a brief greeting towards Mary.

"He seemed well enough, though I will admit my concern for him still lingers."

131

Elizabeth studied her husband's face and the keen sense of awareness in his eyes as he stared ahead at the gardens. "You are worried." She confirmed.

Breaking his reverie, Clifton turned towards her and forced a smile. "I am sorry, love, but yes, I am. I fear he may have good intentions, but none of us know the true strength of this darkness and the power it holds. I am worried. For all of us."

"You are a good man." Elizabeth lightly kissed his jawline and brushed her fingers over his forehead to swipe away his unruly hair.

"I am glad you think so." Clifton added.

"I do think so." Elizabeth stated adamantly, making him smile. "And on that note, I wish to apologize to you."

"Apologize? Whatever for?"

"My behavior towards you in the council meeting."

"Ah." He nodded as if remembering the scenario and Elizabeth felt her cheeks blush at the thought of her ghastly behavior.

"I truly am sorry for lashing out the way I did. I was unreasonable. I should never have demanded my letter from you, especially in front of everyone. I appreciate you giving it to me despite my behavior."

Clifton peered into her pale blue eyes and saw the depth of her regret and he nodded. "I will admit, Elizabeth, I was taken aback and slightly disappointed. However, consider it forgotten. I should have given the letter to you as soon as you awoke."

"No. I think you were in the right."

His brows rose at that statement and had her slightly giggling at his reaction. "What I mean is, I think you did have my best interests at heart, and you were right to protect me from my own stubbornness. I know that whatever lies in this letter will strike a fire within my bones and make me wish to hop to the Realm's defenses immediately. I couldn't very well do that whilst bedridden, now could I?"

"But you would have tried." He added.

"Exactly." Elizabeth agreed. "I am glad you know me so well, Clifton, and that you protect me even when I do not realize I need it."

Clifton leaned back against the bench, his demeanor relaxing, and the worry etched onto his face eased. Elizabeth leaned against him and he gently brushed his fingers over her shoulder as he draped his arm around her.

"So, speaking of this letter." He invited. "Have you read it?"

"No."

"No?" His flabbergasted expression made her laugh.

"I wish to read it together."

Clifton studied her a moment and then kissed her softly, but passionately. "Thank you, love, for considering me."

Elizabeth held the letter out to him and he delicately unfolded the parchment, his finger sliding under her father's wax seal and the page unfolding. "Read it." She said softly, her voice already clouding with tears at the sight of her father's handwriting.

Clifton cleared his throat and began to read.

My Dearest Lizzy,

Oh my dear Lizzy how I will miss you and your smiling face. I pray this letter finds you in good spirits. I know Clifton will have given it to you, for he is honorable. I thank the stars in heaven you will be loved by such a man.

I have also left a letter for Alayna, for which I hope will benefit her as I hope this letter will benefit you. You are on a new path, my dear. A path to be queen, a path we never expected for you. I have no doubts that you and Prince Clifton will serve the Eastern Kingdom well and be a loving king and queen, so I will not waste precious time on such subjects.

I wish to write to you about your role in this Realm. Yes, it is changing, but I also wish to tell you to never change, my Elizabeth. Your strength has made this Realm stronger than you realize. Your love for the other kingdoms and the good you see in all of them will only help our Realm. Your very belief in someone's character has caused a change in the West that will forever shape their future king. Your hope and belief in Samuel makes him stronger as well. Your faith in him encourages him to believe in himself, Elizabeth. Please continue to remain strong in your belief of a greater Realm and the goodness in others. For goodness is what our Realm needs most. Be watchful of your interactions with The Unfading Lands. I know you and Edward have a special kinship, but please, do not be blind to the Lands behind him. They are an ever-increasing threat. I pray your brother remains strong, however, I wish it most for you. You have a vital role to play in the days to come.

Use your intuition. Use your sense of right and wrong. And use your friends where they are strongest. You see things in people that no one else does, Lizzy. Encourage Alayna to recognize those same strengths in them. She will need your help, Elizabeth. She will need your encouragement for her own strength as well. I know you will serve the Realm with your entire heart and being, and I am thankful you have found a man who will do the same. Lancer is a fool if he believes our Realm to be weak. For how can it be if we have people like you?

I love you, my dear. I love you for your courage, your heart, and your strength.

Your Father

Elizabeth swiped her fingers under her eyes to claim the escaped tears as she sniffled. Clifton hugged her to his chest and lightly kissed her hair. "I agree with everything he says." He whispered softly. "You are one of our Realm's biggest strengths."

"I just wish he were still here. I know that is selfish, considering he was in so much pain, but I still wish it so."

Clifton gently rubbed her shoulder. "I know, love. I wish I had gotten to know him better. But we must not dwell on things we cannot change. Instead, we can only focus on what your father taught us and showed us."

"You're right." Elizabeth agreed. "I think he would agree that we must all hold tight to one another and be there for each other. I fear the Realm has yet to see true battles just yet. But I sense them on the horizon."

"Aye, me too."

Elizabeth turned to Clifton and gently cupped his face. "I try not to worry for you. I know you are strong and smart, but I still fear something happening to you."

He smiled tenderly and removed her hands and held them tightly in his own. "Do not worry about what has yet to come. We must not fear the future. We must prepare for it. The more we prepare, the better our chances of success, right?"

"Of course." Elizabeth nodded with a sad smile that Clifton attempted to erase with a delicate kiss.

He pulled away at the sound of trumpets from the front of the castle. "Those are Eastern trumpets." He said. "My father must be arriving." He reached down to Elizabeth and she clasped his hand. She slowly rose to stand on her one foot and Clifton scooped her into his arms with little effort. Sighing, she nuzzled her head against his shoulder in content happiness as he carried her back into the castle to greet King Eamon.

"My goodness is it not a blessed day indeed to see such a beautiful face?" King Eamon stepped towards Alayna and hugged her tightly. "It is good to see you, my dear. How are you holding up?"

Alayna smiled. "I'm doing well. Your son has made sure of that." She waved a hand towards an approaching Ryle and her heart flipped at the joy on the Captain's face at seeing his father. *No doubt Ryle had missed his family*, she thought.

"I believe you become more of a Captain every time I see you." Eamon complimented as he slapped his hand on Ryle's back after releasing him from a warm embrace.

"Aye, I am doing my best, Father."

"I know you are." King Eamon assured him as he moved onto the next person and continued his greetings. His eyes fell upon Elizabeth warmly and he hugged her tenderly as he did the same to Clifton. "Though everyone had just left, I feel as if it has been ages." Eamon reported. He waved towards his carriage. "I must admit I had a stow away. He insisted on checking upon you, my dear." Arnos stepped from the carriage and Elizabeth smiled. "I suppose we will forgive him this once." She grinned as Arnos bowed.

Alayna stepped forward. "Mr. Arnos, welcome to the Northern Kingdom. Your efforts and skills in saving my sister have not gone unnoticed. You are most welcome in our kingdom."

Arnos lightly flushed as he bowed to the future queen. "Thank you, Your Highness."

Ryle smiled at the old man as he followed several servants into the castle. "We are all under one roof again, Alayna, how do you feel?"

Alayna turned towards him, her face glowing from the sunlight and sheer joy. "I am most happy." She admitted softly, her eyes searching his. Ryle lightly brushed his fingertip over her cheek as he smiled, their eyes holding. Alayna felt her knees weaken as Ryle stepped closer to her. A throat cleared and had her hopping back quickly. Her smile transforming into a forced expression as she quickly gathered her skirts and swished into the castle behind the others. Ryle shot an annoyed glance at Prince Isaac who leaned casually against the entry stairwell. "Do you not have anything better to do?" Ryle asked in irritation.

"Not at all. I have yet to find anything to amuse me today until just now." Isaac bantered, sauntering into the castle and leaving the former prince standing baffled on the stairs.

Ryle entered to a bustling castle. Yes, his father had arrived, and with him a new wave of servants and attendants working to find their place amongst the Northern Kingdom's staff. He followed voices into the conservatory as Eamon's eyes widened. "Lancer can no longer cross? My goodness, what news."

"We have saved much of our discussion for your arrival, Father." Clifton stated. "Tonight's council meeting will be quite informative to you and we hope, to us as well."

Eamon nodded. "Yes, well, it sounds like there is much to discuss. Anthony, how goes the West?"

"Ah, good." Anthony stated. "We have recovered from the battles well enough and are working towards establishing a potential future queen for Isaac."

Eamon's brows rose as he turned towards Prince Isaac. The young prince smirked and shrugged his shoulders. "I see." Eamon stated. "Well I wish you the best in your search, Prince Isaac."

"Thank you, my Lord."

"It would seem I have missed much." Eamon continued. "I do hope we can all catch up, but first, I believe I will fetch some rest from my journey and then meet you all at the dinner table." He walked around the circle, hugging his sons and Elizabeth. He bowed to the remaining crowd and exited the room.

"Do you suppose he will be up for tonight's council meeting?" Elizabeth asked Clifton quietly.

He leaned down to hear and lightly brushed his hand over her soft, dark hair. "He has no choice."

"Yes, but I hope we do not come on too strong asking about his past."

Clifton smiled tenderly as he swiped his finger over her worried brow. "Do not fret. He is a king. He has been through tougher situations than a heated conversation."

She sighed and nodded, but her eyes still held trepidation, a sign of Elizabeth's loyalty to his father that made Clifton's heart happy. He was glad she valued his family, and he knew they equally valued her.

"Well, I suppose we must all carry on until dinner. I have much to do. Captain, if you would follow me, please." Alayna turned to leave, and Ryle easily followed, catching the sly smirk Isaac cast his way at his departure.

∞

"Leave us, Jessa." Alayna politely ordered her attendant as Ryle followed her into the council room. He shut the doors behind them and noted they were alone. No Jessa, and most importantly, no Mosiah.

"You wished to speak with me?" Ryle asked.

Alayna circled the table and spread her hand over several maps and parchments. "Yes. I feel I should discuss some points with you before the meeting tonight. I have been looking over a few things in regard to The Unfading Lands and I believe with our new knowledge of objects being able to cross, we may be able to supply Edward's troops with weapons." She turned a specific map his direction and pointed to a spot designated slightly southwest of Elizabeth's clearing. "I fear we may have compromised our position at Elizabeth's location, but if we moved further south, on the border between our kingdom and Samuel's we may be able to move quite freely over the boundary line without suspicion from Lancer. The Southern Kingdom is completely out of Lancer's mind at this point."

Ryle studied the map and then studied Alayna as she leaned on the table, a slight excitement lacing her words as she spoke.

"You have given this much thought." He acknowledged.

Without glancing up, her eyes bounced along the map and she nodded. "Yes, I did not sleep much last night. I feel..." She paused as if searching for the most accurate description of her feelings. "I feel we are close to something, Ryle. That there is something big about to happen. I just know it. In my bones, I know it, and I think if we look hard enough, we may be able to recognize it before it hits us." She finally looked at him and he offered a smile. "What?" She asked.

"Nothing. I just find myself more amazed by you every day." He admitted, noting the small flush that washed over her cheeks. "You seem to be quite on top of Lancer lately, I wonder if you even need my help."

Her eyes widened, and she gripped his forearm. "Of course I need your help! I cannot defeat him on my own. I need your strength and military knowledge to even consider pulling an assault off."

"An assault? Is that where this is going?" He asked curiously.

"Yes. I am thinking it may be our only way to catch Lancer by surprise. He would not be expecting such a thing, not while the kingdoms still appear to be recovering. He most certainly would not expect an assault arising from the South either. That's why I think we must discuss with Samuel the possibilities of utilizing his kingdom."

Ryle chuckled as he shook his head and rubbed a hand over his mouth. "And what army shall we use, Princess? Considering our men cannot cross freely back and forth across the boundary?"

"We use Edward's Uniters. They are mostly Southern guards any way. They are obviously loyal to the Realm and if we can convince Samuel to supply their weaponry, we have an army on the inside already."

"Great, in theory." Ryle stated causing a slight frown to mar her features. "But who will lead them? Edward? Because that will jeopardize his cover. I think we still need him to be Lancer's trusted Captain. I do not think we should expose him just yet."

Alayna sat with a heavy exhaled breath and placed her chin in her hand as she perused the map once more. She then slammed her palm on the table and looked up with bright eyes showcasing an idea. "You will."

"Me?" He asked curiously.

"Yes. You are of Lancer's blood, so you will be able to cross back and forth freely."

"We think." He added, his interjection not slowing down her train of thought.

"Yes, yes, yes, you will." She continued waving her finger at him as she rose and began to pace and talk at the same time. "You will lead the Uniters against Lancer's army. Edward, the Captain of Lancer's guards, will lead the opposing forces, but in a way that gives us the advantage. That way, in Lancer's eyes, Edward is doing his duty to the Lands, but we can still overcome them."

Ryle crossed his arms in thought. "And what should happen if we lose?"

"You won't."

He smirked. "I thank you for your confidence, Alayna, but there are still unknown factors at play here. We are at a

140

disadvantage. We do not know our way around the Lands well enough to offer a surprise attack."

"Edward will orchestrate a route for us."

He shook his head. "Okay, so what if we win? Are we to kill Lancer? What happens then? Does the boundary line vanish? What if it remains? Then the people whom we thought we would be freeing would remain trapped. What is the purpose of this assault if the boundary line does not move?"

"It removes Lancer from power." Alayna passionately explained. "Edward will take his place and it will be a peaceful kingdom. But I am telling you Ryle that the boundary line dies with Lancer. I know it does. It has to."

"Well you have certainly given us some things to think about, haven't you?" He smiled in appreciation. Alayna nodding.

"I know we can do this, Ryle. I know we can."

He gently grabbed her hands in his and brushed his thumbs over her knuckles. "I think we should run this idea by the others tonight. Then, if they agree, we will sort out details with Edward. We also must test my ability to cross. If I am not able to cross freely, I will be stranded on the other side. What use am I then?"

"You will always be of use to me." Alayna stated confidently and lightly kissed his cheek. He gently cupped her face in his hands and leaned his forehead against hers. "I hope so, Alayna. I hope so."

∞

"So you are telling me that Abner has been consulting with your father's realm?" Lancer asked, shock evident on his handsome face, and fire lighting in his eyes.

"Yes. Prince Clifton informed me that Abner mentioned your relations to his realm."

"So now Abner and your father's realm wish to collaborate in my destruction?" Lancer shook his head and then laughed at the idea. "They have no idea who they are dealing with. Especially Abner. He is no friend to them."

"They seem to think so, my Lord." Edward stated, though he did not know if that were a fact. He wished to gauge Lancer's reaction towards Abner or even the thought of another possible threat against him.

"Then they are even more foolish than I first believed!" Lancer shouted. "Abner is no one's friend."

"So you are saying we should warn my sister of Abner?" Edward asked.

"No." Lancer lightly plucked a piece of lint off his sleeve and tossed it aside. "If your sister and the other fools wish to partner with Abner, let them. It only helps us, Edward."

"How so?"

"Because Abner will slowly merge his way into their realm, then turn on them. While the Realm is weak, our Lands grow. Keeping it out of the hands of the Realm and most importantly out of the hands of Abner."

"I see." Edward rubbed his chin as he sat facing Lancer. "Did Abner betray you, my Lord?"

"Yes. He betrays everyone." The disdain in Lancer's voice caught Edward by surprise. The smile on his usual cheerful face had lessened as of late due to his weakening power, and the news of Abner had only made his scowl deepen.

"When you reach out for information about the Realm, find out their connection to Abner. Why is it so important?"

"Yes, my Lord."

"And Edward, I also want you to find out if there is talk of an assault on the Lands from Abner. He is only about conquering. If he were to breach the boundary line, our defenses must hold. He cannot take our Lands."

"I will, my Lord. I will find out."

"Good. Now off with you. I must brood for a bit. Should I need you I best find you strengthening our guards. I wish for all weapons to be at the ready. With Abner inching closer, we must always be on guard." Lancer waved him away.

Edward retreated out the door and into the hallway as he turned to head towards the armory. Edward had not heard much about King Abner in his youth. Just that he was a friendly neighboring kingdom. However, Lancer's fear of the man was evident in his conversation. Edward had never seen Lancer so adamant about preparation for an enemy. He would never have considered an enemy penetrating the boundary in the past. Abner must be more powerful than Edward realized, and much more powerful than Prince Clifton realized if they were in relations with him. Warning bells rang within his head as he walked into the armory. He would definitely share his thoughts and Lancer's words with Clifton. Abner may be their biggest threat yet.

∞

"Good to see you this evening, Elizabeth." Isaac greeted, as he sat at the council table awaiting the meeting that should soon take place. Elizabeth glanced up and smiled. "And you, Isaac. Break any hearts today?"

"No, I'm afraid not. Though I was able to compose a letter of invitation to Katarina of Abner's Realm for the coronations. I will be sending Rupert on horseback tomorrow to deliver it."

"You think it safe?" Elizabeth asked.

Isaac shrugged. "Rupert is a gifted fighter should any hostility arise. Should he not be back by three days' time, I will personally go and fetch him, despite the risks."

"You must really want Katarina here." Clifton chimed in with a knowing grin as he slid into his seat next to Elizabeth.

"It's a strategic move," Isaac began, "as well as a personal one. I feel if Abner accepts the invitation for Katarina, he will send her here as a spy. What he does not know, is that Katarina is not loyal enough for that."

"You know this for sure?" Elizabeth's brows rose in curiosity.

"I believe so. She is the one who told me all his secrets. I do not see her being loyal enough to spy on our kingdom to harm us. She is too kind for that."

"Well," Alayna entered on his last explanation and nodded, "I sure hope you are correct, Prince Isaac. If she harms our kingdom in any way, she will face punishment." Alayna's fierce reply had everyone surprised as she took her seat and smiled in welcome at King Eamon as he sat beside Ryle. "Everyone is here. Let's begin."

"Abner." Alayna began, "King Eamon, I wish for you to tell us all you know about the man, past and present."

Eamon's eyes widened. "Why, my Lady?"

"He is a recent acquaintance of Prince Isaac, and his daughter Katarina a possible ally. She told Prince Isaac of Lancer's past, and we wish to confirm it with you since your wife was Lancer's sister."

Eamon gently rubbed a hand over his face as if perplexed. "I am not sure what all you would like to know. It was a long time ago."

"Katarina speaks of what they term "The Overcoming" in Abner's Realm." Isaac stated. "She said that is when her father, King Abner, attacked Lancer's father, and killed all of his line, or tried to, in order to overtake the realm."

"That is true. Though Queen Erica had already been in the Eastern Kingdom with me for quite some time at that point. Abner had no concern for her however, because when she married me she left and cut all ties with that realm. Including with her brother."

"She was not close to Lancer?" Elizabeth asked.

"Not entirely. Lancer was the spoiled sort. Always belittling her in their father's eyes. She wished to see the world and venture somewhere new. My proposal came with quite excitement because it gave her a chance to break free from that negativity." Eamon explained. "Once we were married, she never wrote or conversed with her brother from that point on. Not by my orders, but by her own choice. She asked that we never speak of her family, and I obliged."

"Why was she so eager to leave her father though?" Melody asked. "She may have had issues with her brother, but her father? Was he not kind to her?"

"He was very kind to her." Eamon explained. "But her father was aging, and his health was fading. His only wish was for his daughter to be loved and taken care of at the time. He wanted her to have an escape from their realm for a better life."

"Lancer never contacted her?" Clifton asked.

"No." Eamon reiterated in slight frustration. "She was adamant that her old life be left behind. Your mother did not wish for Lancer to interfere with her happiness any longer."

"But when Abner overthrew her father, Lancer sought refuge in the East, did he not?" Isaac asked.

"He did." Eamon continued with regret. "He wished for a safe haven, but he did not find one. Your mother turned him out as soon as he reached the castle doors. He never even stepped foot inside the castle."

"Katarina stated that *you* rejected Lancer." Isaac stated.

"No. I was standing next to my wife in support, but it was her decision. I told her we could offer him a night's rest, but she refused. Her brother only brought trouble. He spouted vicious words against her, threatened our growing family, and stormed away. He attempted again the next morning, having spent the night in the village, but your mother refused again. She would not have him bringing his poison to our kingdom. So he fled."

"What else can you tell us about him?" Ryle asked his father with a quizzical expression.

"Not much. I did not know him that well. My trips to his kingdom were brief, and my intentions were for his sister, so I did not see or converse with him much."

"And he never contacted mother again?" Clifton asked.

"No. Not that I know of. She never spoke of him. In fact, when you were just a boy, Cliff, you asked her about her parents because you wanted to meet your grandparents. You were just a toddler then, having just learned the word and what it meant. I remember her specifically telling you that she did not have parents or family anymore."

"So we have no new information." Isaac grumbled. "Great."

"Don't sound so defeated, Isaac. It's unbecoming." Melody scolded from across the table to everyone's amusement, including her brother's. "What King Eamon has told us sheds great light onto Lancer and his past."

"How so?" Isaac waved for her to continue with obvious delight at his sister's outspokenness.

"Lancer was terrible to his sister. She was eager to leave and then a great proposal saves her from her brother's trouble. She leaves him and wishes to never speak of or see him again. Lancer seeks her out a few years later for help, she refuses. He is upset and flees, and then creates The Land of Unfading Beauty. A land where he is the leader. A land where he makes the rules. A land where he is looked up to. A land where he is *wanted*. He has created his very own sanctuary. I think, deep down, Lancer wants to be accepted. I think we could use that to our advantage." Melody turned towards Alayna to see if she understood her meaning.

"You wish to team up with Lancer?" Isaac asked.

"No. I just think that it opens the door to certain possibilities of appealing to him. Perhaps a peaceful treaty of sorts."

Isaac scoffed. "A treaty? With Lancer? A man who created his own kingdom out of pure hate? Peace with *him*?"

Melody shook her head in frustration and then dropped her head to stare into her lap. "It was just a suggestion."

"And a good one." Alayna smiled in thanks. "Melody does bring up great points into his character. Lancer does not like to be ignored or cast aside. I witnessed this the day I stole his horse. I showed my dislike of him and he grew angry. So angry that he turned fresh roses into soot and ash in front of me."

"He what? Why are you just telling us this now?" Ryle asked with a sharp blue gaze pointed at her.

"Because it is relevant now. His very touch has power, which brings me to the next subject of our discussion." She lifted her head and looked at everyone around the table. "Captain Ryle and I were discussing the possibilities of an assault on the Lands."

Surprised looks gave her the encouragement she needed to continue. She explained her plans to everyone while walking around the room. Sighing at the end, she then sat and focused upon everyone's faces as they allowed all the information to sink in. "However," Alayna continued, "After further thought, my concern is that if Lancer were to even sense something amiss, or discovers our weapons crossing he can destroy them by a single touch. So we would need to be most stealthy."

"An assault?" Elizabeth asked again.

"Yes."

"I am not sure that is wise, sister."

"That is why I am asking the entire council, Elizabeth." Alayna stated forcefully silencing Elizabeth's objections.

"What are your thoughts, King Anthony? You have been quiet."

The Western King straightened in his seat and lightly tapped his fingertips against the tabletop. "I find the idea quite devious, yet good. He would not be expecting it. We have resources at our disposal. The Southern guards are loyal to the Realm, therefore loyal to the Southern Kingdom and Samuel. I think they would be encouraged to see their new king interactive with trying to recover them from the Lands and want to fight for the cause. I also think, should Prince Edward indeed help us, then we have no chance of defeat. We should win quite easily and quickly."

"Nothing is ever easy when it comes to war." Clifton stated seriously. "Look at what happened last time. We almost lost Elizabeth and myself. Sending Ryle over the line with a few guards to lead an army he has not trained himself, into a situation with unknown territory… none of that sounds like steps to a successful victory."

"That is why we must prepare." Ryle stated. "We will test my ability to cross the boundary. Should I be able to as well, then we can begin preparations. Weapons may begin to be smuggled across the line. I can spend time with The Uniters and train them. Edward can help us. While Lancer is weak, his sense of the boundary line is weakened. He will not be able to sense us crossing. Now is the time for this to take place."

"And what about you Samuel?" Elizabeth asked the young prince. His facial expression never wavered as everyone discussed the choices his kingdom would need to make in all of the planning. He inhaled a deep breath as he looked to Ryle.

"I will do whatever needs to be done to protect our Realm." Samuel stated confidently. "I should like to be a leader the South can respect, and I should like to serve the Realm in any way I can."

Alayna smiled at Samuel's eagerness and willingness. She exchanged a pleased and relieved smile with Ryle.

"Then it is settled. We shall start our planning." She beamed across the room. "Tomorrow, Clifton and Ryle will travel to the boundary line and attempt Ryle's crossing as well as informing Edward of our plans. We will move forward from there. Coronations are at weeks end. Our trip to the South for Samuel's coronation shall give us insight into the status of his guard there and the weaponry at our disposal."

Samuel nodded.

Elizabeth raised her hand.

"Yes, sister?"

"What happens if Ryle is not able to cross back into the Realm? What if it is not bloodline that makes Clifton able to cross?"

"If I remain stuck in the Lands, I will still continue as planned. Clifton will then be the carrier of the weapons, and I will train the forces on the other side and everything will continue smoothly."

"Yet, we have no idea if the boundary disappears with Lancer." Clifton clarified.

"It will." Ryle and Alayna stated at the same time with equal confidence.

Alayna stood slowly. "I think that is all for tonight. Rest up everyone, the next few weeks shall be busy."

∞

"And what are your thoughts on this?" Elizabeth asked Clifton as soon as the door to their chamber closed. Mary quickly made her way towards Elizabeth behind the changing boards to ready her for bed as Clifton sat on the edge of the bed listening.

"I have my hesitation, but it seems the plan is underway regardless."

Elizabeth poked her head around the divider and stared at her husband's weary face. "Something is troubling you."

Clifton glanced her direction and smirked. "Stop spying on me. You are to be changing instead of giving Mary a difficult task."

Elizabeth playfully stuck out her tongue as she retreated back behind the dividers.

"I am just struggling with all the new information in regard to my mother. I hate that she felt abandoning her own family was the right decision."

"Well look at Lancer." Elizabeth stated. "Would you want him visiting you all the time?"

Clifton's mouth tilted into a small grin at Elizabeth's blunt assessment. "I guess you are right. Though it saddens me she did not have a sibling to love."

"But she had a chance at love with your father, and once she had her own children I am sure her own losses paled in comparison to the joy she found in her new family." Elizabeth emerged around the side of the changing boards, her arm around Mary's shoulders as Mary helped her hop towards her husband. She sat down beside him and lightly rested her hand on his thigh. "It is hard for me to fathom too. Even when Edward left us, I still could not let him go. But we see who Lancer is now… and if your mother knew the hatred and evil lurking within him then, then I believe she was only wishing to protect us all from such a man."

"I believe you're right. She loved this realm. I never knew she was from another realm other than this one. My parents never spoke of their betrothal. And I never asked."

"You're a man. Men never would ask about that." Elizabeth replied playfully.

Clifton chuckled. "I supposed you are right again, love." He ran his hands through his hair as he sighed. He nodded towards Mary and Elizabeth glanced up at her attendant. "Oh, that will be all for tonight Mary. Thank you."

Mary bowed and obediently exited the room.

Elizabeth rubbed a hand over Clifton's back and watched as he stood and began to pace. "We need to be careful, Elizabeth. Edward is our friend now, but my concern is that the darkness is getting to him. Should we seek all his help in aiding us in this battle, I am ashamed to admit, that I am afraid he will turn against us and tell Lancer. I fear we will be ambushed."

She reached out her hands and he took them. She stood to her feet and looked up at his eyes their color like spring grass. "Be watchful then. Should you begin to feel his allegiance shifting, you report it at once to the council. To the council as a whole. Not to your brother. Not to my sister. To the entire council. I fear Ryle and Alayna have teamed together to present this plan in a way to present a united front, however, I think their secret planning has also put us all in a whirlwind of agreement before we are ready. Everyone trusts your judgment. Isaac will too. Isaac, by nature, is suspicious of everyone, much less Lancer and potentially Edward. Take him with you and Ryle tomorrow and let him observe. He is keen on observation."

"You are right. Isaac would be insightful. I believe all of us will go." He watched as hope bloomed in his wife's eyes. "I mean, the princes."

She frowned, and he chuckled. "Sorry love, you are not ready to ride a horse just yet."

"I know." She briefly pouted before easing back onto the bed and sitting. "Though Arnos believes I should be able to attach my falsie by weeks end. The coronation will hopefully be a standing affair for me."

"That is good news." Clifton agreed as he turned down the covers. "Just—"

"Don't overdo it. I know." She finished his sentence making him laugh and then smiled as he kissed her goodnight. Clifton turned and blew out the lantern next to the bed.

"And Clifton," Elizabeth whispered in the darkness.

"Yes, love?"

"Please look out for Samuel in all this as well. Do not let him feel bullied or overwhelmed."

"You know I will."

"Yes. I know." Her voice grew quiet and Clifton heard her even breathing as she slept. He lay awake for another few minutes until exhaustion finally overcame him.

∞

"It would seem you have a letter, Princess Katarina." King Abner walked slowly up the castle steps to the awaiting line of princesses as the Western Kingdom carriage remained out front. Katarina had hoped Isaac had returned but tried to hide her disappointment when her father mounted the steps alone. He handed her the letter. "I wish to know its contents." He stated firmly as she slid her finger under the Western seal.

She smiled at the sight of her name scrawled in his regal handwriting and could not help the small flutter in her chest at the thought of him thinking of her.

Dearest Katarina,

I apologize once more for my abrupt departure from your kingdom. I had intended and now wish I could have extended my stay so as to speak with you more. However, my own Realm currently needs me. I will keep my letter brief and to the point so as to encourage a swift response. I sent a carriage in hopes that you might accept my invitation, and that your father would be willing to part with you for a few weeks.

The coronation of Princess Alayna of the Northern Kingdom and Prince Samuel of the Southern Kingdom are to take place at week's end. I had hoped... nay, I had wished for you to join me in my Realm to help celebrate. I know we briefly discussed my Realm, and I hoped you might wish to see it for yourself.

Please extend my regards to your father and the rest of your family.

Isaac

Katarina read the letter again, only aloud to her father as he paced the entry hall of the castle. She watched him closely as he pondered the invite.

"You will accept."

Her face split into an excited smile. "Oh thank you, Father." She rushed towards him and hugged him tightly.

He pulled her hands away and held her at arm's length. "On one condition, Katarina. You must learn everything there is to know about this Realm. I want to know their plans, their wishes, and their structure. Everything. I realize you are attracted to the prince, but you must not allow this attraction to interfere with my plans. Understand?"

She nodded, though she hated the idea of spying on Isaac and his realm. However, she knew it would be the only way her father would let her leave. And leave is definitely what she wanted to do. She could not wait to see what life was like outside their castle walls. *Had she ever ventured outside the walls? No. Not that she could remember.* How nice it must be to see different lands.

"I will do whatever you wish of me, Father." She stated calmly, earning the satisfied smile she knew would come.

"Very well. You leave tonight." Abner signaled Rupert to give him his response and to ready the carrier for his daughter. Rupert sent a message back to Prince Isaac and awaited Princess Katarina. He knew Isaac would meet him at the boundary between Abner's Realm and Alayna's to intercept Katarina as a welcome. He also prayed that King Abner would allow them all to depart without hindrance, fearing a repeat of their last journey.

CHAPTER 8

Dawn came quickly and before he could fully stretch away his slumber, Ryle found his feet hitting the floor and ready for the day's events. He was nervous, yes, but he knew that if they did not attempt his crossing the boundary line, their plan would be delayed. His main concern was leaving Alayna. Should he not be able to cross freely like his brother, he dreaded not seeing Alayna every day. He would be trapped in the Lands like Edward. Forced to gaze upon his family from a distance. *No.* He shook his head. There was no room to think of such things. His crossing would be successful. He clasped the buttons on his tunic as he straightened. Emerald. The colors of the Northern Kingdom. Colors he wore proudly as his post as Captain of the Royal Guard for Alayna. Though different than the pale blue he was familiar with, Ryle knew he would wear whatever colors he needed to if it meant serving Alayna. He heard a light knock on his door.

"Come in." His deep voice echoed through the room.

Clifton poked his head into the room. "Ready?" He asked quietly, knowing the remainder of the castle still slept.

Ryle nodded and grabbed his sword on his way out of the room. He and Clifton followed the back stairwell Princess Elizabeth had often used prior to her father's knowledge of her visits to the boundary line and her brother. They quietly made their way out of the castle and towards the stables. Prince Isaac and Prince Samuel awaited them, ready and in their saddles.

"It's about time." Isaac baited. "Samuel and I have been here for hours."

Samuel shook his head to contradict the false statement and the Eastern brothers smirked as they vaulted onto their own horses.

"Remind me again why we need him." Ryle stated to Clifton, his younger brother chuckling as they all set out towards Elizabeth's clearing.

When the familiar tree line emerged before them, all princes dismounted and eased through the brush to the other side. Edward was not present yet but a woman with golden hair emerged on the other side. Cecilia. She smiled in welcome, her gaze traveling from one man to the next and she nodded appreciatively at the sight before her. She disappeared for a few minutes and then Edward emerged, Cecilia by his side. His eyes widened in surprise at the sight of all the princes coming to see him. He bowed towards the boundary line and waved a hand for Clifton to cross.

Clifton turned to his friends. "I will be back shortly. Let me check the conditions first." He easily stepped through the veil and Ryle watched his brother closely. No signs of anything amiss, it seemed. Perhaps it was not painful to cross.

Edward greeted Clifton with a hand upon his shoulder. "I am glad you have come. I am glad to see all the princes so united."

"Yes. We have much to discuss with you." Clifton nodded his greeting towards Cecilia. She smiled warmly and waved him and Edward towards a log to sit upon as they spoke. She eased onto a boulder near them and listened closely as Clifton began telling Edward of the possible plans for assault against Lancer.

"So Alayna wishes to utilize the Uniters?" Edward asked with glee. "I am so glad. I am amazed at the young prince of the south offering his armories to us as well."

"Yes, Samuel will be most instrumental. Most of your Uniters are former Southern guards and Samuel feels somewhat responsible for their fate. He wishes to supply them with what they need to aid in their rescue."

Edward clapped his hands and hopped to his feet as he began to pace. "So your brother will cross daily to work with the guards and myself in our quest to defeat Lancer with a surprise attack?"

"Yes. That is the plan." Clifton confirmed.

"And does my sister have an idea of a timeline of when she feels this assault should take place? Lancer's weakened power may not last for long."

"The coronations will take place in a few days." Clifton added. "I imagine a week or two to ensure the guards are fully trained and a military strategy iron clad enough to pass the approval of the entire council. Then I imagine it will happen rather quickly. Do you think this plan is possible?"

Edward nodded. "Yes. Definitely. Lancer will not suspect a thing. He's too focused upon himself at the moment to even think about the boundary line. Especially since he gave me the task to spy across the line. I will report to him only what we want him to know."

"Very good. I am afraid it places you in quite a precarious position. You will need to lead Lancer's army without a hint of suspicion. Do you think you will be capable of this?"

"Yes. I know I will." Edward confirmed. "This is what we have all been praying for all these years." He squeezed Cecilia's hand in excitement and she grinned as he kissed her heartily on the lips. Clifton smirked as he stood and walked back towards the boundary.

"Well then, I guess it is time for us to test my brother's ability to cross." Clifton stepped back through the boundary into Elizabeth's clearing and laid a comforting hand on his brother's shoulder as they stepped towards the foggy line.

∞

"Will you please stop pacing?" Elizabeth cast a tender smile towards her sister as Alayna darted from one end of the room to the other with her arms wrapped around her waist and her eyes boring holes in the floor. "Ryle will be fine."

Alayna's brown gaze shot to her sister. "We do not know that. What if he is not able to cross back over? I... we..." She trailed off and then shook her head. "You're right. He will be back."

"You were so confident last night in his crossing, why the sudden change of heart?" Elizabeth asked, though she could tell her sister possessed feelings for the Eastern prince, she also knew Alayna was too stubborn to admit the fact.

"Well, it wasn't real then. It is real now. He's actually going to cross right now. I guess it just didn't hit me until now." Alayna worried her hands and then walked over to a floral arrangement in front of the main window. She fluffed the flowers all while her gaze travelled outdoors and towards Elizabeth's clearing.

"He will be fine." Elizabeth repeated. "Ryle is of Lancer's blood. He will be able to cross freely."

"She is right." King Eamon's voice drifted into the room as he entered with a warm smile. "And how are you my dear?" Eamon leaned down and kissed Elizabeth's cheek as she smiled. "I'm doing well. Alayna is the one we should be worried about at the moment."

Eamon chuckled. "Ah, a woman's worry. I can spot it a mile away. Come dear, sit." He waved Alayna over to a free sofa as he sat as well. "Everything will go smoothly today, just you wait and see."

"You are not concerned?"

He shook his head. "Not at all. If Cliff believes Ryle can cross without complication, then so do I. Besides, Ryle will serve us one way or another. Whether he remains in the Lands or in the Realm, he will always wish to serve the Realm. To serve you, Alayna." King Eamon's voice held a tone of recognition. Alayna felt her cheeks flush before she turned away to focus on anything besides her feelings for Ryle. *Was it that obvious to everyone?* She rolled her shoulders back and stood. "I think I will await the men at the stables."

"Alayna." Elizabeth sighed in frustration and pointed back to the sofa. "I am not worried. King Eamon is not worried. *You* should not be worried. Now sit. Keep us company. Perhaps some conversation will distract you."

"I doubt it." Alayna admitted. "But I will try."

"Good." Elizabeth and Eamon stated at the same time making them each smile.

"Is King Anthony out and about?" Alayna asked.

"I believe he went to the markets this morning with a few of his attendants." Eamon explained. "I do not expect he will be gone long."

"And Melody? Did she leave with him?"

"No." Elizabeth's eyes held a thrill. "She is walking the gardens with as much worry as you... only her thoughts are with Samuel."

"Samuel?" Alayna's brows rose in surprise.

Elizabeth nodded emphatically. "I think there is something brewing between the two."

King Eamon chuckled at her excitement.

"But he is only sixteen."

"And she only eighteen." Elizabeth added. "It's not that large of an age difference, Alayna. Besides, Samuel acts more a man than some twice his age."

"That is true." Alayna acknowledged. "How does Anthony or Isaac feel of this budding romance?"

Elizabeth shrugged. "I think Isaac suspects something between the two, but he doesn't seem concerned. And King Anthony," Elizabeth playfully grimaced, "I pray he finds out in the most delicate of fashion."

Eamon laughed at Elizabeth's response. "I am sure Anthony will be quite pleased."

"Are you sure?" Elizabeth asked curiously. "He seems quite... insensitive at times."

"Yes, Anthony can be a hard man every now and again, but he wants the best for his children. As do we all." Eamon cast a pointed glance at Alayna and she diverted her gaze.

"Well then I look forward to seeing how the two young ones interact." Elizabeth rubbed her hands together playfully.

"Do not place your nose in their business, Sister." Alayna warned. "Just because you have found happiness with Clifton does not mean everyone else is ready for that next step."

"I know." Elizabeth looked disappointed at her plans being thwarted. "But I can still be excited, can't I?"

Eamon reached over and squeezed her hand. "Of course, dear. I believe the Realm could use a little more happiness spread around, and your smiles seem to do the trick."

Elizabeth grinned and then turned towards Alayna, her sister's mind wandering to the clearing, to Ryle. Though Alayna refused to admit her feelings for the former prince, now Captain, the anxious hold her teeth held on her bottom lip told otherwise. Elizabeth nodded towards Alayna's direction and Eamon turned to witness the princess's attentions. Blinded by her worry, Alayna did not notice the small exchange of smirks between the other two, but instead focused all her hopes and prayers on the small gap within the trees.

∞

Ryle flexed his fingers at his sides, his palms sore from his fingernails digging within his clenched fists. He took a deep breath, felt Clifton's hand on his shoulder, and stepped towards the boundary line. "Is it supposed to feel this way?" He asked quietly, a slight hum of energy lacing through his toes as they neared the line.

"Yes." Clifton replied. "It is not painful, Brother. Trust me."

The two brothers stepped through the veil and into The Land of Unfading Beauty and Edward awaited them. Ryle exhaled slowly as his sharp gaze travelled around the new surroundings. Nothing seemed out of the ordinary, but he could not shake a slight niggling at the base of his neck. An itch that only meant something was not right. Edward walked forward and shook his hand heartily. "You are most welcome here, Prince Ryle." He bowed and waved a hand towards Cecilia. She stepped forward quietly and curtsied shyly.

"It is nice to meet you both." Ryle nodded in greeting.

Edward waved him towards a break in the forest and Ryle and Clifton followed. Ducking beneath branches and thicket, they quickly emerged in a vast clearing filled with men and women of various statures. "This is where the Uniters hide." Edward explained. "Prince Ryle, meet your army." Edward waved his hand over the crowd that began to emerge around Ryle and Clifton. Many men shaking their hands and excited to see faces of authority from the Realm. A hush fell over the forest and Edward pointed to a large stump for Ryle to stand upon. He climbed atop the trunk and rested his hand on the hilt of his sword. "I am Ryle of the Eastern Kingdom, I serve the Realm of Future Queen Alayna!" His voice carried strong across the clearing drawing everyone's attention. "The time has come for us to unite together in overcoming Lancer and overcoming these cursed lands! It is my understanding that you pledge your loyalties to the Realm and that you will fight with us to break down this blasted boundary!" Several cheers erupted, and he lowered his hands to calm the noise. "Over the next couple of weeks, we will be training, preparing, and planning for our moment! Prince Samuel of the Southern Kingdom will be supplying us with weapons and armor! He thanks you for your loyalty and service! We must be secret, stealthy, and serious in our task! *We* are the only hope of our Realm! Fight with me! And let us take back our lands!"

A roar of yells and whistles followed, and several men awaited him as he hopped back to the ground. He shook more hands and met more faces, yet his anxiety over his crossing lingered at the front of his mind. Edward finally stepped in and waved away the remaining troops as he turned Ryle and Clifton back towards the boundary line.

"Now for the fun part." Clifton whispered, nodding towards the looming boundary. Edward, Cecilia, Ryle, and Clifton walked out of the clearing and back towards the veil and Isaac and Samuel quickly rose to their feet at the sight of them.

Ryle turned to Edward with a weighing gaze. "I will be back in the morning at first light. Make sure they are prepared."

Edward nodded. "Of course. We are all eager to prepare." He swiped a hand through his hair and then pointed for Cecilia to head back to the clearing. Once she disappeared, he stepped closer to the brothers. "I do not know if I will be here in the morning. Lancer is quite needy at the moment. Should I not be here, please know the Uniters serve the Realm whole-heartedly. You will have a resilient and loyal army."

"Thank you, Prince."

Ryle studied Edward closely a moment longer, the Northern Prince's demeanor fidgety and antsy. Clifton patted Ryle's shoulder to turn him to leave, his intense gaze never wavering as it moved from Edward to the boundary line. Without hesitation, he stepped forward and easily passed through the veil back into the Realm. A collective breath released from Samuel and Isaac as both Eastern princes emerged on their side of the line. "Glad to see you can cross." Isaac slapped Ryle on the back and smiled.

"Me too." Ryle admitted lightly placing his hand over his chest in relief. He turned a suspicious eye back towards Edward as he offered a small wave of success at his crossing. Edward nodded with excitement and then hurried back through the trees.

"You seem distracted." Clifton stated.

"He just seems off." Ryle's eyes finally turned back to his brother and friends and he shrugged. "I guess that will be for me to investigate further."

"It's the darkness. It makes him a bit distraught. There is no telling when the last time he slept or ate." Clifton explained. "It is one of the effects he said is quite interesting. He says he feels completely fine."

"And you trust him?"

"For now."

Isaac and Samuel listened intently as the two brothers discussed Edward. Isaac's attention then spanned towards the boundary line and he stepped closer to see Cecilia emerge. She offered a small wave as she hurried towards a clothing line near the river and retrieved several articles of clothes and placed them in a basket. "She's a pretty thing." Isaac stated.

"That is Cecilia." Clifton explained. "The woman Edward crossed to be with."

"Ah. Makes perfect sense now." Isaac grinned and turned back to the group paying her little mind. "Shall we head back? Our mission was successful. I imagine you will educate the council on what was discussed in tonight's meeting."

"Yes. I will."

"Did they seem pleased, my Lord? Pleased that I had not forgotten them?" Samuel asked curiously.

"I believe so, Samuel." Ryle admitted and noticed the slight relaxation to the young prince's shoulders. "We will have a strong army."

"But?" Isaac asked, his eyes narrowed as he studied the two brothers.

Ryle huffed in frustration, but tried to tamper down his annoyance, knowing they brought Isaac for his gift of discernment.

"I have potential concerns about Edward. But that is not a discussion for now. Let us reconvene at the castle first. I am sure the Future Queen is anxious to see us."

"Speak for yourself." Isaac mumbled playfully, earning the collective chuckle from the other men as Ryle's neck slightly flushed. Embarrassed at the insinuation, Ryle slapped his reins and galloped a full length ahead of the others as they headed across the highlands back to the castles of the North.

∞

Elizabeth hopped to her foot and balanced herself on the back of the sofa as she heard footsteps emerging at the entry to the conservatory. Her face split into a large smile as Clifton emerged followed by Isaac and Samuel. Clifton immediately embraced her, burying his face in her hair until she softly giggled. "I say! It must have been a good trip." Her eyes then carried to Ryle standing in the doorway, silence deafening the room as Alayna turned from the window and their eyes met. Elizabeth lightly nudged Clifton with her elbow as everyone watched.

"It would seem it is indeed bloodline that can cross." Clifton stated proudly, as Ryle stepped further into the room and accepted the relieved hug from his father. Alayna blinked and lightly shook her head as she walked forward and gently placed her hand on his arm. "I am glad to see you have returned, Captain." Her voice held

164

formality, but Ryle noted the light spark within her eyes that held something entirely different and he smiled as he squeezed her hand. "It is good to *be* back, Alayna."

"I trust we will all receive an earful at the council meeting tonight." Eamon stated with excitement.

"There is much to discuss." Ryle stated, his eyes never leaving Alayna.

Isaac walked by and stumbled into Ryle's shoulder breaking his trance on Alayna. "Oh, terribly sorry. I am just headed to the dining hall for some food. Please... continue." He heard Elizabeth chuckle as Clifton carried her by Ryle and Alayna, and she lightly slapped Isaac on the back of the head at his embarrassing the two.

When they stood alone, Ryle turned towards her once more and grabbed her hands in his. "I am most relieved, Alayna. I must admit I feared I may not return this evening."

"Me too." She agreed. "I am quite pleased myself, Ryle." She lightly stood on her tiptoes as she grazed a soft kiss against his cheek before bypassing him towards the dining hall.

King Eamon lingered in the hall, and as Alayna passed by, he met his son on his way out.

"Tell me you were not spying." Ryle stated with frustration.

"Indeed I was." Eamon admitted with a pleased smirk. "I'm a father. It's my right." He slapped his son on the back in a friendly pat. "You have no need to be embarrassed, son. She fancies you as well. My goodness the girl barely sat a moment today, pacing back and forth worried over you."

"I am sure she was worried about everyone."

"I'm sure that is partly true. However, Elizabeth made quick work of teasing the poor girl, and it seems her attentions were focused upon you." Eamon studied his eldest son a moment and he frowned. "I see you are carrying a burden."

165

"Well there is much about to happen." Ryle's patience with his father began to wane as he neared the dining hall and the smell of a feast made his stomach grumble in anticipation.

"But you do not have to face it alone, Ryle. Therefore, the burden must be shared as well."

"I just—" he paused as a servant passed by them. "I just want this all to be over. No more Lancer, no more Unfading Lands, and no more fear."

"As do we all, son. But matters are only going to intensify in the coming weeks. You must learn to enjoy the present while preparing for the future. Relax this evening. It was a successful day, yes?"

Ryle nodded.

"Then bask in that, and tomorrow we will face what needs to be faced." Eamon squeezed his son's shoulders before entering the dining hall with a warm smile. He nodded towards Anthony in welcome. "How was the village, my friend?"

"It was quite nice. I always enjoy seeing a village rebuild after a war. Things seem to be almost back to normal. A good sign." Anthony reported, nodding his impression towards Alayna's acts of reconstruction in her kingdom.

"Ah, the signs of a good fit to the throne, yes?" Eamon beamed as he lightly toasted towards Alayna. She accepted the praise with gratitude that her father's eldest friends approved of the work she had accomplished. Two successful kings praising her effort, she inwardly sighed in relief as she leaned back in her chair to make room for the servers.

Footsteps sounded from the great hall and a messenger in Western apparel emerged at the edge of the dining room. Tomas walked over to retrieve the letter and then carried it to Prince Isaac. His brows rose in curiosity as he unfolded the parchment. A brief flash of a smile emerged, and he glanced up towards his father. "Katarina will be arriving come tomorrow."

"What wonderful news!" Elizabeth cheered across the table.

"I think I will ride to the border lines and intercept her carriage and escort her the rest of the way." Isaac stated.

"Would you like some company, my Lord?" Samuel asked.

"Aye, that would be most welcome, Samuel. Thank you."

"We will house her on the third level." Alayna announced. "Down the hall from your chambers, Elizabeth."

"Wonderful." Elizabeth winked at Isaac. "I am sure Katarina and I will have much to discuss."

"Actually, yes, I am hoping so." Alayna continued, causing everyone to glance her direction. "We are not to assume she is here without hidden motives. If her father is as ruthless as we have heard recently, then we must remain on guard. You, Sister, have a way with people. I wish for you to befriend her and see what else she may know."

"You mean you would like me to pretend to be her friend?"

"Exactly."

"No." Elizabeth crossed her arms in disappointment at her older sister.

"Pardon?" Alayna asked in shock of being questioned.

"I will not pretend to be her friend, Alayna. From what Isaac has told us, Katarina is a kind woman. I will treat her as such unless she gives me reason otherwise. I do not wish to treat her suspect."

"Just be cautious." Alayna warned with finality.

"I always am, but I think it rude for us to assume she is up to no good, when she has yet to even arrive."

Clifton lightly clasped Elizabeth's hand under the table and offered a small smile. "You are a great judge in character, love. Just befriend her in your special way, and you will know whether or not there is need to be cautious. That is all Alayna is asking. We need you to use that friendly disposition of yours to welcome her, and that incredible discernment you possess to aid us in deciphering whether or not she is friend or foe."

"Well when you put it like that." Elizabeth lightly kissed Clifton's cheek at his subtle way of complimenting her while also bestowing his requests. "He has a better way with words, Sister." Elizabeth stated.

Alayna playfully rolled her eyes and then nodded her thanks towards Clifton at initiating her request in a way Elizabeth would accept. She did not wish to make Katarina feel unwelcome, but she did plan to keep her eyes and ears open to the possibility of Abner sending his daughter as a spy.

∞

Edward paced the boundary line and mumbled under his breath as he began to sort through strategic plans of attack for the Realm to take upon Lancer's army. The day was warm, too warm, and he felt the sweat seeping through his tunic as he inwardly ranted different military tactics. *The only passage would be through the forest on the backside of the castle*, he mused. Ryle would need to circle around without being seen. The trees would provide decent coverage of his movements, giving Edward enough time to move Lancer's army away from the castle. *But how? What reason would he give for moving Lancer's guards?* He scratched his head as he stared off towards the trees. He heard a branch snap and he quickly turned, sword at the ready, until Cecilia stepped through the thicket. "Cecilia love, you scared me."

"I'm sorry, Edward." She lightly kissed his cheek and then cupped his face in her hands. Her eyes stared into his a moment longer and she shook her head. "You are not well, Edward."

"What do you mean? I feel fine." He holstered his sword and lightly nudged her hands away as he continued to pace. "There is something you are not telling me." Cecilia stated. "I wish you would though. I love you. And I can tell something is wrong."

Edward studied her a moment and then reached for her hands leading her to the same log he and Ryle had sat upon the day before. "I am just stressed about coming events, dearest. There is much at stake."

"Not least of all is your life." Cecilia pointed out with concern.

"There is that." Edward forced a smile. "But it is worth it. My whole purpose in these Lands is to bring down Lancer."

"And what about me?" Cecilia asked curiously, her blue eyes sparkling with unshed tears.

"Ah, you are the love of my life, Cecilia. I want us to be free of this cursed place so that we may lead a normal life outside the veil. How I wish to give you the life you deserve. No more hiding in the woods but living in a castle. No more rags for wear, but beautiful dresses of the finest silk. I want to give you those things, but I cannot if we remain trapped in these wretched lands."

"Our time here has not all been bad." Cecilia quietly pointed out. "You are a leader. You are Lancer's Captain, Edward. How do you expect to successfully blindside him when you serve him as well? I fear he will kill you if he learns of your treason."

"That is why he will not. There is no reason for him to. Prince Ryle will lead the Uniters against the army of the Lands. I will be captaining the opposing forces. In Lancer's eyes I will be serving him and performing my duty as Captain to the Unfading Lands. He will never know of my betrayal until the Lands come crashing down around him. By then, it won't matter, Cecilia. Don't you see? He will have no choice but to give into defeat. The boundary line will fall. We will all be set free. Free of the darkness that he possesses. Free from the grip of death he holds upon us."

"It is death that he withholds from us, Edward. We do not die here. That is his gift to us. Eternal youth."

"And it is unnatural. We may have originally wanted this life, Cecilia, but a life that makes us lose our families... is that what we imagined? Did we even think about the consequence of seeing our loved ones die? Time passes and so do they, yet we remain." Edward shook his head. "I do not wish to see another one of my family members die before my very eyes. I already regret not being with my father all those years. Do you not miss your mother? I see you watching her every now and then through the veil. Do you not wish to speak to her once more?"

Cecilia nodded. "I do, but—"

"There are no buts." He cut in. "We can do this, Cecilia. We just have to believe Lancer can be overcome. Hate is what guides him. What if our love for our families and each other is what can defeat him? Our love for the Realm has to be stronger than his hate. It *has* to be. I believe it to be. And I know Prince Ryle believes it too. We just have to think of a way to guide his troops against Lancer's army, so that it is a surprise attack. That is the current dilemma I am faced with. I do not know how I am going to maneuver a strategic position for the Uniters just yet." He squeezed her hand. "Are you with me, love?"

"Always." Cecilia replied with a sweet smile. She lightly rested her head on his shoulder as he continued murmuring about different plans of attack and locations. Her heart was torn. On the one hand, Lancer and the Unfading Lands saved her from an ordinary life that held future promises of bitterness and loneliness. Crossing into the Lands had been the best decision she had ever made. She was with Edward because of that decision. To destroy the boundary line, to destroy Lancer's power... well, she didn't quite want to think of the consequences. She did not wish for her old life as Edward did. She only wished to live a life of happiness with him. Free from her past. He rose to his feet and began to pace, and she watched him closely. She loved him, wholeheartedly. How could she think of losing him in a battle against the Realm, when she could easily keep him here? Where he was safe. Where he was respected. Where he was loved. Nervously, she stood and quietly slipped back through the trees. She would need to think about the coming events in peace, and she only knew of one place to set her mind at ease. The place she originally crossed. The place she first left her old life behind. The place she first embraced her immortality. And the place she first met Lancer.

∞

The carriage pulled to a stop and Katarina jolted at the opening of the door as the Western guard extended his hand inside. "Come, my Lady."

"Have we arrived?"

"Not yet. However, we have a special visit." He smiled warmly as she slowly stepped out of the carriage onto a forest-lined road that held the scent of moss and pine. A scent unfamiliar, but lovely all the same. She brushed a hand over the front of her skirt to try and minimize the wrinkles from her travels until she heard a throat clear. She glanced up to find Prince Isaac standing before her, dressed in his finest tunic and great wolf pelt strung over his broad shoulders. Her breath caught at the vision and she beamed. He bowed and she obediently curtsied, neither stepping forward, but gauging the other from a distance. "I am glad you agreed to come." His deep voice fluttered over her raw nerves and her face blossomed into another smile. "I am excited to journey to your land, Prince Isaac. So far the journey has been quite invigorating." Her eyes then shifted to a young man walking up beside Isaac, his black tunic bearing a double sword crossing beneath his left shoulder. She was unfamiliar with the symbol, but though his colors were of a dark nature, his eyes held a light to them that eased her nerves.

"Ah, this is Prince Samuel of the Southern Kingdom." Isaac introduced. "Or should I say, Future King Samuel." He grinned at his young friend as Samuel stepped forward and bowed politely. "It is an honor to meet you, Princess Katarina."

"Future King." She curtsied, her eyes wide with wonder at all the excitement. "Such a welcome party. I must assume I have officially crossed out of my father's lands into your Realm."

171

"That is correct." Isaac winked and stepped forward offering her his arm as he led her back to the carriage. "I thought I might escort you the remainder of the way."

"That sounds lovely." Katarina's awe remained as Isaac opened the carriage door and she slipped inside. He tossed a nod towards Samuel, the young prince trekking back towards the front of the caravan, as Isaac slid into the carriage as well and shut the door. Katarina's eyes widened at his presence. "Is it alright if I join you?" He asked, noting her shyness.

"Of course, your Grace."

He chuckled and waved away her words. "Please do not call me that, Katarina. Call me Isaac."

"Oh I do not know, my Lord. For standard manners and protocol determine titles to be used. I am a visitor to your kingdom, and as such, I must address you with formality and respect to your title."

Isaac burst into laughter again and then lightly reached forward and squeezed her hand. "Oh Katarina, I do hope you see how different my realm is from yours. And please, call me Isaac. However, if you must remain so formal, just call me Prince Isaac."

She nodded, and her hand tingled from his light grasp. He removed his hand and leaned back in a relaxed posture against the seat.

"How much further until we reach the Northern Kingdom?"

"Only a couple of hours." He stated. "Once we cross into the Realm of Future Queen Alayna, the travel is quite smooth and passes quickly. Did your father give you any trouble in regard to my letter?"

"No. Surprisingly not."

"That is surprising, especially considering his guards attacked me on my way out. Thank you for that warning, by the way."

She blushed. "I am sorry my father sent the men to follow you and to harm you. He was testing you."

"I figured as much. I'm assuming I passed since he agreed to send you here?"

She shrugged. "I am not sure. He is a difficult man to read."

"I imagine so. Yet I will hope he has decided to give me a shot. Perhaps he will find me worthy to escort his daughter around the Realm of Alayna." He winked at her again and smiled as a light blush stained her cheeks.

"Prince Samuel seems kind." She stated.

"He is. Very kind. The very opposite of his father and brother."

"Are they of the harsh sort?" She asked curiously.

"They are dead." Isaac replied without feeling.

"Oh, I am terribly sorry."

"Don't be. They are the ones who initiated the attack on the Realm. Samuel warned us and saved the Realm as we know it. He is a good man and will be an even better king. The South will have a new beginning with him as their leader."

"It is endearing, the way you champion him." She studied Isaac closely as he spoke of the young prince. "You have a soft spot for him."

Isaac smirked. "Somewhat. I believe we all do. Though I have to say I take interest in him for personal reasons as well. I believe he intends to court my sister."

Katarina's brows rose. "Are they to be wed?"

Isaac rubbed a hand over the back of his neck and feigned a grimace. "I sense it one day soon. However, my father does not see what is clearly sparking between the two. I do not know how he will swallow the news."

"Does he not like Prince Samuel?"

"He does. It's just... my sister is a special woman. It will be hard to part with her. I do not think any man would ever measure up."

"That is a sweet sentiment. I look forward to meeting her to see her greatness for myself."

"Ah, you will. You will also enjoy the other princesses as well. Elizabeth is quite the fighting spirit. Should she overwhelm you, just let me know." He smiled at the thought of his dear friend quizzing poor Katarina upon her arrival. He prayed Elizabeth would take it easy upon the gentle spirited Katarina.

"Such powerful women in your Realm. I should like to witness them all. I imagine they are a sight to behold."

"You will fit in nicely." He complimented, noting her slight embarrassment again. He could get used to making Katarina flush. He liked the fact he actually could and made a mental note to compliment her more often.

∞

Alayna's skirts draped over the side of the parapet as she sat outside along the castle wall. The slight breeze teased the tendrils of her blonde hair with the scents of jasmine and fresh earth and she felt her shoulders slowly relax as she leaned her back against the stone wall. *How many times had she come out here as a child to gaze upon her father's lands? Too many to count*, she realized with a faint smile. But that was the difference then. They were her father's lands. Now they were *her* lands. A fact that caused a tightness in her chest and a slight wave a panic to threaten her calm demeanor. She would not give into the feelings of inadequacy. King Eamon and King Anthony both seemed impressed with the conditions of the North, and that encouraged her more than she could say. *But to rule an entire realm?* She lightly brushed a stray curl back behind her ear. *No room for doubts now*, she thought. A battle set upon the horizon of the near future and she could only be prepared for it. She was to remain brave. People looked to her for answers, for courage, and for hope. She must remain strong despite the inner fears of failure that lurked within her mind. Ryle was confident in their decision as well. His trip to the Unfading Lands that morning had proved to be an encouragement. His first day of training showed the Uniters a strong force, and their skill more advanced than any of them had hoped. War would arrive sooner than first planned. Tomorrow she would be announced queen. Then their focus would move to the South. From there, plans would begin to forge and by the time she arrived back in the Northern castle in a week's time, a battle would be underway. A battle that had been brewing since she was a teenager. A fight against what seemed an untouchable enemy. Only through Ryle and Clifton, the untouchable became touchable. She sent up a silent prayer that the brothers would remain safe from harm. Though she had yet to hear the plans for Clifton during the war, she knew that Elizabeth would be devastated if anything happened to her husband.

"I thought I might find you out here." Elizabeth's voice carried over as she slowly walked her way towards Alayna.

"You are mobile again, I see." Alayna beamed as Elizabeth eased next to her, swinging her legs over the side of the parapet and letting them dangle in the breeze.

"I am. Though I am having to get used to the feeling again, I have to say I quite like it." She lightly slapped a hand on Alayna's thigh. "And what brings you out here to your thinking spot?"

"What is there not to think about?" Alayna replied honestly.

"True. I imagine there is much going on in that brain of yours. Coronation, war, love…"

"Love?" Alayna shook her head.

175

"Do not deny your feelings for Ryle, Sister. It is just you and I out here on the ledge, and I know better. Besides, I am quite familiar with the feeling." Elizabeth softly smiled, as Alayna no longer denied her feelings.

"It is complicated." Alayna stated.

"It always is."

"Yes, but this is—" she paused and then softly chuckled in disbelief. "Extremely complicated."

"I admit there are a few things that would need to be worked out, but I have no doubt all hindrances can be overcome."

"Spoken like a true champion." Alayna giggled as Elizabeth placed her hand over her heart and sighed in exaggeration.

"In all honesty Alayna, have you and Ryle discussed the possibility of a courtship between the two of you?"

"What?! No!" Alayna gasped in horror, her head turning to make sure they were indeed alone. "There is too much happening right now, Lizzy. I wouldn't dream of proposing such a thing. Besides, he is Captain now. He is no longer a prince from a neighboring kingdom. I do not even know if a courtship with a guard is possible."

"You are the queen. Can't you make that decision?" Elizabeth challenged.

"Well… I guess I could. But… no. There is too much going on right now. Perhaps when life slows down a bit. Perhaps once we have victory in the Unfading Lands I will think of such matters. By then Edward will have returned and take his rightful place as king, and I will go back to being a princess. Just a princess."

"You believe Edward will be king?"

"It is his right."

"That he gave up." Elizabeth's voice slightly rose in distaste.

"I thought you would be happy about the possibility of Edward returning."

"I am excited about his return. But I do not agree with him being king. You are to take the throne. Father entrusted it to you, Alayna. Edward has been gone for years; our people do not know him. They know you. They respect you. They are prepared to embrace you as queen. Edward no longer deserves the right to rule a people he no longer knows."

Alayna studied her younger sister carefully. "I just assumed everyone would expect me to relinquish the throne once he came back. I did not realize there might even be a slight chance of resistance."

"You assumed wrong. I believe in you, Alayna. And I will help in any way I can. You are not in this alone. Right now, you have a Captain who will fight until the ends of the earth for you, and you have surrounding kingdoms willing to do the same. If that does not show support, then I do not know what does." Elizabeth's blue gaze travelled towards the horizon and she smiled. "Looks like Prince Isaac and his future bride have arrived."

Alayna chuckled. "You sound confident."

"I am. I have never seen Isaac speak of a woman as he does Katarina. I am excited to meet her. Perhaps love is in the air, hm?"

"You are a romantic, Sister." Alayna stated. "You always have been."

Alayna turned her head at the sound of footsteps and Mary walked up. "Ah, hello Mary."

Elizabeth groaned. "He sent you for me, didn't he?"

Mary nodded with a smile. "Yes, my Lady. He just wished for me to check on you. To make sure you—"

"Weren't over doing it." Elizabeth finished. "I swear my husband worries more than a duck over her ducklings."

Laughing, Alayna lightly patted her sister's knee. "He loves you. And someone has to look out for you. Mary and I both know how strong-willed and stubborn you can be." Alayna shot a wink towards Mary as Elizabeth swung her legs back over the parapet and eased to her feet. "Yes, well perhaps I will go find that husband of mine and give him something to really worry about."

"Now that sounds dangerous." Alayna slid to her feet as well and followed as Elizabeth cast a devious smile over her shoulder on their way through the doors.

"Ah, there you two are." King Anthony smiled warmly as he met them on the stairwell and nodded his approval at Elizabeth's mobility. "It seems Isaac has arrived with his Katarina."

"Yes, we saw them approaching the gates." Elizabeth stated. "Are you excited to meet the woman who seems to have stolen your son's heart?"

Anthony studied Elizabeth with a keen eye and then glanced towards Alayna. His original suspicions of Isaac's feelings for Elizabeth flashed across his face as he walked down the steps. "Yes, well I am curious to see his interactions with her." He finally added.

Clifton awaited them at the bottom of the stairs. "And there you are. I see Mary found you."

"Yes, Alayna and I were sitting on the parapet for some fresh air." Elizabeth reported with a light kiss to his cheek.

"That is good." Clifton allowed Elizabeth to slip her arm through his as he escorted her through the great hall towards the main entrance of the castle. Guards opened the main doors, and everyone stepped out onto the landing to offer a formal welcome to their arriving guest. The carriage pulled to a stop and Isaac emerged, a slight nervousness to his grin as he reached a hand inside. A head of long brown hair emerged, the silky curls hanging over narrow shoulders, a slim neck, and a stunning face. Elizabeth felt herself smiling as Katarina's caramel eyes widened in surprise and awe at what stood before her. Isaac draped her hand through his arm and escorted her up the steps towards his father. "Father, this is Princess Katarina."

Katarina curtsied and flashed a nervous glance up at King Anthony. The stately king offered a welcoming smile. "It is a pleasure, Katarina. My son speaks highly of you."

"Thank you, my Lord."

Her gaze then fell upon Clifton and Elizabeth, the Eastern couple posing a wondrous sight for a stranger as they stood with grace and regality. "This is Prince Clifton and Princess Elizabeth of the Eastern Kingdom." Isaac introduced.

Katarina curtsied, and Elizabeth undraped her arm from Clifton and quickly pulled the girl in a tight embrace. She chuckled as she pulled Katarina out to arm's length. "I am sorry to bombard you, Princess Katarina, but I have been most excited to meet you."

Katarina smiled shyly. "That is very kind, Princess Elizabeth. Thank you for such a welcome." Her words were soft, uncertain, as if small kindnesses were unfamiliar to her and Elizabeth caught the diligence in Isaac as he respectfully offered a comforting hand in guiding her to the next people. Clifton lightly patted Elizabeth's back and winked down at her in approval of her greeting.

"And this is Future Queen Alayna." Isaac watched as Katarina hesitated in her curtsy, so in awe of Alayna and the role she would soon possess.

"It is a great honor, your Grace."

Alayna smiled warmly. "And it is a pleasure to have you as our guest, Princess Katarina. I hope you find the Northern Kingdom to your liking."

"I am sure I will, your Highness. Thank you. Thank you all for such a kind welcome." Her gaze travelled over everyone one last time and settled upon King Eamon. She had heard so many stories about the Eastern King, to see his warm disposition in person only made all the rumors and stories more believable. *No wonder Lancer's sister wished to leave her father's realm*, she thought. He seemed kind. They all did. And Katarina was unaccustomed to genuine kindness. She wasn't quite sure how to react.

"My sister, Melody, will show you to your chambers if you wish to get settled and rested before dinner." Isaac stepped away so that Melody could approach. She smiled cordially, and Isaac could hear essence of small talk as the two women wandered off.

"She is beautiful." Clifton complimented. "And sweet."

"Yes. I believe she is." Isaac agreed.

"However did you manage that?"

Isaac turned to the Eastern prince in shock and Clifton laughed heartily. "I am teasing, my friend."

Isaac lightly flushed and then shook his head as Elizabeth emerged next to her husband. "She seems wonderful, Isaac. I cannot wait to chat with her more."

"Thank you, Elizabeth. And I must say it is good to see you up and about on your own."

"Why thank you." She lightly kicked her falsie out from under her skirt. "I feel quite independent again. Not long now and I will be challenging you to that promised duel."

"Is that so?" Isaac baited. "Well I look forward to it then. May the best man win."

Clifton chuckled as Elizabeth stuck her hand out for Isaac to shake in agreement of their challenge. "Indeed." She said with amusement.

CHAPTER 9

Alayna paced. Her emerald silk dress dragging behind her as she turned from one end of her chamber toward the other. "You must hold still, your Grace." Jessa's voice held a slight warning as she tried to lift the train to Alayna's formal gown so the future queen would not trip. "We must add your cape now. It is only a matter of time before King Anthony retrieves you for the ceremony."

Alayna paused, her nerves evident as she nodded stoically. She fingered her father's letter in her left hand and briefly brought it up to her heart. A knock sounded on her door and Elizabeth poked her head into the room. Her sister walked inside with a slow grace, dressed in her Eastern colors of formality and gasped. "Alayna! You look stunning!"

Alayna turned and found the smiling face of her younger sister staring at her proudly. "Father would be so proud of you, Alayna."

Alayna's lips softened into a sad smile. "I wish he was here."

181

Sympathy flashed across Elizabeth's soft face as she smiled. "Me too. We all do. But he is here in spirit." She lightly squeezed Alayna's hand and felt the letter. She pulled it from her sister's grasp and felt the sweaty parchment. "I carry mine with me too." Elizabeth reached into her cape pocket and withdrew her own letter. "We carry him with us. His strength. His encouragement." She grinned as she slipped Alayna's back into her hand. "I know you are nervous, Sister, but you are going to be a wonderful queen. This is the role you were always meant to fill."

Alayna shook her head. "No, it is Edward's position. I am just a substitute."

"No. You are not." Elizabeth stated firmly and led her sister to the chaise lounge to sit. "Look at me, Alayna." She ordered. "You must stop second guessing yourself. No one else does. You were meant to have the role as queen. *You* are the one that is here, not Edward. Edward made his choice, now it is time to make yours. Are you going to lock yourself in your room and skirt away from your duty to this kingdom? Or are you going to raise your chin up, look destiny straight in the eye and meet this new role head on?"

Alayna's lips tilted in a small smile. "You honestly think I can do this, don't you?"

"I imagine I would be quite vocal if I did not, don't you?" Elizabeth teased. "But yes, I do believe you are ready for this. And I also think there is no better person than you for such a time as this." Elizabeth lightly squeezed her hand. "Now, I am going to let you finish dressing and I will go scrounge up my husband and make sure he is ready as well. We are all supportive of you, Alayna. Please remember that."

"I will." She accepted the light kiss to her hair as Elizabeth walked away. She choked back her tears as she felt Jessa tie her cape around her neck and lightly place her tiara upon her head. She studied her face in the mirror. Golden hair, brown eyes and soft lips. She tilted her head and watched as her crown slightly slid. She reached up and adjusted the pin. This would be the last day she would wear her crown as princess. She would soon wear the crown that belonged to her mother. The crown of the queen. She lifted her shoulders and straightened her posture. Alayna, Queen of the Northern Highlands and of the Realm. She shrank back into her chair. Even the title weighed heavily upon her shoulders. *She could do this*, she told herself. Everyone was counting on her. The Realm was counting on her. She stood and softly brushed the wrinkles from her emerald silk dress, the heavy layers of lush fabrics glistening in the lantern light. *The dress was beautiful*, she thought, *finer than anything she had worn before*. But the symbol it represented had yet to rest comfortable upon her. Taking a deep breath and one last glance in the mirror, Alayna made her way to her chamber doors and slipped into the great hall to an awaiting King Anthony.

He smiled as she accepted his arm to walk down the main staircase. She heard the voices of the villagers, those that were able to find a lucky spot within the castle for the ceremony. She rounded the corner and Ryle stood at attention at the bottom of the stairs. When his gaze found hers, she smiled shyly. She felt him studying her, every inch of her, and she wished she could read his thoughts as he obediently followed behind her and King Anthony. She felt his eyes upon her and hoped she did not trip or stumble under the load of heavy fabrics. She rounded the columns of the main hall and stood where Elizabeth had stood not long ago for her wedding. Only this march was to be queen. As she began her walk with King Anthony, everyone bowed as she went, the feeling odd and unfamiliar to her as she wished to tell them to rise and not to kneel. She was just a princess, but deep down a sense of calm washed over her as the sight of the throne, her father's throne, appeared before her. King Eamon stood at attention and held her mother's crown on an ornate pillow in his hands. Ryle moved from behind her and stood to the right of the throne and Elizabeth and Clifton stood to the left along with Isaac, Melody, and Samuel. She smiled at each of them before stepping onto the lowest step of the pedestal and bowed before King Eamon. She remained on her knees as he began the recitation of the king's oath and the promises she must keep.

"You may rise, Princess Alayna." He ordered.

She slowly rose to her feet with the help of two attendants and stood before him. He lifted the crown and held it above her head. "Do you swear your life and allegiance to the servitude of this Realm? Do you promise to lead with courage, dignity, and respect? And most of all, do you vow to honor the people as they will equally honor you?"

"I do." She stated confidently, though her insides were tied, no, more than tied in knots, more like constricted by a snake, she took a deep breath as she felt her old tiara disappear and appear in Elizabeth's hands as King Eamon gently placed her mother's crown on her head. The weight surprising but not unnoticed as she gracefully accepted the responsibility it demanded.

"Queen Alayna of the Northern Highlands and of the Realm." King Eamon's voice carried throughout the great hall as cheers erupted and she turned to face her people. She noticed Elizabeth crying as she clapped and smiled and as Ryle stepped up to help her down the steps, she tightly clutched his arm, so he would not leave her to walk alone. He looked down at her and her imploring expression and nodded in understanding as he began leading her down the center aisle to accept accolades from the villagers. When they had circled into the quiet conservatory awaiting the rest of their family and friends, Alayna finally exhaled and sighed.

"You did great." Ryle complimented. She still held onto his arm and turned to face him.

"I felt that I might vomit if I had to speak any more than I did." The sudden honest outburst had Ryle laughing and Alayna blushing. "I am sorry, that was not supposed to come out."

He grinned as he brushed his knuckle over her cheek. "It just makes you more endearing, Queen Alayna."

"Please do not call me that." She cringed at the thought of Ryle having to be so formal, but knew it was only in respect of his position.

"It is what you are now." He replied softly.

"I know. I just—"

"Just what?"

"I just wish for us to have a familiarity between us. You are my Captain, and we should be friends."

"But you are my queen as well. Your position demands respect and I intend to give it." Confusion clouded his face as she shook her head in disagreement. "Not from you, Ryle. You hear me?"

His blue eyes held her gaze a moment longer and then he lightly bent his head and claimed her lips in a soft kiss. Alayna melted against him as she felt her hands slide up his strong arms and encircle his neck as he moved his lips over hers. He pulled away slowly, his gaze heated and torn. "I apologize, my Queen." The gruffness of his voice belied the look in his eyes and Alayna briefly closed her own. She took a step back. "Do not apologize."

He grabbed her hand and brushed a thumb over her knuckles. "I do care for you, Alayna. I hope you know that."

"I do."

"Good. But we must remember our roles now."

"I am Queen and you are my Captain."

"Indeed. And a Captain does not belong with a Queen."

His last statement hung in the air as disappointment settled upon Alayna's heart at the frustrating rejection. Voices carried into the room as Elizabeth swooped in and hugged her tightly. She lightly touched Alayna's crown and squealed. "It's so beautiful on you, Sister!"

"Thank you." Alayna replied softly, her gaze following Ryle as he stepped out of the way and allowed others to congratulate her. Katarina bowed before her and smiled. "You are the most beautiful queen I believe I have ever beheld."

Alayna smiled at the sweet princess and thanked her as she felt others pulling her in different conversations and directions. She continued to dash quick glances towards Ryle as he circled the room as well, her inattention to several conversations pulling the watchful eye of Isaac as he suddenly realized the slight tension in the room. He smirked as he lightly kissed her hand. "You are a vision in that dress, Alayna. Why if I were worthy, I would try to sweep you off your feet this instant."

She chuckled as he winked at her before slipping to Elizabeth's side. Katarina appeared beside him as they watched Alayna interact with the others. "Do you sense what I do?" Isaac whispered in a hushed tone as Elizabeth nodded. "Oh yes. I imagine we interrupted something special." Katarina listened to the two royals and her curiosity was evident. Isaac smirked and lightly elbowed Elizabeth. Elizabeth turned and grinned. "We believe there is a potential relationship brewing between my sister and Captain Ryle." She whispered conspiratorially to Katarina. Katarina's eyes widened as she studied the two unassuming targets of conversation. "Why do you say that?"

"Oh it is a long story. Let's just say they have a brief history that was interrupted by last year's wars and Lancer's threat. They are both extremely hardheaded and stubborn when it comes to love, but fully dedicated to their positions and roles in the Realm. It's quite frustrating and fun to watch sometimes." Elizabeth admitted, Isaac nodding in agreement.

"Do you think it wise to discuss such matters?" Katarina asked.

Both royals shrugged. "We are nosy." Isaac admitted.

"Indeed." Elizabeth agreed with a soft giggle. "Besides, we only want them to be happy."

"Has a Captain ever married a Queen in this Realm?" Katarina asked.

"No. There has only ever been kings who marry princesses." Elizabeth stated. "They would be the first."

"*If* they were to marry." Isaac added with emphasis. "But we both know that will never happen."

"It's true. And sad." Elizabeth agreed. "But you never know what these new roles will involve for the both of them. At some point, love pushes aside everything else and wins."

"You truly believe that?" Katarina's eyes held wonder at the current conversation and the openness of Elizabeth and Isaac on such matters.

"I do. I am living proof." Elizabeth smiled and then turned her attention to her approaching husband. "My goodness, you have a knack for showing up in conversations when you are the topic."

Clifton's brows rose. "Is that so? I'm sure it was all good things." He smiled towards Isaac and Katarina as he lightly draped his hand around his wife's waist. "We are to make our way to the ballroom." He lightly nudged Elizabeth onward and Isaac and Katarina followed. The celebration of a new queen would last long into the night, and as Isaac passed Ryle and Alayna he smiled knowing the two were only torturing themselves and fighting off the inevitable.

∞

Alayna slipped off her shoes and rubbed her sore ankles as she balanced against the post of her bed. It was long after midnight and her first evening as queen went smoothly. Though she felt awkward with all the attention, she knew the excitement would slowly fade the longer she possessed the position. She was glad everyone seemed elated with her coronation, but the only thing she could think about was Ryle. Their kiss. That perfect moment that ended too soon and with disappointment. Surely, he did not believe in the words of his statement. Yes, he was a Captain, but he was also a former prince. A prince could marry a queen. She growled as she pulled the pins from her crown. *Why was she thinking of marriage?* Annoyed with herself, she tossed the pins onto her vanity and softly laid her mother's crown inside its ornate storage box. Jessa would be arriving any minute to help her change, but Alayna only wished for solitude. She heard the knock on her door as she sat at her vanity, her chin in her hands. "Come in." She called, her miserable expression not changing as she slowly continued pulling the pins out of her hair. A throat cleared, and she jumped in her seat at the masculine sound not expecting her visitor to be a man. She turned quickly, bumping into the vanity table and clumsily turned to straighten the few bottles that began to topple. She then turned to find a tense Ryle standing by her door. "Captain." She stated. "To what do I owe the pleasure?" Her voice stuttered as he took a step towards her. He did not speak. Instead, he lightly cupped her face in his hands and kissed her heartily. Minutes passed, and he rested his forehead against hers. "I am sorry, Alayna. I... had to." He flashed a nervous smile and then dropped his hands as he paced a few steps in front of her. "I do not know how to handle this, Alayna. I have thought only of you all evening. I had to constantly remind myself I was there to protect you, not to swoon over you. We are held to a standard now. A strict standard. I do not wish to tarnish your role as queen, nor compromise your safety due to my own failure of protecting you."

"How would you tarnish?"

"By being a Captain. A guard. A service position. I am not worthy to court the queen. It is unheard of. Scandalous."

"But you are a prince of the East."

"Was. I *was* a prince of the East. I forfeited that position and right. I am royal by blood but not by position any longer."

Alayna reached for his hand and lightly threaded her fingers with his. "We do not have to rush into anything, Ryle. We can keep this quiet for the time being until we both figure out our new roles. There is no reason for us to fight what we both feel, right?"

He held her creamy gaze and lightly kissed her forehead and sighed. "It is wrong, Alayna."

"No. It is not. I am Queen now. I make the rules." She smiled haughtily, hoping her jesting would break forth a smile, but it didn't. He continued to frown.

"I would never put you in the position of compromising the respect of the crown."

"I know. And I do not believe you would be. Perhaps we could discuss this with your father."

"No. No, we should not discuss it with anyone. We should not even let this happen. I should not have even come to your room. What was I thinking?" He scolded himself as he hurried towards the door. She hurried after him. "Ryle, wait!" She called as she caught him by the elbow. Her eyes held a hint of desperation as he turned. "I do not wish for you to leave just yet. Please. We can figure this out."

He lightly removed her hand as Jessa knocked and walked in. Surprise evident on her face as she saw the Captain standing before Alayna. His gaze followed the servant a brief moment before finding Alayna's. "It is time for me to, Alayna." His voice was soft, and she felt the tears begin to cloud her vision. He brushed his hand over her cheek. "Sleep well, my Queen." He held her gaze a moment longer before he departed with regret. Alayna turned to the sound of Jessa's excitement and praise over the coronation as she quickly made work of helping Alayna ready for bed.

Alayna sighed as Jessa finally left and she blew out the light of the lantern. Lying on her pillows in her luxurious bed, Alayna felt her heart slightly break at the thought of Ryle's refusal. He battled feelings for her just as much as she did for him. *Why did she give in to his kisses? Why did she ache for more, yet at the same time wish to never see his face again?* The thought of both making her heart ache. She was not to be distracted by thoughts of love. *Did she not have a war about to be waged? A war against a fearful enemy who could ruin their Realm? Yes, her thoughts needed to focus upon the Realm, not her own selfishness.* Her role as queen meant her life now revolved strictly around the safety and success of their Realm. She did not have a place in her life for love or a family of her own. Yes, her father accomplished both of those things. But times were different. Her time was different. Though her heart longed for more with Ryle, she knew he was right. Their positions demanded their attention and anything distracting could cause them to fail in the protection of their Realm. Though she hated accepting her fate of being alone, she knew it was right. And she would always do what was right. Her eyes closed, and she blocked out images of Ryle and the feelings his kiss stirred within her, and instead filled her mind's eye with Lancer, his horse, his anger, and her desire to defeat him.

∞

Three days. Three short days had everyone traveling to the Southern Kingdom for Prince Samuel's coronation. Samuel became the topic of conversation. Samuel became the focus of everyone's attention. And Samuel was quiet, anxious, and terrified of what lay ahead as his carriage emerged in front of the Southern castle. It was as he remembered. Dark, foreboding. He took a deep breath as he stepped from the carriage. No one awaited him. No servants. No villagers. No guards. No one. All was quiet. Eerily quiet as the other royals emerged from their own caravans. Isaac walked up beside him and laid a comforting hand on his shoulder. "Do not be discouraged, my friend. All good things take work."

"Yes. I know." Samuel replied quietly. "It is as I left it."

"And now you have returned to change it." Isaac stated confidently. "With the help of friends. Come. Show me your home."

Samuel climbed the steps and opened the large wooden door. The creaking echoed throughout the vacant castle. The musky scent of dust, death, and abandonment hung heavily in the still air as Samuel's hopes slowly began to diminish. Elizabeth stepped into the main hall and looked around. She walked over to the front windows and pulled back the heavy drapes, light flooded the room and caused everyone to turn her direction. "What?" She asked with a small smile. "The new king has returned. Let's shed some light into this place." Alayna smiled at her sister and followed suit. Katarina and Melody joining her as they quickly opened up all the remaining drapes in the main entry. "Much better." Elizabeth swiped her hands together to shake off the grime from the heavy curtains. Her gaze surveyed the room. "It is a grand hall. The floors are spectacular." She commented on the dirt covered floors that showed faint signs of intricate detailed paintings and engravings. "I imagine once we hire some servants, the floors will gleam."

Everyone turned towards Samuel and noted he had moved ahead of them into the great hall where his father's throne sat. A blackened stain of dried blood remained from that dreadful day Prince Eric, his own brother, killed their father. Samuel fell to his knees and hung his head in his hands. Melody stepped forward and stopped as Isaac placed his hand on her shoulder. King Anthony studied his daughter closely, his eyes narrowed in question as she looked up at him.

Clifton slowly walked towards Samuel and knelt before the throne as well. He heard the young prince softly clear his throat so as not to let on that he was crying, and Clifton lightly placed a hand on his shoulder. "There is much to overcome, Samuel." His deep voice calming and encouraging. "You will have your work cut out for you. But you have friends to help you. We are all in this fight together."

"I know." Samuel's voice was faint, uncertain, and sadness swamped his demeanor.

"It is hard to lose someone we love." Clifton continued. "Especially a parent. But your father would be proud of the man you have become and the king you will be. The South deserves a fresh start, Samuel. They have been through much. They have gone a year without an authoritative presence. Mosiah has kept watch over your lands and the castle, along with several Northern guards, but it is your turn now. It is your place."

"I fear I am not ready for such responsibility." Samuel admitted quietly.

"We never feel ready, my friend."

Samuel looked at Clifton closely. Yes, the Eastern prince had been tossed into the role of future king as well. He had never planned to inherit the throne, much like Samuel. Eric was to be king. Not him. Much like Ryle was to be king instead of Clifton. "It is comforting to know that you relate with my position, Prince Clifton. However, you are older than I am. More experienced. People will not trust a child."

"You are no child, Samuel, and they will see that. You are the rightful heir to the throne, and you will take it with authority. An authority they will respect."

"But they have seen such darkness from my family. I fear their distrust of me. Of another Renaldi."

"You are a man of the light, Samuel. The darkness of the South was revealed through your brother, but you... you decided to oppose that darkness. Darkness vanishes with light. Be the light for your people to see. And they will see it, Samuel. Oh, they will see it. And when they do, it will give them hope." Clifton slowly stood to his feet, followed by Samuel. He lightly squeezed Samuel's shoulder and turned towards their remaining friends and family. He nodded in recognition of their sympathetic looks, and when Samuel turned, those expressions changed to encouraging smiles.

"The armory is in the East Wing." Samuel stated. "I do not know if there are any weapons remaining, but we must check."

"We will get to that." Alayna stated. "But first, I think we must bring in the servants from the North to set this house to right." She walked to the front doors and opened them to an awaiting crowd of faithful servants to the North, and they flooded inside. Samuel watched as Mary, Elizabeth's attendant, quickly directed several servants up the stairs and towards one wing as Jessa, Alayna's attendant, quickly directed maids towards the opposite. Mosiah entered and nodded his greeting. "Welcome home, Prince Samuel." He bowed. "If you will follow me, please." Samuel slowly stepped forward and solemnly followed the former Captain as he led him towards the back of the castle. Everyone followed. "I can only imagine the state of our gardens." Samuel muttered as Mosiah reached for the doors. He pulled them open and Samuel's eyes widened at the sight of the crowd of men. Cheers erupted as black tunics spread over the expanse of the gardens. Dead flowers and shrubs encompassed the landscape, but a cheerful army awaited him, the number greater than any of them imagined. The cheering exploded louder as the other royals stepped out onto the back landing. Surprise covered all of their faces at the loyal group in front of them and Samuel eased down the steps to accept handshakes and greetings. Pure wonderment filled his expression as he slowly relaxed at the joyful welcome.

"Seems our future king has quite the army." Clifton murmured to Ryle.

"Indeed. I must say, I am surprised." Ryle turned to Mosiah. "How did you manage this?"

Mosiah smiled. "When I first arrived, they were living in front of the castle in tents and huts. It seems that those loyal to Prince Eric burnt most of their homes if they did not show allegiance to the fight against the East and North. They have yet to fully recover in the villages, but those loyal to Samuel and to the throne of the South and the Realm, remained protective of the castle. It did not take long to convince them of the young prince's honorable character, and they are willing to serve him."

"These are great numbers." Ryle commented. They both watched as Samuel walked through the crowd attempting to learn names and embracing old acquaintances. "He will be the greatest king the South has ever possessed." Mosiah stated confidently.

"I believe so too." Alayna stepped up and added. "It pleases me to see this, Mosiah. Good work."

"Thank you, my Queen."

"Captain?"

"Yes." Ryle turned towards her. "How about you take Mosiah to the armory and see what we have to work with for our upcoming battle against the Lands."

"Yes, your Grace." Ryle and Mosiah bowed before exiting and headed into the castle.

∞

Lancer watched as the Prince of the South patrolled the boundary line with several guards and the newest Captain of the Royal Guard, Prince Ryle. *So the South would have a new king,* he thought. *A young king.* Lancer sneered as he imagined the possibilities of manipulating Samuel's allegiance to the Lands like his brother. He chuckled at the thought of Prince Eric's delusion of grandeur before the first war. He thought he could join up with the Lands and defeat the Realm. The idea made him laugh. However, that very belief caused the South's downfall. If this young prince was like his brother, Lancer knew he could easily sway him. Especially since the Southern Kingdom was extremely weak and almost uninhabited from the war and self-destruction it placed on itself. He caught sight of Queen Alayna as she rode by on a horse, wait… *His horse*, he realized. He growled in anger as he stepped towards the boundary line. He found a rock upon the grass and tossed it through the veil and it landed near the hoof of his horse. The horse jostled a moment as Alayna's gaze wandered towards the boundary. Surprise lit her gaze as she spotted him, and she slowly smiled as she stroked a hand over his horse's neck. She pulled her reins and slowly slipped to her feet, causing everyone to halt. She walked towards the boundary line and stood before him, her gaze hard and unwavering. She lifted a hand in a light wave. The Captain of the Guard quickly dismounted and ran towards her side and pulled her back from the line. "You must be careful, Alayna. Objects can now pass through the line. What if he had a sword that reached through?"

"He's not going to hurt me." She stated calmly and pulled her arm from his grasp. "Trust me. He is just spying to see what all is happening here in the south." She stepped towards Lancer again and considered him. His mouth began to move as he shouted at her. She placed a hand to her ear and smirked which made him angrier.

"I will kill you!" Lancer yelled. "Do you hear me?!" He knew she could not hear him, but the yelling felt good. It felt freeing, and he wanted her to see his intentions. His intentions of destroying her and all she held dear. He watched as her eyes widened and he turned to find Edward emerging from the tree line to his right. His smiled broadened and he draped his arm over Edward's shoulder. "Ah, Edward. I'm so glad you could join me. I was just having a conversation with your sister."

Alayna lifted her hand in a small wave of uncertainty at her brother and Edward nodded. "She wears my mother's crown. The coronation must have taken place." Edward stated.

"Looks that way." Lancer agreed. "They have been surveying the Southern Kingdom the last few days. It seems the young prince thinks he can become king." Lancer laughed. "We may have a new ally soon."

Edward knew that would not be the case at all but held his tongue. Alayna took a step back from the boundary line and nodded her head in dismissal. Ryle helped her onto her horse and she turned to Lancer once more as she happily slapped her reins and began trotting away.

"That is your horse, my Lord." Edward pointed out.

"Yes. She taunts me with it." Lancer's voice held a sharp edge and Edward watched as the others passed. Elizabeth saw him and though her eyes held excitement she did not wave for fear of giving him away. *Wise, Lizzy*, he thought. He felt the inward relief of seeing her alive and well. "Your family disgusts me, Edward. They must be stopped."

"What do you suggest? We cannot attack them because we cannot cross. Plus, our armies are preparing for Abner... or are you not worried about him anymore?"

"I will never forget Abner." Lancer gritted his teeth as he began walking back towards his current horse and climbed into his saddle. "I am headed towards the Western boundary line next to see just how threatening Abner will be."

"Why would he be in the West, my Lord?"

"It is closest to his realm. If he has spies, they will be in the West."

"And what happens if we do find Abner has intentions of an assault? We cannot take the fight to him either. And I know my sister's realm would never dream of crossing the boundary, so why do we assume Abner would risk crossing too?"

"Abner will do whatever it takes to overcome the Unfading Lands. He would cross quite willingly if it meant a war with me." Lancer's voice slightly fell as his eyes clouded with uncertainty.

"But we are strong, my Lord." Edward reassured. "Abner could not defeat us. And his army would be trapped and at a disadvantage."

"Never underestimate him, Edward. Never. We prepare for the worst."

"If he has intentions. I do not believe Abner a threat, my Lord. Though he seems to have established relations with my sister's realm, I do not see why he would even care to venture here. I think our intentions should be focused elsewhere." Edward shifted on his feet, hoping his idea of shifting focus was rejected, yet hoping it was believable enough that Lancer assumed his concern as genuine.

"We remain focused upon Abner and your sister's realm. The fact Abner is establishing relations with your old realm shows his true colors, Edward. He sees them as weak. He will conquer them. And as soon as he does, he will target the Lands next. We must have a guard ready. I must have my full power back. My lack of strength is going to be our downfall if the darkness does not return to me fully." He clicked his tongue and the horse turned to leave the small clearing. Edward glanced up at the empty trail opposite him. He had just seen his sister's entire royal court, and he could not greet them.

He shook his head. He missed them terribly and seeing Alayna as queen sparked a slight tinge of jealousy in his gut that he tried to tamper down. He gave up the throne to come to the Land of Unfading Beauty. He deserved his role now, and she deserved hers. But he felt the sting in his heart of being overlooked. *They could have held off on crowning anyone until he was back in the Realm.* The thought fluttered through his mind quickly, but still settled upon his heart. *No. He would not allow the darkness to turn him against his family.* He had a good life with Cecilia, and when the boundary line fell, and they were free, he would stand beside his sister in support, as Edward Prince of the North, and Cecilia his princess.

∞

Abner read the letter from Katarina once more and sighed in frustration. "Is everything alright, dear?" His wife asked quietly.

"It will be." He ran a hand over his beard and read over his daughter's words for a fourth time and his anger grew even more. His daughter did not provide one ounce of information in regard to the Realm's military structure or strength. All she spoke of was the kindness of Prince Isaac and all the other royals. She was falling for the Western Prince, and he could not have that if Isaac was not to be useful for him. He hated when his plans did not evolve how he wished. Katarina was to provide him insight into the weaknesses of the Realm and win over Isaac to support Abner's quest to overcome it. Now was the time since Granton was dead. *How could his daughter not see that?!* He slammed his fist on the arm rest of his throne and stood. His response would need to be harsh and demanding, as was his usual tone with Katarina, but he needed her to know the importance of her role in his future plans. His plans failed if she did not succeed. He needed Isaac's allegiance so that he could freely move forces across the Western Kingdom. He sat within his personal chamber and wrote vigorously. His hand cramping from the forceful exertion as he let his anger spill forth. Katarina would shape up or he would send for her to return. No questions asked.

He inquired of Lancer and what she knew of the Unfading Lands. She did not mention them in the first letter. He needed to know the relationship between the Realm and Lancer as well. Where did the boundary cross the Northern Kingdom? Where did the Eastern boundary lie? Important questions that Katarina had better answer. As he folded the parchment and sealed it with wax, he yelled for a messenger and sent it on its way with a brisk warning that if the messenger did not return with an adequate response, his life would be forfeit, and Princess Katarina was to blame. The messenger, fearful for his life, hastily made his way out of the castle and on his way.

Abner rose and walked towards the window and watched as the messenger and his horse travelled out of the castle walls and faded into the horizon. His gaze washed over his beloved Valleylands and he smiled to himself when remembering the Overcoming. The fall of Lancer's household, and the coward Lancer running for his life. It humored him to think of Lancer creating his own realm. However, the power that Lancer stumbled upon seemed unrealistic. *How could such a weak man have such power? And why would power choose such a pathetic vessel?* Matters that he aimed to answer. Matters Katarina better provide answers for. In the meantime, he would prepare his army. For if he attacked a realm or the Unfading Lands, he rather didn't care which came first. He just ached for bloodshed and victory. And he would have victory. It was in his nature to win. And he never knew a time he didn't. Minus Lancer's escape. *However, the poetic justice of demolishing his realm a second time would be quite pleasing,* he mused. He stepped away from the setting sun and made his way down to the dining hall. His eagerness for Katarina's response inspired his appetite and he felt pleased in the days that would lie ahead.

∞

"Ha! You are dead again." Prince Isaac holstered his sword as his chest heaved from exertion.

"I did not die," Princess Elizabeth corrected, "I merely lost my other leg."

Isaac threw his head back and laughed. "I'm sure your husband would love to have a wife with two wooden legs." He teased as he bent over to collect his red cape from the burgundy chaise. He made swift work of fastening it around his neck and turned to find the princess doing the same. He watched as her pale blue cape puddled around her feet and she tucked her sword into its sheath that Mary held. "My husband loves me with one wooden leg, I do not see why another would be so awful."

Isaac grinned. "Very true. You could be hairless, toothless, and legless, and the Prince would still fall all over himself when it comes to you."

Elizabeth beamed. "I know." She sighed in happiness at the thought of Prince Clifton and the marriage they had so swiftly accepted less than one year ago. *How her life had changed the last year,* she thought. The Unfading Lands threatening the Realm, the Southern Kingdom revolting, her father passing, her marrying, and her sister, Alayna, being crowned Queen... she shook her head at the overwhelming nature of it all.

"Are you to be useless now that I've mentioned the prince?" Isaac jested.

"Not at all." Elizabeth walked over to the stairwell, her limp barely noticeable, and held her hand to her lips. "Clifton!" She yelled.

"Really?" Isaac winced and lightly tapped his ear in mock annoyance earning him a smug grin from Elizabeth. Footsteps waltzed to the edge of the stairs. "My Elizabeth? What is it, love?" Prince Clifton stood alongside his brother, with his brow etched in concern.

"I wish to inform you that Prince Isaac killed me twice today." Her voice held distaste at the topic and had all men laughing.

"Is that so? Why, perhaps I should seek my revenge." Clifton began trotting down the steps towards his beautiful wife and met her on the last step. He lightly kissed her lips as her sparkling blue eyes danced before him.

"No, no revenge just yet." Elizabeth penned Isaac with an amused gaze, "I wish to keep him around a little bit longer."

Isaac swiped a hand over his brow. "Phew." He sighed. "And here I thought I would be sent packing and have to leave dearest Katarina." He shot a wink to the pretty princess as she walked towards them after watching their parry.

"We wouldn't dream of sending you back just yet, Isaac." Elizabeth draped her arm around Clifton's waist as she spoke, the handsome future king and queen of the East looking regal and kind. "Besides, my feet have been itching to parry with you these last few months."

"Don't you mean *foot*?" Isaac corrected, his lips tilting into a smirk.

Elizabeth laughed until she could barely breathe, Clifton and Isaac looking at her in amusement. "Oh my goodness," she wiped the tears that streamed from her eyes, "My... I have no idea why we tolerate you."

He bowed. "And I you, Princess."

She leaned up and kissed Clifton's jawline. "I think I will go find my sister. I believe she was meeting with Samuel for a bit before the council meeting."

"Aye, of course." Clifton's emerald gaze traced over her delicate face once more before he released her to climb the stairs and he continued his way into the main hall with Prince Isaac.

"She has recovered well." Isaac acknowledged.

"Indeed, she has." Clifton replied.

"I promise I did not engage her fully on her feet today."

"I thank you for that. I am glad she feels up to the challenge of sword play, but her balance still falters every now and then." Clifton added.

"Has Ryle said anything in regard to the armory?"

"Not yet. I believe he is saving his assessment for the council meeting tonight. Samuel and Alayna are in there now."

"I see." Isaac surveyed the room around them. "It is a dark place, is it not?"

"Yes. Though I feel with the right leadership Samuel can make it anew." Clifton answered. "And perhaps a thorough cleaning."

Isaac chuckled. "There is months' worth of dirt and grime that is slowly being scraped away. I believe it could possibly be a beautiful castle once the servants are finished."

"I believe so too. Though I am fearful to leave Samuel so soon. He will be crowned tomorrow and then we head back to the North. I know my brother will remain, but his daily visits to the Lands will occupy his time. I wonder if I should linger to help Samuel."

"I think Samuel will be fine. Mosiah is staying as well. And with Ryle and Mosiah seeing to him, I believe he will be just fine. Besides, I feel you and I will be needed in the North before too long."

"What do you mean?" Clifton asked. "Do you have a feeling something is about to happen?"

"I'm not sure. All I know is that while we begin plans for the war against the Lands, you and I have yet to find our role. Are we to raid with Ryle as well, or is he just leading the Uniters against Lancer? Are we to stay behind? Or do we help?"

"You would cross knowing there was a chance you could not come back?" Clifton asked curiously.

Isaac shrugged. "If it was to serve the Realm, of course. Though I much like our Realm, I want to demolish the Lands just as much as the next person."

"Aye, we are in agreement on that. I do not know my role for the upcoming assault either. I wish to fight, of course, but what of

Abner? How do you feel about him? Should we worry about his intentions?"

"That's just it. I don't know. I had a feeling we would have already been feeling some movement from him, but nothing seems to have emerged. My father travels back to the West after Samuel's ceremony tomorrow. He assured me he would alert us if there was any movement across the West."

"That's good." Clifton watched as Melody entered and was warmly greeted by Katarina who stood across the room surveying the large intricate paintings along the walls. "Your sister seems quite active in helping Samuel."

"I know. I think it will be hard for her to leave him here tomorrow as well."

"Does she travel back with your father or will she remain in the North with you for a while?"

"The North. Father finds her interactions with Elizabeth and Alayna encouraging for her. I also think Melody deserves a place to be heard. The council meetings have provided her that. It's been good." Isaac nodded a greeting towards his younger sister as she glanced his direction. Her smile widened as she glanced up and spotted Samuel trotting down the staircase towards their hall. "And that is another reason I wish to keep her with me." Isaac acknowledged.

Clifton turned and spotted the reason for Melody's smile. "They would fit quite nicely." He stated.

"Yes. They would." Isaac agreed. "I don't believe my father is fully convinced, either that or he is personally choosing to ignore it for the fear of handing over his little girl. But Melody would make a great queen. She and Samuel a positive match."

"I am surprised you would be so willing to part with her."

"I'm not completely heartless, Clifton." Isaac chuckled. "I wish her to be happy, and I see the sparks between the two."

Clifton slapped him on the back and smiled. "And what of Katarina?"

"I wish her to be happy too."

"Good." Clifton smirked as Samuel was intercepted by Melody and immediately began leading her across the room.

∞

"I am so thankful we are all here and able to assist Samuel during this transition." Alayna's voice carried through the small council room. Though not as large as the Northern Kingdom's, the room held a heavily carved wooden table and had adequate seating for everyone, minus Katarina who remained in her personal chambers. Alayna had purposefully not invited the visiting princess into their meeting, her trust having yet to be earned, as well as matters of this Realm not concerning her personally. She knew Isaac was slightly disappointed at her earlier dismissal of the proposal, but she knew he would quickly get over it. "We have been here for several days now, Samuel, how do you feel about your kingdom thus far?"

Samuel straightened his shoulders and offered a grateful smile. "I thank you all for your help. There is much more work to be done within the castle and surrounding villages, but I am encouraged by the loyalty of most of our people and that of my guard. I believe the South will develop quite successfully over time."

"Agreed." Alayna stated warmly. "Tomorrow is the coronation ceremony; over which King Anthony will preside." She nodded towards the Western King and he acquiesced with a slight nod. "Afterward, though I long to stay for a few more days, I fear we must all head back to the North. Though King Anthony will head back to the West and King Eamon to the East. Captain Ryle and Mosiah will remain here in the South to aid in the development of your kingdom and in the Uniters' army across the boundary. Your armories proved well stocked, and we believe the transference of weaponry should begin immediately."

Samuel nodded in understanding.

Isaac raised his fingertips from the table and Alayna glanced his direction. "Yes?"

"Prince Clifton and I were just discussing this today… what is to be our role in this upcoming assault against the Unfading Lands? Are we to remain in the North? Or are we to cross the lines and fight as well?"

"That is for Captain Ryle to decide, Prince Isaac. I believe you will remain in the North due to your inability to cross the boundary freely. However, Prince Clifton may need to assist in leading the Uniters."

Disappointment washed over Isaac's face. "I am willing to cross, my Queen. Should I be needed, I will gladly cross to fight. I am one of the strongest fighters in the Realm."

She held up her hand to ward off any further argument. "Like I said, Captain Ryle will see to your role."

"Well there goes that." Isaac mumbled, catching the steely look from Ryle across the room.

"Has there been a strategy that's been mapped out?" Clifton asked.

Ryle leaned forward in his chair at the far end of the table. "Edward and I are meeting in two days' time to finalize our routes and plans. Then we will reconvene and discuss battle plans in the North."

"And what of Abner?" Elizabeth asked. "Are we to be concerned about him?"

Alayna shrugged. "So far Abner has not proved to be a threat. Therefore, I will not treat him as one. Our focus is the Lands."

"We should be cautious with Abner." Isaac warned.

Alayna blew a frustrated breath and turned towards Isaac. "Just because you lost your temper with a man willing to have you escorted safely back to the North and attacked his guard does not mean we have to be on guard for a war. He sent his daughter to come and see you, for goodness sake. I do not believe he would do such a thing if he wished to harm us."

"Believe what you want, Queen Alayna," Isaac added. "But I am telling you the man is not amiable towards our Realm."

"Duly noted. Now moving on." Alayna firmly moved onto the next topic at hand and addressed the issues of the Southern Kingdom's staff at the castle and the newly hired crews that would serve under Samuel. The topic bored Isaac and her lack of faith in his feelings towards Abner ate away his calm demeanor. He caught Elizabeth's pointed gaze and shook his head at his own disappointment in Alayna's ignorance.

Elizabeth cleared her throat and Alayna turned towards her. "Did you have something to add, sister?"

"Yes… though it is in regard to Abner."

Sighing, Alayna lightly pinched the bridge of her nose and then waved for her to continue. "Fine. Go ahead."

"I am in agreement with Isaac." Elizabeth stated.

"Of course you are." Alayna combatted and then heaved a frustrated sigh at her outburst. "I'm sorry, please continue."

Elizabeth's eyes narrowed at her sister as she continued. "I am just saying that Isaac does not go around accusing people of distrust. For him to adamantly proclaim mischief with Abner, I believe we should not take it lightly. Perhaps Abner's intentions in sending Katarina was not just for her potential relationship with Isaac. What if he wished her to be a spy after all? I am not saying she is, but what if? Then his intentions are not pure, and he becomes a threat as well. I think, that while we focus upon the Unfading Lands and our battle to come, we must not reject the possibility of a threat coming from another Realm either. Isaac should remain in the North if both Clifton and Ryle are to raid the Lands. We need someone who can lead our armies if an attack were to happen."

"I think that is over contemplating a simple matter." Alayna began. "We cannot stretch our attention to multiple battles or thoughts of battles when our real enemy lies behind the boundary line. Abner has shown no signs of a threat to us, minus his disappointment with Isaac at his departure. But look at how he departed? I would have been upset too. So we stick with the original plan and Isaac will be sent where Captain Ryle deems best." She waved her hand as if to cut off further comments. Elizabeth flashed a worried glance towards Clifton and he lightly squeezed her hand to let the matter drop for the time being.

"Now, let us all try to sleep as we prepare ourselves for the celebration of Samuel for tomorrow. Good night." Alayna dismissed them and exited the room first, followed by Ryle.

"Thank you for the defense." Isaac stated.

"I will try to speak to the Queen." King Eamon stated. "I am in agreement in regard to Abner. He is not to be trusted."

Clifton lightly clasped Elizabeth's hand and draped it through his arm. "Come. Let us go to bed. The matter is left in capable hands now." Elizabeth lightly kissed King Eamon's cheek in thanks and waved her good byes.

King Anthony, King Eamon, Samuel, and Isaac remained. "I will come to your aid in the North should Abner decide to make a move while we are in the Unfading Lands." Samuel stated to Isaac.

Isaac patted his young friend on the back. "Thank you, Samuel. Though I may be overreacting, my gut tells me something is about to happen."

"Mine too." Anthony chimed in. "That is why I will be leaving directly after the coronation tomorrow. If Abner is to make a move he will have to cross the Western Kingdom. Should I see any suspicious behavior, I will send word."

"Thank you, Father." Isaac stated.

"It is imperative we keep you in the North, Isaac." King Eamon explained. "There must be a military leader there should something happen while Clifton and Ryle are gone. Mosiah will be here in the South with Samuel should you need them, but the North will be left vulnerable. You must remain there."

"And what happens if the newly inducted Captain wishes for me to join them in the Lands?" Isaac asked.

"Let me take care of that." Eamon stressed. "I will consult with Ryle over this decision. He will trust my judgment of Abner."

"And yet, he does not trust mine."

"I believe he senses something as well, but he wishes to appease the Queen with a victory beyond the veil."

"But will a Northern army follow a Western Prince?"

"They will have no choice if the need arises." Anthony draped an encouraging hand over his son's shoulder. "Until then, how about we all catch some sleep." The other men nodded in agreement as they headed their opposite directions for the restless night ahead.

CHAPTER 10

King Anthony placed the baroque crown upon Samuel's head and accolades flared throughout the grand hall of the Southern Castle as he stood to his feet and turned to meet the faces of the many villagers, servants, guards, and attendants who claimed him as their king. He began the long walk down the center aisle towards the exit, his black cape dragging behind him as Queen Alayna walked beside him dressed in her own formal attire. The sight was rejuvenating for a kingdom long without hope, and as the front castle doors opened and Samuel stepped out onto the main landing, an uproarious and celebratory crowd erupted outside as well. He was king of the South now. His turn to change everything he had hoped to change in years passed. He inhaled a deep breath of fresh air as his gaze sought Melody beside her father. She offered him an encouraging smile and he felt his shoulders straighten as he embraced the new role of kingship.

Clifton stepped beside him and bowed as he congratulated him once more. "The crown suits you, my King."

Samuel lightly flushed in awkwardness. "I hope to one day prove that statement true, Prince Clifton. Thank you."

"You will." Elizabeth stated confidently as she lightly kissed his cheek. "I am so proud of you, Samuel. I feel as if I may cry I am so happy for you. I will refrain however for fear of embarrassing you." She laughed as she linked her arm with her husband and stepped to the side and allowed room for Isaac. Isaac extended his hand and Samuel shook it. Isaac pulled him slightly closer. "Melody will remain with me in the North." His voice was low, and Samuel shyly caught the amused scrutiny of Isaac. "I just thought you might like to know that. Considering we may be seeing much of each other in the next few weeks."

"Thank you, Prince Isaac." Samuel replied stiffly making the Western prince chuckle. Katarina linked her arm with Isaac's as he proudly escorted her towards his father and sister. Samuel gazed out amongst the cheering crowd and the surrounding lands of his kingdom and an appreciation swelled in his chest. He would protect his kingdom no matter the cost, and he would serve the Realm with his entire heart and being, of that he had no doubt. His ability to rule however, continued to overwhelm him, but he squelched the inner doubts and embraced the friendships that would long help and guide him in his new role. His eye wandered towards the boundary line and he sensed Lancer's presence. Perhaps the evil leader lurked behind the veil and watched the celebrations. Perhaps, just maybe, he feared what he saw happening in the South. A revolution. A new beginning. A threat. Yes, he prayed Lancer realized his days were numbered, and he prayed that he could assist in the biggest battle of their time and for once, perhaps the South may witness a victory.

∞

The darkness swirled around their ankles, and Edward silently prayed Lancer did not see the slow weaving of the darkness up his legs and into his palms. Currently his eyes were closed, and Edward knew Lancer's only focus was himself within the reflection chamber. This was the first time they had shared the space since Edward had taken in the darkness. And feeling it now seeping into his core, the temptation to succumb to more power was almost more than he could bear. He watched as Lancer's head snapped up and his eyes opened, the black, dilated pupils in his eyes slowly fading back to normal and the darkness in the room slowly fading. Lancer took a deep breath and then sighed. "I feel better. Coming in here together has made me feel stronger. Perhaps you are what has been missing. I have not seen the darkness in weeks, but perhaps you are slowly becoming more open to it, Edward, and it senses your willingness." Lancer smiled in relief as he straightened his tunic. "I feel completely rejuvenated."

"You feel strong, my Lord?"

"I do."

"Should we test your crossing the boundary?"

"Oh no. Not yet." Lancer admitted. "I am not yet back to my full power completely. I just feel slightly better than I did. I am pleased you were more open to the darkness, Edward. It pleases me to see you trying. Though I am sorry it has yet to enter you. I am telling you, Edward, when it does, you will feel completely transformed. It makes all things new. Better. You will see."

"Yes, my Lord." Edward inwardly cringed at the thought of more darkness within him. He already struggled with what little he possessed, and yes, he had seen the current side effects. The easiest agitation, the prolonged insomnia, the lack of desire for food and water. His mind divided into two different people. The Edward from the Realm and the Edward from the darkness. Slowly he felt the dividing line blurring, he just prayed it lasted until the battle against the Lands. Perhaps the boundary line would fall before his body and mind completely gave into the evil desires of the darkness. His hatred for Lancer seemed to fade every day, and his longing for youth and life seemed to grow with every second. He feared the loss of his own soul should he have to remain in the Unfading Lands much longer. He was slowly becoming more and more like Lancer, and he could see it happening. Helplessly. He knew Clifton sensed it as well yet remained hopeful. He did not want to lose that trust, or his role to help the Realm would cease to exist and then he would truly be lost.

"Did you hear me, Edward?"

Edward shook his head to clear his thoughts. "I'm sorry, my Lord?"

"I asked if you wished to come with me to the Western boundary."

"Oh. I would, my Lord, but I need to work with the guards should we need them against Abner."

"Ah, good plan. I will let you do that then. I, on the other hand, am going to see if I notice anything amiss in the West. I have a terrible feeling about that man." Lancer admitted.

"I will do my best, my Lord, so that you will have nothing to fear should he even come close to us."

"Good man." Lancer smiled as he walked towards the door. He turned at the last minute and grinned. "I may not be back tonight Edward. I think I wish to take a journey along the boundary lines. The East, the West, and the North. I have surveyed the Southern line, but the others could use some attention. Should I not return, I will be back tomorrow. I wish to have a report for you in regard to the West."

"Thank you, my Lord. That saves me the journey."

"Well I want your attentions focused on our safety, so it is the least I can do. I thank you for your service, Edward. I know it must have been hard to see your family in the South, but I assure you your loyalty will only be rewarded."

"Thank you, my Lord." Edward watched as Lancer's retreating back disappeared out the door and down the hall. He slowly relaxed his shoulders and looked down at his palms. Again, he felt the tingling sensation from the sacrificial cuts, but the healing powers of the Lands had erased the wound completely. He knew it was the darkness that lingered within him. Tomorrow he was to meet Ryle at the Uniters' camp, and he needed to warn him of Lancer's journey around the boundary lines, so their weapon deliveries would not be discovered. By weeks' end, a battle would commence. *By weeks' end he would be free,* he kept repeating to himself. *Free.*

∞

"It feels nice to be back." Elizabeth glanced around the Northern castle in a wave of nostalgia.

"You were only gone four days." Clifton reminded her.

"I know. It's just always nice coming back." She tugged on the top clasp to his tunic. "Don't frown, Cliff, I miss the East too." She lightly kissed his lips and earned a smile.

"I'm glad."

"You two love birds are seriously annoying sometimes." Isaac bypassed them in a hurry towards the West's wing of the castle.

"What has his gait in a stumble?" Elizabeth asked curiously as Alayna entered not long after Isaac. "Oh." She stated quietly. "They must have had words."

"Or the lack of words from Alayna may be bothering him as well." Clifton added.

"I worry about her tunnel vision."

"She will come around, love. You will see. My father spoke with Ryle and Alayna last night before his departure and they have both agreed to leave Isaac in the North as a precaution while we attack the Lands."

"But only to appease King Eamon, not Isaac." Elizabeth pointed out.

"Still, it is a small step and a much needed one. We will accept what has been given."

"I do not like the thought of you fighting within the boundary lines of the Unfading Lands. What if something happens to you?" Elizabeth looked up and lightly cupped his face. Clifton kissed the inside of her palm and smiled tenderly. "Then I will heal."

She lightly shoved him against the chest and groaned in frustration.

"What was that for?" He asked on a laugh.

"Because you can still die over there, Clifton. Do you not think Lancer knows that beheading you will kill you?"

"I know, love, but that is not going to happen, so do not dwell on it."

"You do not know what will and will not happen, Clifton."

"You are right; however, I trust our guards. I trust my brother. I trust *your* brother, and I trust myself. We will all be careful and have our wits about us."

She sighed as she hugged him tightly. "You better, or I will personally come across that line and beat you myself."

She felt the rumble in his chest as he chuckled, and she smiled, breathing in the scent of him, the strength he seemed to carry in his very being.

"Perhaps I may steal your prince a moment, Princess?" Isaac waited at the edge of the stairwell for their private moment to come to a close before he approached. Elizabeth raised her head and nodded. "I suppose, but not too long Isaac, for I have plans for my husband."

Both men raised their brows in surprise at her statement.

She laughed. "Oh for goodness sake, not that. I meant with our current conversation... never mind." She waved them away in a teasing gesture as she climbed the steps towards her personal chambers on a giggle.

"Well," Isaac cleared his throat and stifled a grin as Clifton laughed. "I did not mean to interrupt, no matter her meaning."

"It is alright, Isaac." Clifton patted him on the back as they began to walk towards the conservatory. "What ails you?"

"Ails? Is it that obvious?"

"Quite so." Clifton admitted.

Isaac rubbed a palm over his tired face and then sat in a free chair as Clifton sat across from him. The Eastern prince carried his relaxed posture wherever he went, much like his father, and Isaac stemmed the slight peak of jealousy at Clifton's ease and comfort he brought to every situation. "I wish to travel to the edge of the Northern and Western border tomorrow."

"What for?"

"I wish to just check on… things." Isaac finished.

"You mean you wish to make sure there are no signs of Abner's men?"

"Yes. Though I wish to do this without the knowledge of anyone else in the castle. I do not wish to cause an uproar towards my suspicions."

"I see." Clifton pondered Isaac's statement a moment. "And where shall you be if someone asks? Because Ryle and I will be in the Lands tomorrow training guards with the new weapons."

"That I am out riding, I don't know." Isaac shrugged. "It's not a lie. I just need to make sure that Abner has not already sent men through the Western Kingdom and into the North."

"And how will you know?"

"I have people I trust that survey the borderlines. They will know if new faces have passed through. I figure it will then give us a firmer inclination of whether or not my hunch is correct."

"I do see that benefit." Clifton stated. "I think it a wise move. However, I wish you would tell the Queen. I understand your reasoning for not telling her, but she would be furious to know you went without her knowledge."

"I do not believe she could be any madder at me than she is right now." Isaac reminded him.

"That is true too." Clifton's lips tilted into a slight smile as he ticked his tongue against his teeth in a thinking gesture. "Okay, I will not say anything. But set out early. I do not wish for the Northern Kingdom to be exposed too long without a military leader present."

"Thank you, Clifton." Isaac shook his hand.

"Now, if you will excuse me, I wish to go finish my conversation with my wife."

"Conversation… riiiiight." Isaac baited earning the smirk from the Eastern Prince he knew he would receive as Clifton briskly made his way up the stairwell.

Isaac chuckled to himself as he watched Clifton's eagerness and shook his head. The man was a fool in love when it came to Elizabeth, and for once, Isaac did not feel jealous. He turned at the sound of footsteps and Katarina emerged, her face pale, and her eyes damp. He hopped to his feet quickly.

"Katarina?"

Just her name made the princess melt into another fit of tears and she tried to swipe a hand over her face as Isaac pulled her against his chest. "What is the matter?" He pulled her away to look in her face, and he smoothed the hair back from her cheeks as her brown eyes implored him to believe what she was about to say. "I am sorry, Isaac."

"Sorry? Whatever for?" His gaze rose and spotted a messenger dressed in clothes from Abner's Realm and he looked back at

Alayna. "My father has sent me a letter, and I fear I do not know how to answer him."

"Is that all?" His voice was light, and he offered an understanding smile.

She shook her head and his smile faded.

"I fear that I do not know how to answer him, because I have failed him. But I fear of showing you its contents because I do not wish you to think ill of me."

"I never would, Katarina. Please." He motioned for her to sit and eased down beside her. "Tell me what it says."

She handed him the letter with shaky hands and he quickly unfolded it and began to read.

Katarina,

You have failed me. What is this first letter? It is nonsense! I sent you to bewitch the Western prince and you have failed. I sent you to learn more about Alayna's Realm, and you have failed. I do not wish to read this fluff! What am I to use of this?! Nothing!

I need to know where the boundary lines appear across each kingdom. I need to know the Realm's intentions with Lancer. And I need to know the strength of their guard. How am I to plan anything if I do not have all the facts?! You stupid girl!

Send me the answers to my previous demands and these or the messenger before you will die for your lack of loyalty. Should I receive anything less than what I've requested, he will not be the only one punished!

Your Father

Isaac glanced up and Katarina dropped her face into her hands and her shoulders began to shake. "Forgive me, please?"

Isaac looked to the messenger standing in the shadows, his face ashen from the worry for his life. He then lightly smoothed a hand over Katarina's soft hair. "Look at me, Katarina."

She slowly glanced up and he lifted her chin with the tip of his finger. "There is nothing to forgive. From the sounds of this, you did not do his bidding in the first place. Which means your task of spying on our Realm was a failure. A failure I am most grateful for, not only for the sake of the Realm, but for myself. It encourages me that your intentions are pure. That I... that I might mean something to you."

She tried to speak but he slid his finger over her lips to stop her words. "Will you trust me with this?"

She nodded.

"Good. We will present it at the council meeting tomorrow night. Together."

Her eyes widened in fear. "Oh please no, Isaac. I fear Queen Alayna will dispense of me immediately. I could not bear the thought of everyone thinking me a traitor."

"But you aren't a traitor, Katarina. By giving us this letter, you have prepared us for a possible threat."

"I do not know if she will see it that way."

"I will make her see it that way." He stated firmly. "Trust me. And trust that we will answer this letter so as to protect you and your messenger." He nodded towards the scared man across the room. He squeezed her hand. "Are you willing to face the council with me?"

He felt her hand shaking in his. Fear. Uncertainty. She nodded, and he softly kissed her cheek. "You are quite the princess, Katarina." He whispered softly. "Come. Let's take a stroll in the gardens before dinner to gather our thoughts and calm down a bit." He stood and extended his hand to her, her acceptance of his gesture and her trust in his character establishing a new wave of appreciation between the both of them. *A role reversal for him*, he mused. He no longer felt the cad he had long been, now he had the respect of fellow kingdoms and the trust of a distressed princess. *How long had it been since anyone trusted him with something so precious?* A year ago, he would have said never. Now, the new turn in his life and character had seemed to gain the attention he had always hoped for and he prayed he was able to carry the new responsibility.

∞

Ryle and Clifton stepped through the clearing and Edward intercepted them with a broad smile and a quick wave of his hand for them to step into the trees, his eyes surveying the area behind them as if looking for intruders. The two brothers exchanged a cautious glance and then followed willingly into the Uniters' camp. "I am glad you have arrived." Edward's voice was low. "Lancer is patrolling the boundary lines the next few days, so we must be cautious. Are all the weapons here or do we still have more deliveries?"

"This should be all." Ryle replied studying Edward closely. "You feeling alright?"

Edward ran a hand through his dark hair and shook away his annoyance knowing the captain was genuinely concerned. "Yes. Well, I had to join Lancer in the reflection chamber last night. The darkness… it is difficult to contain. But I am fine. It just takes me a bit to catch my bearings afterwards. However, I must tell you that Lancer did receive some of the power last night. He said it was the first time in weeks the darkness has even emerged in the chamber. I know it was because I was in there." Cecilia walked up to greet the two brothers and Edward paused in his conversation to smile at her. She fluttered away as quickly as she had come, and Edward inhaled deeply. "Lancer did say he did not feel completely back to his full power, but we must not underestimate what power he does have. The man is still powerful."

"Agreed." Clifton stated. "It is imperative that the assault take place at weeks' end. We cannot afford to waste the precious time he is weaker."

"The plan is before dawn on the eve of day after tomorrow." Ryle explained.

Edward nodded, his head bobbing faster and faster as he crossed his arms over his chest and tried to contain the excessive movement. His body uncontrollable at times due to the power wishing to surge through his veins. "I believe that will be a good time frame. A surprise attack is the Realm's only hope. Should Lancer find out, there is no way the Realm can defeat his army. They are too strong. Right now, I have his focus targeted at Abner, so a blindside attack from the Realm is not even on his mind."

"Good. It sounds like things are lining up perfectly then. We have the routes planned, the guards are trained, and we feel confident." Clifton nodded, pleased with the surrounding army and the plans that were falling into place.

"I hope you two know that I will have to fight alongside Lancer's army." Edward reminded them. "I at least have to appear to be in his favor, though if opportunity arises I will take care of some of our guards as well. But he will be watchful, especially of me."

"We understand. We will ensure none of our guards assault you, only the other guards. That way you will not be forced to fight against a fellow Uniter." Ryle placed a hand on Edward's shoulder and felt the nerves radiating beneath his skin. "It will go smoothly, Edward. You have done well."

A relieved smile washed over Edward's face and he looked to Clifton. "I am eager to be with my family again. I have missed them."

"And they you." Clifton explained. "Elizabeth is beside herself wanting to join the fight and to also make preparations for your return."

Edward grinned, "Yes, well Lizzy was always my biggest champion."

"Hold onto that thought, because your coming days will be difficult. We can already see how the darkness is affecting you, Edward. There is no sense denying it. However, we have faith in your loyalty to the Realm. We know you will aid us in our victory." Clifton noted the slight flush to the prince's face at being called out, but that the reassurance in their belief meant much to him.

"We are ready then." Ryle confirmed. "Cliff and I will arrive back in the camp tomorrow night and we will be ready to ride out against Lancer and his guard at dawn. You are sure you can have his guard on the Western Boundary line?"

"Yes. He already has me stationing guards there to keep watch over any potential movements from Abner, so it will not take much to convince him that I have seen more action on that side and we will need more troops."

"Perfect." Ryle extended his hand and Edward shook it. "Until tomorrow night then, Prince Edward."

Edward nodded and caught Cecilia's gaze from across the clearing. Her eyes held worry, and he attempted a smile that she slowly returned. He turned and watched as the two brothers made their way out of the camp and back through the boundary line. *Two days. Just two more days,* Edward told himself.

∞

Clifton returned to the castle late in the evening after conversing with Ryle in Elizabeth's clearing for final military plans and strategies. Ryle had headed back towards the Southern Kingdom and Clifton walked into a darkened castle with only lanterns to light his way up towards the Council meeting. He knew he was late and he prayed Elizabeth was not too worried for him. He stepped into the room and saw relief wash over not only his wife's face but everyone else's as well. He noted the presence of Katarina next to Isaac and greeted her with a nod as well. "I am sorry to be late. Last minute preparations took a bit longer than intended."

Alayna waved away his apology. "No worries here, Prince Clifton. We are glad to have you back. Everything ready?"

"Yes. I believe so. We could not be any more prepared than we already are."

"Good." She turned her attention to Isaac. "Prince Isaac wished to share something with all of us." She sat in her chair and Isaac rose to his feet. He gently squeezed Katarina's hand in reassurance. "I know Ryle and Samuel are not here to add their insight, but I feel I must share what news I do have so that we may be prepared for certain possibilities." He reached for the letter Katarina had entrusted to him and he saw her visibly tense in the seat beside him. "Katarina received a letter from her father upon our arrival back in the North." He handed it straight to Clifton, knowing the Eastern prince would read it with an open mind in regard to their previous conversations. "Abner had wished to use Katarina for information into our Realm, our military, and boundary lines and interactions with the Unfading Lands. She refused, and he is now threatening the life of the messenger and Katarina. I implore you all to see reason. Abner is no ally. He is a threat to our Realm, and I believe he is making plans for his own assault."

Alayna sighed heavily as Clifton handed her the letter from Abner. Isaac watched as her face remained stoic as she read. She lowered the letter and looked at him to continue. "He does not know of our plans to attack the Lands, but perhaps if he did he would join with us in the assault and it would divert his attention towards Lancer instead of the Realm."

"We do not know he isn't already focused upon Lancer as well." Alayna stated.

"But he has always hated Lancer." Isaac continued. "If he sees our Realm as weak, he will attack us first. Once he has overtaken our Realm, then Lancer is the only man standing in his way of taking over all the lands. It is us or Lancer first, but we will both face an attack sooner or later."

"We must not count our chickens before they hatch, Prince Isaac." Alayna interrupted. "I highly doubt Abner would attack our Realm while his precious daughter is staying with us. Yes, he threatens to punish her, but not to kill her. This letter shows him to be a disappointed parent."

Isaac's eyes widened at the absurdity and his jaw tightened. "Your judgment is clouded." He forced out through gritted teeth. Alayna stood swiftly and raised her chin. "We have no other proof of Abner's threat, until we do, our focus remains on Lancer!" Her voice rose, and she tossed the letter towards the middle of the table.

"I do have proof." Isaac combatted. "I traveled the borderlines of the Western and Northern Kingdoms this morning and spoke with various watchmen. There have been several groups of Abner's men that have made it through. My father did not make it back to the West in time to implement border barriers. Abner has successfully moved troops into our Realm. It is only a matter of time before his target is chosen."

Alayna shook her head. "No. We will not let anything interfere with our plans against the Unfading Lands. We have waited too long for this opportunity, we will not pass it up."

"My purpose is to protect our Realm while Clifton and Ryle lead the fight against the Unfading Lands." Isaac interrupted her, and he could tell she did not like it, but he continued. "How am I to do my task if you will not see reason?!" He slammed his fist on the table and began to pace.

"You are just angry that I will not let you fight in the Lands." Alayna began, but her voice stopped when she saw the venomous gaze Isaac shot her way, a chill passing over her arms at the anger she saw lurking beneath his eyes.

"How dare you think I am of childish jealousy when I am trying my best to awaken you to the possibility of an attack!" He rounded his chair and began walking towards her, his finger pointed towards her face. Clifton rose and slipped between them. "We must all calm down for a minute." He softly ordered and lowered Isaac's hand and then turned towards Alayna himself. "I believe we must take Abner's threat seriously, Alayna." Clifton slipped back towards his chair once Isaac did the same. "Though our attention will remain on our current battle plan against the Unfading Lands, I believe it wise to allow Isaac to establish some precautionary plans for protection just in case Abner were to make a move while our attentions are diverted."

"I agree." Elizabeth added.

"Me too." Melody stated.

Alayna's eyes bounced around the room and landed on Katarina. "And what of her?" She pointed to Katarina. "Are we to forget she was sent here to dig up our secrets?"

"And she has refused." Elizabeth reminded her sister. "Perhaps we can all put our brains together to draft a letter to her father. One that will spare the messenger's life but also Katarina. It may be an opportunity for us to divert Abner's intentions."

"Alright." Alayna sighed. "I will leave that in your care, Elizabeth, with the help of Isaac. Clifton, I do not want you distracted by this. Your attention is Lancer."

"Yes, my Queen."

"Come tomorrow evening, we may have an entirely different Realm in our care." Alayna allowed a smile to break through. "The boundary line will fall, and Edward will return. Let us sleep on those hopeful thoughts for tonight."

Everyone nodded in agreement as they headed their separate ways towards their chambers. Elizabeth lightly gripped Isaac's elbow in the hall until he turned. "I will see to the letter, Isaac, and to Katarina. I wish for you to make plans for the safety of our kingdom. For if Abner attacks, it will be here. And if he is days ahead of us, I would not be surprised if his men have already immersed themselves within our villages. His target will be the castle."

"Those are my thoughts as well." Isaac muttered. "His only aim is to overcome and kill. He wiped out Lancer's entire family, I see him easily wishing to do the same here. That would be the quickest way to stake claim to a Realm."

"I agree. I trust you with this." Elizabeth offered an encouraging smile. "Now trust me with her." She nodded towards Katarina, and he nodded. "I do, and I will. Good night Elizabeth."

∞

Lancer watched as several men appeared along the other side of the boundary line of the Western veil of the Unfading Lands. They could only be Abner's men. It had been ages since any of the Western villagers came so close to his boundary line. The thought of Abner made his blood run cold. *He could not overcome him again. He had created this Land and he would not let anyone take it from him. The darkness was his. The power was his.* He clicked his reins and continued onward towards the Northern boundary line. The journey through his lands always lightened his spirit, but lately the weighted cloud of uncertainty hovered over him. He was weak, and it had been so long since he had that feeling he wasn't sure how to handle it. The only reason could be a surge in power in the Realm. The unification after last year's war must have built a temporary burst in their strength. He knew it would eventually fade. And though the boundary line had shifted further in and he had lost some ground, the loyalty of his people remained strong. As he neared a familiar path along the line, he spotted a familiar blonde head that he had not seen in quite some time. An uncertain smile flashed up at him as she curtsied. He halted his horse and dismounted. "It has been a long time, Cecilia."

"My Lord." She greeted.

"You fall in love with my Captain and I never hear from you again." He teased lightheartedly as he peered through the fog of the line and spotted Cecilia's mother washing linens in a large basin of steaming water. "Your mother is hard at work I see."

"Yes, she is."

"Does she see you often?"

"No, my Lord. She never looks towards the line."

"But you come to watch her?"

"Every now and then to check on her." Cecilia admitted.

"That's an honorable trait." Lancer breathed in deeply as he continued to watch Cecilia's mother scrub the grime away from whatever filth lingered upon the delicate cloth. "Do you miss your old life?"

"No."

She answered quickly and with a firm disposition it made him smile. "I am glad you have found the Land of Unfading Beauty a great place to be, Cecilia."

"It is the reason I came here today. Edward had mentioned you would be riding around the boundary lines to help him." She made sure to offer praises within her language so as not to cause unwarranted anger towards Edward. Lancer grinned. "I have been keeping him busy."

"So he has told me." She looked up at him. "I wished to speak with you in regard to some movement I have seen along the boundary line. I have yet to mention it to Edward, because he seems so adamant to protect the Lands against Abner. I do not wish to distract him."

"And what have you seen?" Lancer's brow rose as he walked towards a large boulder and sat so that Cecilia would feel more comfortable in sharing with him. The petite woman often shrank back from imposing figures and he was pleased that Edward had fallen for one of his most faithful followers. The young girl had also fallen hard for the former prince, a pleasing unity that Lancer approved of.

"I believe the Realm is planning an attack upon the Lands, my Lord."

"And what makes you believe that?" He asked with curiosity in his voice.

"I have seen the new Captain of the Realm training troops in the South."

"Perhaps he is just trying to rebuild what was destroyed in the last war." Lancer added.

"No, my Lord. You asked Edward to converse back and forth with the Realm to see what he could discover, and though he has yet to discover anything amiss, I have. I conversed with the Queen once, and she was quite insistent about an attack. I believe the Southern army is being trained to assault us."

"But why would they risk crossing, knowing they cannot cross back and forth?" Lancer asked.

"Because they are confident in their victory, my Lord. Captain Ryle can cross freely because he is of your blood. I have seen him attempt this and succeed."

"My blood?"

"Yes. Your nephew."

"Yes, I know who he blasted is, Cecilia." His voice rose, and he tampered his anger down when he saw her slightly fidget to leave. "I apologize. Yes, I know Ryle is one of my nephews. I did not realize my blood was powerful enough to allow them to cross when I myself cannot seem to."

"Perhaps their crossing is what has put a hold on yours, my Lord." She offered the explanation without thought and he nodded. "You may be right, Cecilia. But why would they wish to attack me knowing they cannot win and most certainly that it will be death for them all should they even attempt it?"

"Abner." Cecilia provided. "He wishes to attack as well from the looks of it. I think the Realm hopes his distraction will pull your attentions elsewhere so that they might be able to sneak into the Lands and take you blindly."

Lancer bolted to his feet. "That is absurd! How has Edward not heard of these plans?"

"Because they know he would tell you, my Lord. Edward is loyal to you and his family knows this. Though they have conversed with him through the veil, they do not speak of delicate matters because they know his allegiance truly lies with you."

"Thank you, Cecilia, for bringing this all to my attention. I will patrol the boundary of the South once more to see if a threat stirs."

"I would think it would venture from the East, my Lord."

"Why do you say that, when you clearly just told me they were training in the South?"

Well because your attention is focused upon the West right now. Though they train guards in the South, I believe they will attack you on your blindside in the East."

Lancer tilted his head and considered her a moment. "I am grateful for your loyalty, Cecilia, and your watchful eye. Edward truly is a blessed man. I will do my own investigating now. But have no fear, nothing is going to happen to our Lands. You have my word."

"I know, my Lord. I trust you."

The simple words swelled his chest in pride and he felt empowered. "Take care, Cecilia." He slipped his boot into his stirrup and lifted into his saddle. He redirected his horse and headed towards the Southern boundary line to see what he could witness himself.

Cecilia exhaled her pent-up breath and slipped onto the boulder Lancer had just vacated. She felt better for telling him of the attack. Though she did not confirm it as a definite, she felt she did her part by giving him the seed of suspicion. She also made it sound as if the Realm was using their own army, not one Edward had prepared. She did not betray her Edward. Smiling, she lifted her face up to the sunshine and let the heat warm her face. She loved the Unfading Lands, and she loved Edward. Now that Lancer would know of the Abner diversion, he would be able to protect the Lands against the Realm's attack and she and Edward could stay here. Satisfaction filled her heart and she giggled in happiness at the thought of forever.

∞

"Sit with me, Katarina." Elizabeth welcomed the timid princess with a warm wave towards a small table and chairs in the gardens, the fresh air needed after a stuffy breakfast and heartfelt goodbye to Clifton as he left to join up with Ryle in the South. This evening the brothers would venture into the Unfading Lands and organize their troops for the following morning and the attack that would take place soon after. She sighed as Katarina eased into a chair and accepted the glass of wine from Mary as the attendant laid out a tray of small vittles for the women to enjoy while they talked. As if Katarina could eat anything. Her stomach tied into multiple knots just thinking of the conversation she and Elizabeth would soon be having, and she prayed the Eastern princess did not lose taste with her.

"So I figured we would write this letter to your father early this morning and accept our morning cakes outside so as to gain more privacy. It will also provide ample time for your messenger to make it back to your father's realm before nightfall if he rides fast enough." Elizabeth smiled as she reached for a blank piece of parchment and laid it before Katarina. "Now, what should we tell him?"

Katarina lightly shrugged her shoulders and Elizabeth noted the light quiver to her chin as her brown eyes remained focused on the blank paper before her. Elizabeth reached over and lightly squeezed her hand. "Take a deep breath."

Katarina glanced up and nodded. "I suppose I should tell him some information about your realm."

"Good starting point. What do you think he will want to know? He said something about our boundary lines with the Unfading Lands, did he not? I don't see why we cannot be truthful about those. There's no secret there." She began reciting the different land markers and dividers throughout the realm for Katarina to record and nodded when she read over the princess' words. "Your father hates Lancer, right?"

"Very much so."

"Perhaps if your father knows of our attack on the Unfading Lands he will be pleased with our Realm." Elizabeth suggested.

"I do not know, Princess. My father only cares about consumption. He wants more, more, and more, no matter what land it is."

"But still, perhaps he will see the benefit of defeating his old foe once again and help us in the fight or at least lose his distaste for our realm enough to let us defeat Lancer without worries of an attack from him."

"Perhaps." Katarina stated unconvinced.

"Put information in your letter about our plan to attack the Unfading Lands in the coming days. Just mention that we will be destroying the boundary line and plan to set everyone free. You do not have to mention any other details than that. That way he sees we are proactive against Lancer as well, but also he will not know enough to hinder our plans."

Katarina wrote intently as she tried to encompass a nonchalant attitude in her words and to also withhold details that could negatively affect Isaac and his realm.

"Can I ask you something?"

Katarina looked up at the curious blue of Elizabeth's gaze and nodded. "There's something I do not understand. My father and the other kings as well have always mentioned your father as a friendly neighbor to our Realm. Why is it he hates us now? What changed?"

"It is not that he hates you." Katarina stated quietly. "When your father was alive, King Granton was a strong king. Your royal guard was strong and intimidating. My father kept peace with your father for fear that if he did not, he could not beat King Granton. He always said your father would be the only man to defeat him. So he never tried. When your father died, your Realm weakened… or at least, in my father's eyes. He does not see your sister, or a woman for that matter, as strong enough to rule a kingdom, much less a realm. He feels that his perfect opportunity to consume more lands and become a more powerful king would be now. It is nothing personal to him. He is just greedy."

Elizabeth shook her head. "He underestimates us greatly."

"I believe so too." Katarina briefly smiled. "He underestimates many things."

"And what of Lancer? Why has he not tried to attack Lancer before now?"

"Your father. In order for my father to invade the Unfading Lands his troops would need to cross your father's realm. And King Granton did not want to start a war against Lancer when no one understood the power behind the veil. My father does not care. He believes he can defeat Lancer as he did before."

"And once he defeats all of the surrounding lands he just wishes to reign as a supreme king over everything?!" Elizabeth's voice held an edge of disgust as Katarina nodded.

"I know it sounds sickening, but I believe my father *is* sick to some degree. He does not wish to be anything but powerful. The fact Lancer contains a mysterious power drives him insane with jealousy. The fact your father reigned over an entire realm with little to no conflicts drove him mad. He does not wish for anyone to be better than he is."

Shaking her head Elizabeth took a sip of her wine. "It must have been hard growing up with such a man."

"He has his moments where he is kind. There are not many, but there have been a few."

Elizabeth smiled warmly. "Well I am glad he allowed you to come and visit us."

"Me too." Katarina lightly blushed as her thoughts wandered toward Isaac and what he would be doing at that current moment.

"I can see your mind has journeyed to another place." Elizabeth grinned. "Perhaps one that includes a handsome prince from the West?"

Trying to hide her embarrassment, Katarina shook her head and quickly took a drink from her cup.

"Oh it is quite alright, Katarina. I have been there." Elizabeth giggled. "Isaac is a good man."

"Yes, he is. He was quite kind to me when he visited my father's realm. I was pleased when he sought me out by letter."

Elizabeth studied Katarina closely, the long brown hair that draped over her lean shoulders, her brown molten eyes, creamy skin. Yes, the princess and Isaac would make an attractive pair should they take that final step. Elizabeth's smile widened when Katarina leaned closely towards her.

"May I ask you something now?"

"Of course."

"You and Isaac seem to be close friends."

"We are." Elizabeth agreed.

"Has he ever mentioned his mother, the queen?"

Elizabeth's brows rose. "No, why?"

"I was just curious is all. I know that the Eastern queen passed, may she rest in peace. I also know that your mother has as well. I am so sorry for your loss."

Elizabeth nodded.

"But I have never heard anything about a queen from the West. Did she pass years ago?"

Elizabeth shook her head. "No. In fact, she is very much alive. However, she does not venture out of the castle."

"I see." Katarina looked confused.

Elizabeth leaned back in her chair and nodded for Mary to clear their plates. "You see, Katarina, I do not know much about her. She is not spoken of, and my father always told us to never ask. Queen Isabella suffers from an unhealable illness."

"Oh, I am so sorry for Isaac and Melody. How sad." Katarina lightly placed her hand over her heart. "I did not mean to pry into such delicate matters. I just noticed she was not here with King Anthony when I arrived, and yet I recalled never hearing about her either."

"I have never asked the king nor his children about the queen." Elizabeth continued. "I imagine if they wished for me to know, they would tell me."

"You are right. I will not ask then. I wished to make sure I would not offend, but since the matter is so delicate I will refrain from questioning Isaac."

Elizabeth folded the parchment and handed it Mary. "Please give to Katarina's messenger, Mary. Make sure he knows the meaning of haste."

Mary nodded.

"Thank you for helping me write to my father. I am sure the letter will appease him greatly and will spare the life of that poor servant."

"I hope so." Elizabeth stood, and Katarina followed suit.

"In all of my questions and all of your help with my problems, I have yet to ask how you are doing, Elizabeth. With the departure of Clifton and all."

Elizabeth chuckled. "Oh, I am doing fine I guess. I know he is where he needs to be and that is what matters. I could no more lock him in our room and throw away the key than I could tell the sun to stop shining. The man has set his mind on protecting our Realm and he will."

"All of the princes seem that way. All are honorable in their different ways. And kind."

"That they are." Elizabeth smiled. "Prince Samuel is braver than he gives himself credit for and he will be an extraordinary king for the South. Prince Ryle, now Captain," Elizabeth corrected, "loves this Realm so much he forfeited his right to kingship so as to serve the Realm's throne. Clifton has smoothly transitioned into the role as future king of the East and I think he will be perfect, but then again I am quite biased." She winked at Katarina on her last comment and the princess softly chuckled. "And Prince Isaac will be a noble king for the West, once he fully believes he can be."

"I think him quite noble. Why would he not?" Katarina asked curiously.

Elizabeth laughed. "Because he is too stubborn. He is a good man who punishes himself for his past. I slowly see him letting it go and moving on, but he has obstacles hindering his progress every now and then. But he will come around. Clifton and I believe in his goodness, because we have seen it and experienced it."

"How so?"

"He saved our lives."

The princess' eyes widened. "He did?"

"Yes." Elizabeth continued. She stopped from their walk back to the castle and lifted the corner of her skirts, her wooden leg peeking out. Katarina gasped. "Oh my! Princess, I did not know! Are you alright?!"

Snickering, Elizabeth dropped her skirts. "I am. Thanks to Isaac. And Clifton lives because of Isaac as well. You see, in last year's battle against the South, I would have died but Isaac saw to it that I would not by chopping off my leg. It was badly wounded and was in the process of killing me when he did so. And Clifton," Elizabeth shook her head at the memory. "He was stabbed through the chest. Isaac could only save one of us, so he dragged Clifton across the boundary line into the Unfading Lands so that he might heal there, and he quickly brought me back to the castle."

"My goodness," Katarina muttered.

"Yes, it was quite exciting. In a tragic sense."

"And yet you all live and are dear friends."

"Yes. The experience has brought us all closer to one another. That is why our Realm is strong."

"I can only imagine how wonderful it must feel to have such friends and such a kingdom." Katarina sighed as they entered into the castle. Elizabeth lightly squeezed her new friend's elbow. "Perhaps one day you will." She smirked as they rounded the corner into the conservatory to see Melody cross stitching patterns into thin linen towels.

CHAPTER 11

"All lined up?" Ryle asked Clifton, pulling his reins next to his brother's horse. They had marched several hours already for the morning to arrive along the Eastern boundary line. They needed to attack from behind, and though he could tell the riders were somewhat tired, their hearts were full of passion and fight. They had rested a couple of hours and now it was time. Clifton nodded. "I believe so. All men are accounted for." Ryle nodded in approval as his eyes scanned the army of Uniters. He raised his sword into the air and rode back and forth along the front lines. "Gentlemen! It is early! It is dark! And we have readied ourselves all night! But now is the time!" He watched as riders straightened in their saddles and tucked their shields next to their sides. "Our time has come to defeat these Lands! Let no man stand against us! The Realm of Queen Alayna will be victorious!"

All the men cheered as they raised their swords in unison. Ryle lowered his sword and pointed ahead. "Let's go!" He slapped his reins and began to ride hard towards the Western boundary line. Today their fate would be decided. Today their Realm would start a new chapter, and today people would be freed from Lancer's control.

Hooves pounded on the dewy earth as they covered much land and crossed the Rollings River. They had to reach the Western boundary by dawn in order to attack at their strongest. Edward assured him that was the time his daily training sessions took place with Lancer's guard. The only way to attack all of Lancer's guards at once, and completely in secret. They would not be in formation but scattered. Not all would have weapons, and that would only work in the Realm's favor.

As they neared the small divide in the trees that Edward had described, Ryle slowed his horse to a walk and the men followed suit. He then halted everyone. "I will ride ahead and verify the layout." He muttered to Clifton. "Keep them in the trees." Clifton nodded in understanding as Ryle silently slipped to his feet and made his way through the thick forest towards what would soon be the designated site of the Realm's future. Clifton took a deep breath. The air was still, too still, and a sense of unease traipsed up his spine. *He was just nervous*, he tried to convince himself, but he knew something was off. Could be nothing, but something definitely felt off. He surveyed the trees surrounding their army trying not to draw attention to himself. He did not want to cause unwarranted worry. He saw nothing moving. The wind seemed to stand still, the leaves of the trees frozen in place as if they were too scared to move. He listened carefully and heard nothing minus the horses shifting on their hooves.

"When do we ride, my Lord?" The guard to his right whispered. Clifton raised his hand to silence the man. "When Captain Ryle returns." The guard obediently fell back into place and into quiet as he patiently waited for Ryle to step back through the trees.

The calm before the storm, Clifton believed. The eerie feeling of unease continued to swim through his veins and into his chest. He tampered his breathing and took slow deep breaths. He would wait for Ryle a bit longer then he would go looking for him. There was no reason for him to not be back by now. His horse whinnied and stomped its hooves at what Clifton sensed as a direct reflection of his own apprehension. He lightly patted the horse's neck. He heard a twig snap and his head turned to the side to find Ryle trying to make his way through the thick brush.

"Well?" His voice was quiet as his brother climbed back upon his horse.

"They were just starting to arrive. I say we wait until the first peek of the sun through the trees, then we attack." Ryle smiled as if he were completely unaware of the thick weighted atmosphere surrounding them. "It is our time, brother." His whisper edged with excitement. "They are completely unaware."

Clifton nodded and swallowed the lump in his throat. *His brother was confident, why was he not?* He forced a smile as he pulled his sword and held it at the ready. Minutes felt like hours as he watched his brother adjust the straps of his armor and ready himself for battle as well. Ryle turned to the guard next to him. "Remember, we must aim for their heads. The only way to kill here is to decapitate. Otherwise they will heal and continue to attack us. Aim for the heads. Spread the word quietly." He heard the man turn to the guard next to him and whisper the command, the confirmation of their training to refresh their nervous minds.

"You ready?" Ryle asked.

"I will follow you." Clifton replied.

∞

"The guard looks good, Edward." Lancer praised, riding alongside Edward as the guards took to their stations for their morning training.

"They are strong, my Lord. A formidable army, ready to face Abner if necessary." Edward watched as several of the guards climbed into their saddles. He wrinkled his brow in confusion. "What are they doing?" He whispered more to himself than to Lancer.

"Oh, I hope you don't mind. I took the liberty of throwing a new station into your training routine." Lancer beamed. "I wished to incorporate a full rehearsal this morning."

"Rehearsal?" Edward asked. "I don't understand."

"Well, Edward, our attention has been on Abner, meanwhile your very own sister has been plotting against us. Your army is not training today, Edward. We are taking them on a trek through the forest." Lancer smirked at Edward's shock.

"Is that wise, my Lord? I thought you were concerned about Abner? I have heard nothing about an attack from my Realm?"

"I have a feeling, Edward. Trust me." Lancer flashed his charming smile and Edward felt panic rise in his chest as Lancer began lining up the guards on horseback. All were wearing full armor. *How had he not noticed that before?* Edward cringed. Somehow, Lancer found out about the Realm's attack and Ryle would be walking into a trap. He felt the pang in his chest of anger and fear. *What had he done?!* There was no way to warn them. He prayed the Realm and the Uniters were strong enough, though he inwardly knew they were not. He watched as Lancer turned towards him. "Shall we ride, Edward?"

Edward clicked his reins and pulled up beside Lancer. "To the West!" Lancer called out. He then watched as pure shock covered Edward's face. "Calm yourself, Edward. Your family really had it coming to them, did they not? They honestly thought they could defeat me, the darkness, my Lands." He scoffed. "They deserve to be humbled. Are you with me?"

Edward's face hardened, and his eyes flashed with anger. "I'm with you." He stated confidently, though he prayed his heart would be strong enough to fight against the darkness instead. He had to appear to be on Lancer's side, but defeat had already swamped him and now he felt the slight rise in his veins of a different nature. A venomous nature that only wanted blood. Uniters' blood. He gritted his teeth and a small growl escaped his lips as he blinked his eyes closed for a moment to fight off the thought and feeling. He needed to focus. Lancer was the enemy. *Lancer was the enemy*, he repeated to himself. But as he saw the flash of a blade in the trees, thoughts of helping the Realm fled from his mind.

∞

"Do you hear that?" Clifton quietly asked as he strained to listen to the early morning air. "Hooves." He turned to Ryle with a grim expression. "They are coming for us. We should leave now, Ryle."

"No. We will fight. His guards are training this morning. It is just the sound of their training routines."

"With horses?" Clifton's whisper was harsh with disbelief. "We have been discovered. We must flee and attempt our assault at a different time."

"No." Ryle's voice rose as he stared at his younger brother. "We will fight. We have planned for this."

"And we have been betrayed." Clifton's voice began to carry as well as he let his worry get the best of him. "I know we do not want to accept that fact, but someone has betrayed us, and we are sitting ducks. We must flee."

"We will not flee." Ryle's lips formed a firm line as he raised his sword and heard the Uniters do the same. He clicked his reins and took off out of the trees at a full gallop. Clifton had no choice but to follow, and as soon as they appeared through the trees, a full army of Lancer's guards awaited them at the ready. Clifton watched as arrows whizzed by his head and several men fell. He spotted Edward riding alongside Lancer and cringed at the thought of killing Elizabeth's brother, but his betrayal clawed its way into Clifton's heart and he wished him to suffer. Ryle led the pack and Clifton spotted his brother cutting down two Unfading guards in one swipe. His brother's heart was in this fight, his pride was in this fight, and Clifton took a deep breath and swung his sword, the familiar drag of human flesh and bone making his stomach sink.

Ryle cringed as he felt the spurt of a man's blood splash across his face and he turned his horse in enough time to see an Unfading rider swinging his blade. He blocked the blow with his shield and felt the impact as he tilted in his saddle. His horse remained steady, but the guard quickly regained his composure and swiped the straps of Ryle's saddle sending Ryle to the ground. He found his feet in a hurry and blocked three blows by the time he was able to correct his stance and attack with his own sword. He felt a gash in his right shoulder and did not bother looking down as he knew it would slowly heal. He dodged another sword and felt the strength of the blow against his shield and he stumbled over what used to be a Uniter guard. The parry he faced surprised him as the man's strength bore down on him and he felt his muscles quivering in exertion with every swing of his sword. Blood, dirt, sweat, and iron flooded his nostrils as he spun away from the next blow and landed his blade on the backside of the man's neck. A precise slice that took the man down in a single stroke. His chest heaved as he surveyed the surrounding battle ground. He spotted Edward fighting against one of Lancer's guards, Lancer completely unaware of his Captain's actions. *Good. Edward was still on their side.* The small comforting thought fled quickly as he felt an arrow land in the middle of his left thigh. He yanked it out and growled at the pain as he charged the next Unfading guard he spotted.

Clifton had made his way closer to Edward. The Northern prince fought against both Uniters and Unfading guards as if he could not make up his own mind or decipher his enemy. Clifton charged him from behind and tackled him to the ground. Edward scrabbling underneath him to fight off the attack. He rolled to his back and froze as his eyes focused upon Clifton's face. "Traitor!" Clifton yelled as he backhanded Edward across the face and felt a small sense of satisfaction as a spray of blood squirted from his lip. Edward pushed against Clifton's chest and gripped the wrists that housed the strong grip around his throat. "It-wasn't-me." Edward's voice rasped as he struggled to free himself from the vise like grip. Clifton released him and grabbed his sword, holding Edward at the tip of it. Edward did not aim to rise. "You have to believe me."

Clifton shook his head and brought his blade above his head. "I will forever be plagued by your death." His words were forced through a grim set of lips as regret flooded the Eastern Prince's usually kind gaze. Edward's eyes widened and flashed over Clifton's shoulder, causing Clifton to turn swiftly slicing his sword through the air and the form of an Unfading guard fell behind him. He turned back to Edward, but the Northern Prince was up on his feet fighting against two more of Lancer's guards.

Clifton would let him live for now. He did not wish to kill Edward if what he said was true. Panting, he began parries between two guards and managed to kill both men. His strength was fading, and their numbers were growing slim. He sprinted towards a group of Uniters and fought alongside them. "Get to the clearing the first chance you get." He barked the order and several of the men nodded when they had a chance. Clifton sought out Ryle and caught his brother's gaze briefly, signaling to him for retreat. Ryle shook his head and blocked a blow. Clifton covered the ground in swift steps as he brought his sword through the man from behind and Ryle finished him off. "We must retreat, brother!" He shouted over the clash of blades and screams. Ryle continued fighting, his eyes crazed with passion as he assaulted one guard after another. Clifton yanked his arm back once he finished off his latest foe. "Retreat!" He yelled. "Retreat!" He screamed it again so those around him would hear and repeat the order. Ryle shoved away from Clifton's grip and had no choice but to follow his guards back into the woods and the race towards their hideout, with a prayer Lancer's men did not follow.

∞

Edward watched as the last of the Uniters scurried away and into the forest and he raised his fist into the air to signal victory and all of Lancer's men cheered in response as Lancer appeared from his hidden alcove and smiled alongside Edward. "Well done, Edward. Well done!" Edward inwardly sighed in relief that Lancer had not seen several of his attacks on Unfading guards, and he played his part as loyal Captain well as Lancer rode through the battlefield with victorious waves of his sword. He reached Edward's side once again and halted. "You realize, Edward, that you will need to pursue their remaining army and kill them?"

"Yes, my Lord."

"Because the two princes are the only men who can cross the boundary line. The rest are trapped here. I want them all dead." The smile on Lancer's face turned into a snarl. "No one comes into these Lands with the expectation of defeating me without facing the consequences. Show Eamon's sons what true defeat feels like. Make them watch the death of their followers."

"Yes, my Lord."

"Then I want all of these bodies gathered up and burned. There is no sense for our people to have to look at such unsightly carnage." Lancer straightened in his saddle. "This victory was good for us, Edward. I imagine the strength of our Lands will reestablish and we will gain ground. For now, I believe I will celebrate in my reflection chamber. When you have a moment, meet me there."

Edward nodded and watched as Lancer rode away with a personal detail and left Edward with the mess. His gaze washed over the bodies before him, some friends, some enemies. He silently sent up a prayer as he tried to think of a way to hide the remaining Uniters. He also prayed Clifton believed him when he denied sharing their plan. He knew it wasn't him. He had consciously made an effort to steer clear of such conversations with Lancer unless absolutely necessary for that very fear of revealing too much information. Someone else had to have told him, or perhaps the darkness betrayed Edward. *Perhaps the fact he had yet to fully succumb to its power somehow revealed itself to Lancer. No.* Then Lancer would know of Edward possessing the darkness, and he seemed to still not notice. Edward cleared his mind and took a deep, regretful breath as he watched Lancer's army pulling bodies into a large pile. Death was hard. Death of large numbers devastating. Death of friends... he dropped his head as an overwhelming sadness filtered through his heart. He had killed two of his fellow Uniters. Two men going to their death believing the worst of him. He tried to stifle down his self-loathing, *but what was to become of him if he turned on his friends?* He remembered the struggle. He remembered the way the darkness empowered his very blade and turned his eyes blind to those he fought. He had no feeling. No control. Until Clifton shook him from his trance. The Realm had been defeated, and with it, so had Edward.

∞

Elizabeth sat on the parapet, her legs draped over the side and her skirt blowing in the light breeze.

"You must come eat, Ms. Elizabeth." Mary anxiously suggested. "You are no good to Prince Clifton if you are weak with hunger."

Elizabeth tossed a tender smile towards her attendant. "I am sorry Mary, but I have no appetite. I will not eat until Clifton returns."

"Yes, my Lady." Mary bowed and remained in the shadows as Elizabeth continued to survey the surrounding horizon waiting for the first glimpse of her husband's blonde hair. She saw nothing. The boundary line remained, which meant they were still fighting against Lancer. Sighing she leaned back and worried her hands in her lap. She tried to imagine the difference Lancer's defeat would make in the Realm. The people that would immerse back into the kingdoms they left long ago. Would their age catch up with them? Would they live in the kingdoms they once left? So many questions, and little answers, until the veil actually fell. Elizabeth straightened quickly and slightly teetered on the edge, her hands gripping the parapet as she stabilized and strained to see what appeared on the Western horizon. Slowly, her blue eyes widened with panic. "Mary!" She called.

Mary stepped forward. "Yes, my Lady?"

Elizabeth swung her feet over the landing and gripped Mary's shoulders. "Find Hector immediately. Tell him to ride to the Southern Kingdom for King Samuel. We need the Southern Army at once. Abner is here. Go!" She shoved her attendant towards the castle doors and Mary sprinted ahead of her. When Elizabeth entered, she yelled as loud as she could. "Isaac!" She hurried towards the stairwell, her limp more pronounced as she hastily tried to walk and jog at the same time. "Isaac!" Her voice pitched with panic as she gripped the banister. Katarina appeared at the bottom of the stairs with Melody. "Elizabeth? What is it?" Melody asked in concern at the Eastern Princess's distress.

"I need Isaac! Where is he?!"

"I believe he is in the conservatory." Melody pointed over her shoulder and Elizabeth immediately swished by her. The two other princesses gathering their skirts to follow.

"Isaac!" Elizabeth screamed.

Isaac appeared in a sprint and slid on the floor as he saw her appear the opposite direction he was running. "Elizabeth, what is it?" He allowed her to grab his arm as she tried to catch her breath. Her eyes full of terror. "Abner. He's on the Western Horizon. Army." She panted.

Isaac stepped back and darted towards the window and peeked out at the edge of the highlands. Sure enough, a vast number of troops were lined up at the ready, and they were not his father's.

"I've sent word to Samuel." Elizabeth stated, "but for now we are on our own."

Katarina began to shake, and Melody clasped onto the princess' hands as she eased her into a chair. "He will come straight to the castle." Katarina muttered. She then looked up at Melody with imploring eyes. "He will come here!" Her voice rose in panic and Isaac grabbed Elizabeth's hand and pulled her to the side. "I will gather the guard. I want you to barricade yourself and all the female attendants in the highest room of the castle. Understand?"

She nodded.

"Good. And Elizabeth," he paused his eyes surveying her sweet face, "don't forget your sword."

Her eyes narrowed in determination as she turned to the other two princess' and gave them the same order to gather maids and attendants in the bell tower. She then made her way to her chamber, Mary intercepting her on the way. "Hector has gone, my Lady. I also sent James to the Eastern Kingdom. I did not send a messenger to the West for fear of capture."

"Good thinking, Mary, thank you. We must gather everyone we can. I need my sword from my chambers. Fetch it for me and meet me at the tower door." Mary nodded and darted up the stairwell.

Elizabeth spotted all the men attendants and servants arming themselves and creating barricades to all the doors as Isaac sprinted towards the armory to rally the guard. She thanked her sister for forfeiting her wishes and keeping him here. *Her sister!* Elizabeth hurried out to the gardens where her sister had mentioned she wished for peace and quiet. She spotted her, unaware, as she sat with her back to her. "Alayna!" Elizabeth tripped on the stone pathway and fell to her knees, her palms scraping against the small stones. She grunted and stood quickly, Alayna horrified by her sister's grace. "Elizabeth, what on Earth?"

"You must come inside. Now." Elizabeth began pulling her towards the castle and Alayna resisted. "I will not. I told you I needed my peace out here for a few hours."

"You don't have a few hours!" Elizabeth yelled in frustration. "Abner is marching on us this very instant!"

Alayna's face paled. "What?"

"He is coming from the West. Isaac is fetching the guard. The castle is being bolted down, and word has been sent to Samuel and Eamon. Now come! I will explain more once we are inside."

Alayna followed, gathering her skirts as Elizabeth led her up the many staircases towards the bell tower. "Get inside." Elizabeth lightly shoved her sister's back into the room with the servants and maids, all looking terrified. "Lizzy, what are y—" The door closed in her face and she heard Elizabeth yell through the wood. "Bolt the door!" And Alayna heard the sound of the heavy wooden barricade latch.

Elizabeth sank against the doors to catch her breath. Her leg throbbed, but she knew it was not the time to think of herself. Her father's castle would soon be under attack and she would die defending it from such a man as Abner.

∞

"We must go, brother." Clifton sat on the large boulder in Elizabeth's clearing and watched as Ryle lay in exhaustion upon his back in the grass. The sun was at full attention in the sky. *Noon*, Clifton realized, their journey into the Lands, the battle, and the death had all taken less than six hours. Ryle's breathing began to even and he eased up onto his elbows. "I do not wish to go back just yet."

"We must. We must inform the others and come up with a better plan." Clifton stood and began sheathing his sword onto his horse. "We lost, Ryle. Accept it." His voice was gruff, and his forwardness would more than likely make his brother angry, but it was the truth.

"And what of the other Uniters?" Ryle asked.

"They will continue to hide."

"If we were betrayed by someone, and it was not Edward, then their location is already at risk. They will be killed." Ryle's face twisted into a pained grimace as he fought for control of his emotions and the anger that ravaged his insides.

"It was a risk they were willing to take." Clifton stated. "We pray they remain safe, but in the meantime, we must head back to the castle and regroup."

"No. I will not go as of yet. We need to think of another plan before we face everyone. We need to show there is another way to defeat Lancer." Ryle stood and began to pace around the clearing and Clifton swallowed his frustration. He tilted his head as he listened closer to the sound of what appeared to be hooves. "Do you hear that?"

"Hear what?" Ryle asked and paused a moment. He shook his head. "You are probably just imagining things. The sounds of battle remain long after the fight."

Clifton shook his head and slipped into the trees leading out of Elizabeth's clearing and he froze as he gazed upon the Southern army heading at full speed towards the North. A horse pulled up beside him and he looked up into the familiar face of Samuel. "What is the meaning of this?" Clifton yelled over the pounding upon the earth.

"Abner marches from the West. Word was sent for reinforcements."

Clifton's gaze hardened, and he nodded. "I will gather Ryle and we will meet you there!"

Samuel nodded and kicked in his heels, his horse racing to gain back the ground he had lost from the front of the pack. Clifton hurried through the trees and found his brother sitting on the boulder with his head in his hands staring at the ground.

"Your sulking will have to wait." Clifton barked, climbing up into his saddle. "Abner marches on the North."

Ryle's head snapped up. "What?"

"You heard me. We have to move." Clifton turned without waiting and heard his brother mounting his horse as well. When Clifton emerged from the trees, Samuel's army had already covered considerable ground and would be arriving at the castle in mere minutes. Ryle appeared next to him as they rode hard and fast towards Alayna and Elizabeth.

∞

Isaac raised his shield as arrows pelted against him and the royal guard. Several men collapsed, but most were protected by shields or coverings. The first level had to hold, or the castle would be lost. The royal guard was strong in skill but lacking in numbers since the battles from last year. Without reinforcements, Isaac knew they could not hold Abner's army off for long. He spotted black tunics making their way across the highlands and thanked the heavens for Samuel's haste. He prayed he arrived soon enough to help protect the inner courts.

"Hold your ground!" Isaac yelled. "Hold your ground!" He watched as the first of Abner's guards reached the outer castle walls. "Archers! Take your aim!" He raised his hand. "Fire!" He heard the rush of arrows swim through the air and meet most of their targets. "Ready!" He yelled again. "Fire!" Round two, and several more guards went down. Abner's numbers continued to multiply, and Isaac could not imagine the reason for an army so big except for conquering. The gates to the inner courts pounded open and a flood of guards seeped into the market square. A clash of green and red tunics with shields echoed around the castle. "Maintain your ground!" He shouted and ran down the side parapet to reach the next landing. He found his footing quickly and raised his sword to protect a royal guard from behind and then rotated in time to block another blow to his right shoulder.

"We are surrounded, my Lord!" A guard called to him as they clashed blades with two red tunics. "The castle is surrounded."

"The South is coming and so is the East. We must hold them off long enough until our help arrives." Isaac turned and realized he was speaking to no one as the man's glazed eyes stared up at him and his chest poured with blood. Shaking his head at such a loss, he jumped over several bodies to come to a stop at the edge of the railing. The South was already fighting for them on the first level, but the inner courts were breached. Protection of the main castle doors was paramount, and Isaac slipped into the castle to make his way there. His footsteps echoed throughout the western wing of the castle as he headed towards the front entrance. Elizabeth was rushing down the stairs. "What are you doing?!" Isaac yelled at her. She froze and waved her hand in the air frantically. "I cannot find Katarina or Melody. They were to round up the maids and meet me at the bell tower. The maids arrived but they have not."

Isaac ran a hand over his worn face and grabbed her elbow pulling her out of the way of oncoming royal guards taking formation behind the castle doors. "Listen to me, Elizabeth." His eyes bore into hers and he could tell he had her full attention. "The castle is going to be breached. You *must* get to safety. Do you hear me?"

She nodded. "But what of Melody and Kat—"

"They will find you. You need to protect the Queen, your sister."

"Isaac, I—"

"Go. Melody and Katarina will either make it to the bell tower or they are on their own now. There is no time. Go!" He barked as pounding began against the large wooden doors and he darted towards the action. Elizabeth surveyed the scene around her and outside the windows she could see the battle underway. Mustering what little courage she had left, she began making her way up the stairs just as the doors burst open.

CHAPTER 12

"Elizabeth!" Alayna pounded on the locked doors of the bell tower. "Open this door this minute! You cannot lock me in here! Elizabeth!" She gave up with a frustrated blow of her bangs and walked over to the small opening of the tower and peeked out. Shock tore into her at what surrounded her father's castle and she quickly pulled herself away from the sight. She heard a rustle outside the door and it opened briefly to allow several more attendants to pass through. She quickly stalked over. "Elizabeth!" She squeezed through the crowd and slipped into the hall just as Elizabeth reached the top of the steps. "Get back inside!" She screamed at Alayna waving her hand frantically as several arrows landed behind her sister. Alayna gasped as she felt a hand pull her towards the doors. Melody with wide eyes pulled the Queen into the tower behind her. Elizabeth sighed in relief at seeing the Western Princess, but Katarina could still not be found. Elizabeth turned and held a shield at the ready as she heard footsteps making their way up the stairwell. Two guards from Abner's Realm smirked at the sight of her and she spotted Katarina hiding in an alcove behind them with wide eyes and Mary coming up the stairwell behind them. Mary slid to a stop but caught the men's attention and one of them turned,

spotting Katarina huddled in the corner. Mary darted forward, her hands grabbing the hilt of the man's sword as he rose to strike Katarina. Scrambling to keep her hold, he backhanded Mary across the face, sending her to the floor. Elizabeth parried with the other guard, her arms aching from lack of use and she scolded herself for not practicing more. She felt a slice along her left thigh and felt the man's strength behind his next blow as he thought he would slice her leg. His blade temporarily snagged against her wooden peg and she noted the man's surprise as she advanced without flinching. He yanked, and his blade came free just as Elizabeth stabbed him through the heart. Katarina screamed as the other guard made his way towards her and Mary hurried, pulling herself across the floor to her feet to dive at the man's legs. The man kicked and turned just as Elizabeth brought her blade around. He moved just in time, his sword finding its way into Mary's stomach and Elizabeth's just grazing his shoulder. Her eyes drifted to her faithful friend and servant, Mary's sweet gaze slowly dimming as her blood began puddling over the floor. Elizabeth felt the sting of tears as she kicked out and nailed the man in the middle of the chest with her peg, the force taking him by surprise as she drove her blade deep into his own stomach. She jerked and twisted as he leaned forward, his grip loosening and his blade clattered to the floor. She held his dark gaze as his life slowly drained from him, and she made sure he understood the pain which she inflicted was out of vengeance. When he finally collapsed, and Elizabeth removed her sword, Katarina slid to her knees beside Mary and cupped her face, the front of the princess' dress covering with blood. "Leave her. She is lost." Elizabeth yanked Katarina to her feet and pulled up the barricade to the bell tower and shoved Katarina inside. She caught the brief terrified gaze of Alayna as she closed the door and the sound of the bolt slid into place.

Footsteps carried up the stairway and Elizabeth braced herself for further attack, but her eyes widened at the sight of Samuel and Mosiah. Samuel spotted Mary on the cold floor and his face filled with regret.

"You came." Elizabeth's words barely a whisper as she enveloped the young king in a tight embrace.

"I came as soon as your messenger reached me." Samuel nodded to the two guards. "There will be more. I suggest you join the others in the tower."

"I can fight." Elizabeth assured him.

"I know you can, Princess, but now is not the time. You have done your part." Samuel turned as several guards emerged and he and Mosiah began engaging. She remained where she stood, her sword dripping in blood and her gaze drifting to dear Mary. *She would never find a more loyal friend*, she thought, and she wished she could take a moment to weep for the loss of such a lovely person but knew that moment would need to be postponed. She reached under her skirt and grabbed her dagger and threw it with exact precision at the guard that had just reached the top step. Samuel turned briefly and nodded his thanks as Elizabeth stepped forward to join in the fight with him and Mosiah.

∞

"We must push the remaining forces back towards the boundary line. Once across we can let Lancer handle them." Ryle grunted as he shoved off of one man and into another, his blade appearing through the man's back.

"That would take too long." Clifton dodged a strike to his chest and pulled the man's face down to meet his knee, the satisfying crunch of the man's nose sending him to the ground.

"It is the only way. Father cannot possibly reach us until nightfall if we are lucky. We cannot hold much longer if we do not divert Abner's army."

"Then go!" Clifton yelled. "Grab some guards and go! We will stay and cover the castle."

Ryle nodded and began sprinting down the stairwell towards the Eastern wing of the castle where he found the second wave of royal guards preparing for their emergence into the battle. "Arm yourselves, gentlemen! Our plan is changing! We force them towards the boundary line of the Unfading Lands!"

The guards nodded and began riding out of the inner courts and through the walls of the castle, their numbers taking Abner's army by surprise as their assault on the Eastern side came to an adjustment in tactics. Abner's men began rerouting towards the front entrance and Ryle and his guards continued driving them back. *Even if it was just one portion*, he thought, *they would send these men across the line*. His men funneled the red tunics into a single push, striking down the stragglers as they rode with force across the highlands. Abner's army continued pouring in from the West and Ryle's hope of utilizing the boundary line would only work if they stopped the continual assault against the castle.

Ryle rode up next to one of his guards. "Divide. Push them from the West to the South. We must force them from all directions towards the boundary line."

"Yes, Captain." The man began his run along the split and a slow curve began to shift the royal guard into two halves. One headed towards the boundary line past Elizabeth's clearing. The other as a barricade between the Northern castle and pushing them further south. The veil grew closer and Ryle felt the brief flurry of satisfaction as he saw the first few men escape into the Land of Unfading Beauty. Their lack of knowledge into Lancer and his hatred towards Abner, a sudden point in the Realm's favor. The men would be dead within minutes due to their sporting Abner's coat of arms. He spotted Edward on the other side, weapons at the ready with Lancer's guard lined up along the boundary line. *Lancer was prepared for Abner after all*, Ryle mused. He turned on his horse as the first wave of soldiers were sent to their death on the other side of the line and he rerouted his guards to begin pushing against another chapter. He would repeat the cycle all day and night if he had to, in order to bring down Abner's numbers so the Realm had a fighting chance.

Clifton finally reached the main entrance of the castle and ran inside to pure chaos as bodies fell from landings and blades clashed and echoed throughout the inner halls. His gaze travelled up towards Isaac midway along the stairwell and he fought his way towards him. He reached the Western prince and blocked Isaac's blade as he spun with fury to kill the next man approaching. His face transformed from anger to relief at the sight of Clifton.

"About time you showed up."

Clifton felt his lips tilt into a brief smile as they both immediately turned to sounds of more boots. "The women are in the bell tower. We have secured this landing. Samuel and Mosiah are securing the top landing of the castle as we speak. If we can continue forcing out Abner's men we can regain the castle." Isaac shoved a guard towards Clifton's blade and the two men worked together to finish clearing the stairwell and the men who dared journeyed up.

When they reached the bottom step and the surrounding halls were clear, Clifton nodded in satisfaction. "Ryle is pushing outside forces towards the boundary line. He thinks Lancer will kill Abner's guard as soon as they cross."

"I sure hope he's right." Isaac's chest heaved as he swiped a hand over the sweat that threatened to drip into his eyes. "I want to find Abner. This ends with him."

"We find him together then." Clifton and Isaac headed towards the back of the castle. "If we can hold off the forces long enough for my father to arrive with reinforcements, then we can achieve victory." His voice shook as he ran, and Isaac looked at him in amusement. "What?" Clifton asked.

"Your positivity sometimes sickens me." Isaac chuckled at the absurdity and Clifton did as well as they made it through the doors and quickly found two horses that would carry them to their next target.

"Edward, let none of Abner's guards remain alive once they cross. I will not have Abner tainting my lands!" Lancer screamed as he stood back from the line and watched as red tunics flooded into his precious realm.

"Yes, my Lord!" Edward yelled, his voice wavering as he brought his blade across the man's neck. He shoved the body behind him and felt the brunt of a large shoulder in his chest, the next man knocking him to the ground to try and escape from Edward's clasp. Growling, he shoved the man off of him and sent him flying several feet back. The man's eyes widened in surprise at Edward's strength, and Edward slowly felt the rush through his veins, his pupils dilating, and his chest heaving. He swiped his blade through the air and the man's body staggered a moment, headless, and fell to the ground. Edward turned then, the new strength, the new power enriching his body with pure venom towards his enemies as he protected the Lands from Abner's invading men.

Lancer watched in awe at his Captain and the skill in which Edward moved and the passion behind his fighting. *He chose the perfect man*, Lancer realized. And all his doubts of Edward's loyalty disappeared as each stroke of his blade protected the Land of Unfading Beauty from Abner's poison. His gaze then ventured towards another wave of red tunics being pushed towards the boundary line, minus one. He spotted a green shield battling in one on one combat, the Prince of the East that dared to invade him just that morning. Lancer kept to the shadows and grabbed several guards on his way as he watched as Ryle continued to nudge the guard closer to the boundary line. *All he had to do was cross,* Lancer thought. *One step and he would be in the Lands again.*

Ryle blocked the blow to his face and felt his shield fly to the ground and a sword pierce through his chest. He felt a tingle filter down his arm and he struggled to maintain his grip on his sword. His vision blurred, and his feet staggered. He glanced over his shoulder towards the boundary line, the thought of passing through for a quick healing crossed his mind, but his strength was fading. He dragged his blade behind him as he attempted to make the trek. He dodged a blow to the shoulder and almost fell to his knees as the pain in his chest continued to spill blood through his fingers. He pressed as hard as he could against the wound and reached the light hum of the fog that had grown familiar the last few weeks as he trained the Uniters. He felt the grass beneath his cheek as hands pulled him completely across the boundary line, the wound from his chest leaving a dark trail behind him as he was carried away from the clatter of swords and shouts.

∞

Isaac signaled for Clifton to circle around the backside of the small cluster of ranking guards surrounding Abner. Clifton nodded and signaled for several of their fellow guards to aim their arrows to the backsides of Abner's protectors. He lowered his hand and the first sweep of arrows hit their targets taking the guards by surprise. Abner adjusted in his saddle long enough to see a galloping Isaac riding towards him with sword at the ready. Clifton rode out immediately from the opposite direction, the two princes both targeting the same man.

Abner smirked as he swiped his blade towards the Prince of the West and Isaac's blade clashed with his. Clifton rode quickly past the distracted King and aimed his blade for the straps of Abner's saddle sending the arrogant king to the ground. Isaac dismounted quickly and ran towards the man tackling him before he could even rise to his feet. Fists pummeled against the older man's face as he reached the dagger at his side and drove it beneath Isaac's ribs. The satisfied pull against flesh causing Isaac's fists to pause in their assault. He glanced at the man's hand and then drove another hard fist into the king's face as Isaac pulled the dagger out of his side himself. Clifton fought the remaining guards, his watchful eye keeping Isaac within sights as the Western prince slammed Abner's dagger into the king's heart with all his remaining strength.

"You... have no idea... what you have done." Abner's breaths were ragged as his eyes slowly faded and his breathing stopped. Isaac slid to the ground next to the dead king and felt his own wound betraying him. His eyes closed as darkness clouded his vision and all he could think about was how Katarina would be free.

Clifton dove towards Isaac and pressed his ear to the prince's chest, pulling his arm over his head and lifting Isaac onto his shoulders. He draped Isaac over his horse and hurried towards the castle. Abner's men were retreating, and the sound of hooves riding in from the East awakened the hope Clifton knew would come in the sight of the Eastern flags flying on the horizon. His father had arrived, and this battle would be over soon. He reached the castle doors and rode straight inside the castle as Samuel and Mosiah were running down the stairs having cleared the final landing. Samuel momentarily froze at the sight of Isaac's limp body but immediately helped Mosiah pull him down to the floor and carry him straight into the conservatory. "My father has arrived." Clifton panted. "Help has come. I will ride out to meet him and finish this. Remain here."

Samuel nodded and watched as Clifton hurried away and his attention rested on Isaac's pale face. "It is not your turn, Prince Isaac." Samuel stated as he placed pressure on the wound as Mosiah began treating it. "Wake up." As he nudged further pressure into Isaac's side, Isaac's eyes flew open on a gasp and he blinked several times as he groaned in pain. "Hold still, Prince." Mosiah ordered.

"S-Samuel." His voice was ragged. "M-Melod-dy?"

"She is safe in the bell tower." Samuel replied, helping Mosiah stop the bleeding.

Isaac relaxed and felt his head swim as he heard the familiar voice of Elizabeth filter into the room and his thoughts. He felt her hands on his face as she lightly tapped his cheeks, but he could not will his eyes to open. "You'd better not die, Isaac, or I will kill you myself." She barked in a grumbled tantrum as she poured what felt like hot water over his wound. He jolted from the pain but felt the numbness take hold and he surrendered to the dark.

Alayna made her way down the stairs slowly as she surveyed the destruction before her. Bodies littered the halls and staircases and she heard several gasps behind her as the attendants and maids made their way to freedom as well. Her eyes searched what few faces she saw but she caught no sign of Ryle. The castle doors were now closed, and guards began clearing away the butchery before them. She heard rustling within the conservatory and found Elizabeth knelt beside a still Isaac. She heard Melody gasp and rush by her to her brother's side as Arnos appeared next to the Western prince.

Samuel straightened at the sight of Alayna and bowed. "It is over, my Queen. The Realm was victorious, though I must say I'm not sure if true victory could be achieved by anyone in such matters as this."

She squeezed his arm in thanks as she continued into the room. "Is he alive?"

"Barely." Arnos stated, his brutal honesty a harsh reminder of what could be.

Katarina walked into the room and she slowly made her way towards Isaac, her shoulders lightly shaking as she stroked her hand over his hair. Elizabeth squeezed her hand. "He is a fighter, Katarina. He will make it." She rose to her feet and walked towards her sister. Alayna's gaze sweeping over Elizabeth looking for injury. She pulled Elizabeth into her arms into a tight embrace. "You scared me to death, Lizzy." Her words a wavering whisper as her brown eyes clouded with tears.

Elizabeth pulled back and held her sister's shoulders. "I am fine."

"Clifton?" Alayna asked.

"I do not know." Elizabeth stated. "He has not arrived back yet."

"Ryle?"

Elizabeth shrugged, and Alayna's face fell.

"We have lost many, Alayna, and there will be time for grief, but for now, we have many who need our strength." Elizabeth whispered. Alayna studied her younger sister in awe and squeezed her hand in thanks. "You are right, Lizzy."

Elizabeth nodded as she turned towards the sound of boots in the main hall and Clifton emerged with King Eamon. She found the chair next to her as she collapsed in relief at the sight of him and he rushed to her and hugged her tightly to his chest. She felt tears running down her face and tried to swipe them away, but she noticed Clifton's face held the same. She looked up at King Eamon and he sweetly brushed his hand over her hair as he faced Alayna.

"Ryle?" She asked him.

"I have not seen him just yet, my Queen."

"Abner?"

"Dead." Clifton stood back to his feet, lifting Elizabeth to her own and hugging her towards him. "Isaac killed him."

Katarina's head popped up at that announcement and her gaze travelled back to the prince before her as she tenderly brushed Isaac's cheek with her fingers.

"It is over." Clifton stated.

∞

Edward entered the reflection chamber and shielded his eyes from the bright flames that licked up the sides of the walls. When he adjusted to the change, he caught sight of Lancer with his back to him and his arms raised. He was calling the darkness and Edward cringed at what power might come to him now that they aided in destroying his one true enemy: Abner. He turned at the sound of Edward and his smile twisted into one Edward had never seen before. "You are just in time, Edward. I would like you to meet our guest." He stepped to the side and Edward gazed upon Prince Ryle tied to a chair before Lancer with a gag tied within his mouth, his appearance weak, torn, tired, and tattered from the fights he had endured. Edward tampered down his anger towards Lancer as he approached, and Lancer laughed in glee.

"It seems we just captured a prince of the East, Edward. Though he disguises himself as a guard of the North, I know exactly who he is. He is my nephew. I would recognize Erica's eyes anywhere." Lancer leaned towards Ryle's face and slapped him.

"Why have you captured a prince, my Lord?" Edward asked curiously, Ryle finding his gaze and gauging his movements with a cautious eye.

"What a silly question, Edward!" Lancer chuckled as he walked behind Ryle and lifted his face to stare at Edward. "Isn't it obvious?" When Edward made no move to reply, Lancer rolled his eyes and tossed Ryle's head to the side. "The Realm thought they could attack me one minute and then be my ally the next. And this particular prince," he pointed his sword beneath Ryle's chin, "he thought he could use our boundary line for his own personal gain. Not only to heal himself but to drive Abner's men into my realm."

Edward watched as Ryle remained alert and wary of Lancer's movements as the ruthless leader continued circling around him. "Eamon will be so disappointed." He tisked his tongue as he lightly sliced a gash into Ryle's forearm. The Eastern prince never flinched, but instead shot lethal barbs with his eyes.

"What do you plan to do with him, my Lord?" Edward asked, stepping closer towards Ryle's chair.

"Kill him, of course. But not right now. I do not want to be too hasty. He will come in handy soon."

"How so?"

Lancer grinned, and his eyes flashed black as his voice grew deep and dark. "I imagine Eamon will do most anything to have his precious heir to the throne saved. It is only a matter of time before your old Realm attacks again, and when they do, we will have another fighter on our side." He rested his hand on Ryle's shoulder and Ryle jerked to try and pry himself from the man's clasp. Lancer laughed, the sound echoing through the reflection chamber as Ryle watched dark swirls of cold, smoke like fog began to cloud around his chair and slither up his legs. He flashed panicked eyes towards Edward, but Edward remained frozen at the sight before him. Ryle closed his eyes and took deep breaths to try and stop the fear from overcoming him. He did not want the darkness. Not one ounce of it. He felt the cold leave his calves and he opened his eyes to see the darkness swarming and wrapping around Lancer's body, seeping into the man's palms. Edward continued to stare, and Ryle watched in horror as the black tendrils creeped across the floor to Alayna's brother and began doing the same.

The epic battle continues…

Redemption Rising

Part Three in The Unfading Lands Series

Where will YOUR allegiance lie?

ABOUT THE AUTHOR

Katharine E. Hamilton started her writing career nearly a decade ago by creating fun-filled stories that have taken children on imaginative adventures all around the world. By using her talents of imagery and suspense to illustrate the deep, underlying issue of good and evil within us all, Katharine extends the invitation for adventure to adults everywhere. She finds herself drawn time and again by the people behind her adventures and wishes to bring them to life in her stories.

She was born and raised in the state of Texas, where she currently resides on a ranch in the heart of brush country with her husband, Brad, her son, Everett, and their two furry friends, Tulip and Cash. She is a graduate of Texas A&M University, where she received a Bachelor's degree in History. She finds most of her stories share the love of the past combined with a twist of imagination.

She is thankful to her readers for allowing her the privilege to turn her dreams into a new adventure for us all.

All Titles by Katharine E. Hamilton
Available on Amazon and Amazon Kindle

The Unfading Lands Series
The Unfading Lands
Darkness Divided
Redemption Rising

The Lighthearted Collection
Chicago's Best
Montgomery House
Beautiful Fury

Children's Books
The Adventurous Life of Laura Bell
Susie at Your Service
Sissy and Kat

Find out more about Katharine and her works at:

www.katharinehamilton.com

Social Media is a great way to connect with Katharine. Check her out on the following:

Facebook: Katharine E. Hamilton

Twitter: @AuthorKatharine

Instagram: @AuthorKatharine

Contact Katharine: khamiltonauthor@gmail.com

www.ingramcontent.com/pod-product-compliance
Lightning Source LLC
Chambersburg PA
CBHW031610240626
47153CB00002B/699